ALONE IN THE FORTRESS

ALONE IN THE FORTRESS

So quick bright things come to confusion. - W. Shakespeare

By Joseph Wurtenbaugh

iUniverse, Inc.

New York Lincoln Shanghai

Alone in the Fortress

iUniverse, Inc.

For information address:
iUniverse, Inc.
2021 Pine Lake Road, Suite 100
Lincoln, NE 68512
www.iuniverse.com

ISBN: 0-595-29540-1 (pbk)
ISBN: 0-595-66013-4 (cloth)

Printed in the United States of America

CHAPTER 1

▼

The saying goes that everyone has one novel in them. So I suppose this would be mine. I do believe it's a little better than most—that's my prejudice, obviously, but I think I'm right. My one novel is a true story about true love, which is a rare thing in this world. It took place in real time, as the world measures time, not long ago, amidst the trappings of everyday reality. It is not a fairy tale. It does not begin with the phrase *once upon a time* and for sure it does not end with the words *lived happily ever after*.

I start in this way to give fair warning—for I have found a paradox exists concerning stories like mine. An enormous number of persons who have no patience with fairy tales nonetheless continue to believe in fairy-tale endings. But real life is not like that, and this is not a story about anything else but real life.

And while I am in this iconoclastic mood, let me dispel some more illusions. This is not a story about young love. When I first met Mira, I was 48 years old. I'd fathered two children, and I was separated and about to be divorced. Mira was twelve years younger, divorced as well, and she'd gone me one better, bearing three children. So there aren't any balconies, no moonlit gardens, nothing at all like that. You can also forget fire escapes and bleak urban playgrounds if you're partial to modern retellings of the old story. The beginnings of this one were far more subtle and more mundane—a Special Ed class, an UnSuperbowl party, two concerned parents, all located in a pretty suburb some 30 or so miles south of San Francisco. If you are not expecting true love to appear in such an unlikely setting, join the club.

Neither did I.

At the time it all began, I had been separated from Linda, the mother of my children, for about a year. It had not been my decision, either wholly or in part. It was hers, entirely unilateral and announced entirely without warning. She had come home one evening and without further ado, told me she wanted out. Perhaps I should have expected it—after twelve good years, we had had a very rocky five, what with the deaths of two parents and the gradual discovery of the true severity of Nicholas' condition. Sex had all but disappeared, passion had vanished entirely. There was a lot of morose, lonely drinking (mine), a lot of brooding depression (mine), and a lot of free-floating anger (hers). Still, even though we may have gone dead in the water, for over sixteen years we were strong couple, an exceptionally strong couple. We had built a perfect suburban life, with a large suburban house, two children, two careers, solid financial security, all of the middle class trappings. We shared the same basic values, we both loved Elizabeth and Nicholas—I had always assumed that we'd get by, one way or another. What dry rot had set in seemed manageable.

But Linda had her own ideas. On a rainy March evening, not coincidentally on the first anniversary of her father's death, she had walked into the family room, sat down on the couch beside my reading chair, and told me flat out she wanted a divorce. Though there were clues for months (I could see clearly after the fact) I went into shock. With a woman like Linda, there is no such thing as a tentative decision or a trial balloon. If she was anything less than certain, she would not have said anything at all. So I knew at once that the decision was irrevocable and final.

We went through the motions. Linda is a woman's woman; she lives at the center of a vast network of female friends and acquaintances; she thrives on their good will and good opinion. She could not show her face in that company if we did not at least try out some form of marriage counseling. So two weeks after she detonated the bomb, we found ourselves at a marriage counselor, who proved to be a woman of middle years, a licensed clinical psychologist, recommended by one of the more trusted members of the female Mafia.

The counselor asked a few questions and got a few answers and a few shrugs.

"I think this is manageable," Dr. Dotrice—Marianne Dotrice—said at last. She was thoughtful and reflective. "You two don't seem to have nearly the issues that most divorcing couples have. We can accomplish something here."

"No, we can't," Linda answered immediately and decisively. "I've had it with this man. I don't want to be married to him any more." This was Doctor Dotrice's crash course introduction to my wife's will of steel. Despite knowing better, I'd had my own illogical hopes up to then—after all, we *were* at a marriage counselor—but they died at that moment. Linda got up and left the office abruptly. She didn't slam the door, but she might as well have. The marriage counseling had lasted all of fifteen minutes.

So that was that. You can't force someone to live with you if they don't want to. We found a realtor. The realtor found a two bedroom condominium about four miles away from the five bedroom house I'd built us with my software money. Linda raced around, trying to quiet her conscience by decorating my new digs to a fare-thee-well. She did a good job, too, although a bit on the feminine side. All this frenzied activity mercifully distracted me from the reality of what was happening. But then the day did arrive, six weeks later, when—unimaginably—I found myself actually moved into the condominium, surrounded by the clutter of all my useless things, cut off from the people who mattered most to me. The distractions ended then, and the full weight of the event crashed down upon me. My ideal suburban life had been blown to smithereens. It was a warm day in May, but I felt cold and numb and afraid.

The dispassionate tone with which I'm recounting all this is something of a fooler. At the time it was massive trauma, the largest and most difficult of my life. The governing emotion was fear, a fear that went way, way beyond any regrets I had over a lifestyle that I could already see was dead a long time before the obituary was written. It was not fear for myself. It was fear, sheer terror actually, for my children, primarily my older, my bright, beautiful, magnificent Elizabeth, then just three months short of her tenth birthday. There is a danger in the perception of a pattern in events; too often the pattern, like beauty, exists only in the eye of the beholder, in what is only the ordinary chaos of chance, the way an apparition can appear suddenly amidst the flow of light on glass, a quick, glimmering reflection that takes on form and menace. But spectral or not, the pattern was real enough to me. It pervaded my days, it haunted my nights. If scene setting is what I am doing, pay attention, for this is center stage stuff. At its core were two or three sepia photographs some sixty years old.

Back in 1933, in Pittsburgh, in what these days would be called family court, my mother, then aged ten, dressed in her nicest Sunday dress, had gone into a judge's chambers and been asked which parent she preferred to live with. The sepia pictures were of her, taken that day, a marvelous little girl. She'd been well rehearsed as to an answer that probably would have been the same without any rehearsal—her mother. She walked out of the courtroom, said goodbye to her father—and never saw him again in her life. She grew up to be a diffident, unhappy woman, strong and vital, but brittle and anxious, bound hand and foot by invisible thread, constraints that only she could see or feel, against which she thrashed and writhed her entire life. Her angry outbursts were sometimes provoked, more often not, but always disproportionate and out of balance. I bore the brunt of it; I was her only son. The decisions made that day in 1933 echoed and reverberated deep into my adulthood, affecting every aspect of my life and masculinity.

When my time came to choose a wife, it was possibly by chance—but more likely not—that my bride-to-be was the product of a violent and unhappy marriage. She too had gone into a family court, this one on the Great Plains of Iowa, at age ten, and chosen a home. Linda was more fortunate than my mother; she did see her father on infrequent occasions. But the relationship was distant and hostile, and the only emotions she ever expressed toward him were bitterness and contempt. Then he was dead, and the depth and anguish of her grief astonished me. But how could it have been otherwise? She was his first-born daughter, she had loved him deeply, painfully, and secretly, and his death brought her finally the freedom to voice it openly. Nor—of course—did the negativity vanish with the expression of love. Instead it found a new direction. As the once-despised dad descended into the grave, he ascended into sainthood. All of the free-floating anger she had directed at him in life now became mine to enjoy and savor. The dawning of a day on which I would learn that I had built my marital house on sand became inevitable.

And now Linda had pulled the plug, with Elizabeth at age ten for all practical purposes, and thus about to take her turn as the next in succession of an endless line of bitter, deserted women, eaten up by mute anger and inarticulate love. Elizabeth had always been a quiet, contemplative girl; now she brooded in her room and waited for the other shoe to drop. Alone in my barely furnished condo, late at night, I brooded as well. *How long? How many?* I did not accept the timing of the divorce as a coincidence. Nightmare visions afflicted me, of the Kelsey family locked into an eternal recurrence, never free, a hand from the grave always around one ankle of the runner, build and in the same motion unbuild, over and over and over again, forever. I became determined that my mother's fate and Linda's would not become Elizabeth's, that the pattern would be broken, that my precious daughter would remain untouched and unharmed, whatever the cost to me.

Thus Elizabeth. But there was also Nicholas to consider, my second child, as afflicted as Elizabeth was blessed. What precisely was the medical cause of his problems no one knows; it is another neurological mystery. All that I can say is that his mother and I knew we had the problem before he was one year old. The books call his syndrome PDD (for Pervasive Development Disorder), a distant, low-rent cousin of autism blended with ADD. What it translates into in day-to-day life is difficulty in learning to walk, to talk, and all the rest. We had done well to be on top of it so early; Nick began in special education shortly after his second birthday. At that time, not yet six years old, he was already in his fourth year of public education. He had made amazing progress. But he did not function like a normal child, and never would.

He was not retarded; Nick was a bright, alert little boy, a marvelous little boy actually, unusually well-attuned to the physical environment around him. His problem lay in the processing of the data, not the intake. That made him both frustrated and frustrating. In dealing with him, there was a constant sense of soup overflowing the bowl, of a huge, capable grasp that lay just beyond his reach.

I did not have the same degree of concern of emotional harm to Nick that I did for Elizabeth. There was no pattern of paternal abandonment of sons in my family, and to some extent his condition shielded him from the worst. But I was concerned. Nick might not have possessed Elizabeth's social acuity, but neither was he oblivious. Causes did produce effects in Nick; events would often disappear into some cavern in his soul, apparently lost in the void, and then reappear a few weeks later in some odd, totally unexpected way. He, too, was at grave risk.

These two human beings were the sun and moon of my life. Whatever else might occur, whatever the cost to me, I was determined that Elizabeth and Nick be shielded to the maximum extent possible from the traumatic effects of the separation. How this could be accomplished I was not immediately certain. I was in another country; divorce is unknown in my family. I could only rely on my instincts.

This, then, was the nature of the fear that tormented me. I did not mourn the loss of my house, or lifestyle, or community reputation for more than a trifling instant, a few days. I would live; worse things happen to people every day. But the thought that demons would prey on Elizabeth and Nick all their lives because of the inability of Linda and myself to resolve our own problems, that they would be damaged to their core by events for which they were not responsible and over which they had no control—these possibilities tormented me.

What to do? How to respond to this situation? To that subject, I devoted all my emotional energy. It seemed to me that the devastating effects on children of a marital break-up took two different forms. The first was abandonment, a loved parent simply disappearing. This was the principal means by which the colossal harm that my mother had suffered was visited upon her. The second was anger, the child's life and being becoming the battlefield on which two people too immature or enraged to worry about long-term consequences engage in their petty war. This was the fate my soon-to-be-ex-wife had suffered. My hope lay in the fact that both these effects were controllable, and to be precise could be controlled by me.

It was critical that the children's lives be disrupted as minimally as possible. I was insistent that the children dwell primarily in our large home, the only home they had ever known. I would reside a short distance away, always available, and if possible with them daily. An arrangement of this type would have been unworkable with many estranged couples, but we were civilized to a high degree. Moreover, even during the highest, best days of our marriage, Linda was gone frequently. She was many miles more social than I, active in a variety of social and political organizations that either bored or annoyed me, particularly the political. At the practical level, we would be living not too much differently than we had before, except for the separate residences.

So much for the abandonment aspect of the problem. As for the anger element? A much simpler matter, a much simpler solution. It is not possible to do battle with one who will not fight, one who is prepared to provide an infinite number of the soft answers that turn away wrath. This sort of person was the person I determined to become. No dramatic transformation was required, as I am not a quarrelsome person in the first instance. Linda and I had always had a tranquil relationship. I was resolved to keep that quo status, no matter how great or infuriating the provocation.

My plans seemed to me sensible and realistic. But they were vigorously and bitterly opposed from the outset by the mother of my children. Simple decency requires I place these matters in larger perspective. Linda is not going to figure too well in her brief appearances in these pages, for the elemental reason that all these events occurred during the years of the greatest turmoil in her life. This is hardly a coincidence; it was her crisis, and my need to cope with it, that set the entire chain of events into motion. But she was and is a kind, decent woman, dedicated to our children and—by the way—extremely attractive. For most of our marriage, we were a strong, loving couple, with shared values and enormous mutual respect. I was always faithful to her, and I have no question of her fidelity to me.

But she was no more able than I had been to free herself from the dead weight of family history. In a fundamental sense, her insistence on divorce was a symbolic gesture. What she truly wanted was freedom from her past, which of necessity required freedom from her present, since the past was implicit in it. The demons that were released at her father's death, the same ones with whom I had become acquainted five years earlier at my mother's passing, whispered in her ear late at night that she had been cheated, that the life she should have led had been stolen from her. She yearned for an entirely new life, a fresh start, a chance to sweep the board clean of all the misplaced pieces and begin the game again.

Her interest in divorce thus was not limited to me, but extended to Elizabeth and Nicholas as well, though she would never have admitted that fact to herself. At her heart of hearts, she wanted a clean slate, free from all three of us. She would never have actually abandoned the children; she loved them. Her heart's desire took the form of a demand for a degree of freedom that was not actually reconcilable with the responsibilities of parenthood. Her thought was that I'd buy a house, she'd keep our big house, and Nick and Elizabeth would shuttle between on a weekly basis.

Nuts to that, said I—children need a home base just like adults. The thought of the three of us crowded into a condominium or a three-and-two, while Linda wandered like a ghost through a five-bedroom house, struck me as preposterous. I'll see my children at your house, *their* house; our problems are *not* going to become their problems. *Nuts to that*, said my erstwhile beloved. What will people think? What will my friends say? What about my privacy? *Nuts to that*, said I (my turn again)—if you value your privacy that much, *you* go live in the goddam condo.

In the end, I won. I always did when the kids were concerned. And—as I expected and predicted—she was gone often that first year, weeknights and weekends, finding herself or losing me or whatever. As my on-site parenting amounted in practical terms to unlimited free babysitting, Linda must have privately decided that it wasn't all that bad an idea (although that was another thing she would never have admitted out loud.)

Thus was my life defined in the year following the separation. I treated my condo like a motel room rented by the hour. I'd come home from the D.A.'s office, change, and drive over to what I called the Big House, (the other prosecutors had a lot of fun with the name), read with Elizabeth, commune with Nick, then leave at 10:00 to sleep, rise, and start again. Weekends were more kids, with the occasional day off, never more. I had little or no time for myself. But I had no greater expectations. I was fully aware that I was socially marooned. It was a life-style I had adopted voluntarily, and the isolation was no more than the price I had expected to pay.

But there was more to it. There always is. No one adopts any life style for only one reason, and I was no exception. Most of the people

who knew anything about the situation saw me as a noble, self-sacrific-
ing person, and there was a solid element of truth in that. But in reality
my motives were not that pure. In the words of a popular song of the
30's, I was through with love. The collapse of my marriage had left me
weary and demoralized, sick to death with frustration and disappointment. All alone in my condo, all that long, long year, I paced and
brooded and wondered about myself. I didn't try to initiate a social life
because I didn't want a social life. I wasn't interested in affairs, or
involvements, or dalliances, or dates, not arranged or blind or set-up or
for coffee or lunch or for anything. As far as I was concerned, all any of
it ever led to was heartache and misery, and a colossal waste of energy
of which I already had too little.

So my paternal heroism was real enough, but that noble quality also
served to conceal much that was not noble at all, a monumental timid-
ity and self-doubt. I immured myself in the four walls of my condo
because I was unwilling to face anything that would disrupt my inertia.
As far as I was concerned, that part of my life had ended, and thank
God. The idea that my adventures were not over, that they had scarcely
begun, that there were events I could hardly imagine waiting just
beyond the horizon—in particular, the discovery of the one woman I
would come to prize above all others—that thought never occurred to
me. I would have scoffed at the very notion of destiny of that sort if it
had.

And with that, I'm done with scene setting. It's time to begin the
story.

CHAPTER 2

▼

As it happened, Destiny, Kismet, Fate, call it what you will, that force
at which I laughed and which I was determined to avoid, was laughing
behind its hand at me from the beginning. I was determined to avoid
involvements for the sake of my children. But if I hadn't been as
focused on my children as I was, I would never have met Mira. It was
my conscientiousness as a parent that started it all.

All this began about nine months after I'd moved into the condo.
Nick at that time was three months shy of his seventh birthday, but he
behaved more like a child half his age. He was unable to play or social-
ize effectively with anyone. He had all manner of need, but by far the
most important was socialization. Disabled children are as different
from one another as they are from normals. But there is one thing they
all have in common. *If only he could play appropriately! If only he had
someone to play with!* That's the mantra of all parents with children in
this situation, as I had come to learn. Everyone is aware in principle of
how much children learn from one another. But it is only those who
live with a child who *can't* learn from other children who know how
true that truism really is. An ultimately vicious circle is at work here.
To the extent my son could not play with others, he spent more time
alone. The more time he spent alone, the less he learned to play. With
kids like Nick, the puppy catches its tail, over and over and over again.

Without acts of resistance to the natural progression—truth be told, often despite acts of furious resistance—all the child-development dominoes fall in reverse order, and the descent into the solo universe continues relentlessly, with nothing but sadness and despair.

So resist I did. During those years, I came up with all sorts of socialization plans for Nick—outings, excursions, movies, trips to amusement parks, horseback-riding lessons. Most of them fell flat on their face; all the other kids would rush ahead to experience whatever was new and different, and Nick would hang back by himself, maddeningly content in his own little private world. But occasionally there'd be a partial success, and, even when not, I was convinced that something seeped through by some sort of psychological osmosis—Nick's personality was a semi-permeable membrane, not the total shield of the truly autistic. In any case, if I didn't try for him, who else would?

It was one of those socialization schemes that led to my meeting first Crockett, then Mira. The professional football team in our area had had a much better year than I had, winning the NFL conference championship. I like spectator sports, quite a bit, actually, but as for the NFL, I am not a fan. I am in fact, an active, dedicated un-fan. I loathe the violence and spectacle, the ceaseless hype. When the Super Bowl was a couple of weeks away, I thought I spied an excellent opportunity to do something for Nick. The idea was that I would organize an 'unSuperbowl' party, which would give the fan parents of children who shared the Special Education class with Nick a window in which they could enjoy the game. I had a location in mind. There was an estuary not too far from the school, a little park that bordered on marsh land, where ducks and waterfowl nested. A visit out there, to feed the ducks, armed with a lot of stale bread and some balloons and toys, could be made into a fairly good excursion for Nick and his buds. So I sent invitations to every member of Nick's Special Ed class, to school with him in his back pack. This wholesale invite was not quite as broadly generous a gesture as it might at first appear to be. There were only seven of them.

I had learned a lot since Nick's birth, knowledge I never wanted or had dreamt I'd need. The community that Nick and I belonged to, of the disabled and those who love them, is large, all around the 'normal' community and invisible to it, far larger than the uninitiated have any idea. Every parent in it starts out with the hope that a Magic Day will dawn some morning, that a pill will appear or an operation be discovered, or that the problem will be outgrown and history. It never happens. Sooner or later, a different day comes, a grimly real day when that fantasy has to be squarely faced and abandoned. A lot of families abandon hope as well on that day, and descend completely into inertia and listlessness. As it happened, nearly every family in Nick's class apparently fell into that category. I received only one response to my invitation, from someone named Crockett Watson, the father of a classmate of Nick's named Alicia.

"Hi," he said over the phone, "I'm Alicia's dad. That's a generous gesture of yours."

"No sweat," I answered. "I don't like the Super Bowl. Too glitzy."

He laughed. "As a matter of fact, neither do I. I'm a soccer coach, and that's my big competition. So I'm planning to join you, if you don't mind."

"Not at all."

"Always kinda liked ducks."

We met out at the park that Sunday afternoon. We were lucky with the January weather; the day was sunny, the air brisk but not too cold. Crockett brought all three of his children, not just Alicia. His two sons, her younger brothers, were normal. We started off well, but some basic flaws in my plan became apparent almost immediately. For one thing, I hadn't brought nearly enough stale bread for our purposes. It was all gone in a quarter hour, leaving a lot of disappointed ducks and—I worried at first—some disappointed kids. But Crockett's boys were able to find ways to amuse themselves, and Nick and Alicia at least remained in the same vicinity. It would have been wonderful if they'd played co-operatively, but children of their kind never do. They played in parallel, in their separate zones—in their separate worlds, to be more accurate. At least they were minimally aware of each other's existence. With Nick you settled for what you got.

Crockett was a decent looking man in his mid-30's, 10 or 12 years younger than I, four or five inches shorter than my six-one. We wiled away what was a fairly boring afternoon with the ususal variety of male chitchat. I knew he was divorced due to separate addresses on the class roster. I asked casually about his ex-wife.

"Her name's Mira," he answered.

"What's she do?"

"Commercial real estate. She manages office buildings."

"Are you two on good terms?"

"Oh, yeah." He shrugged. "We get along."

At about 5:00, we said our good-byes, with the kids muddy, but not too muddy, and everyone in decent spirits. It worked out to be a reasonable day, though I was disappointed by the low turn-out. *Try, try again*, I said to myself, not for the first time, not for the last. Crockett seemed like a nice enough fellow, but he hadn't made any particular impression on me. I didn't expect to see him again, outside of classroom meetings, and I didn't particularly care.

Two days later, I returned home from my job doing justice for the Great State of California to find the message light on my answering machine blinking. I pressed the button.

"Mr. Kelsey—"

" Normally I try to avoid superlatives; they are generally an indication of either a poor observer, a lazy writer, or both. But this is one occasion on which my notions of stylistic delicacy have to give way to simple truth. After just two words, I knew I was listening to the most perfectly modulated, most beautifully melodious speaking voice I had ever heard in my life.

"—this" is Mira Watson. I just wanted to thank you personally for the outing on Sunday. Alicia has been talking about nothing but ducks for two days now." She laughed, a laugh of marvelous clarity and lightness. "At least it's an improvement over water tanks." From which mysterious comment I gleaned that Alicia was as obssessive in her way as Nick. "So thank you."

I am an aural man—I always have to spell that adjective out when I meet someone new—sound influences me far more than sight. I have been nearsighted nearly all my life, I can't rely on my eyesight at all, but my hearing is unusually acute. I can't remember now whether I was enchanted immediately. I know for certain I became curious immediately about the possessor of that wondrous voice. Over the next few days, I speculated from time to time about this unknown woman—what she was like, what would happen if I met her face-to-face. But I didn't do anything about it. The walls of my fortress were still high, the interior comfortable, I had no wish to venture out , and not enough reason to do so. So I marveled, and wondered, but I did nothing.

Destiny, not at all content with that state of affairs, then stepped in and gave the matter a nudge. Crockett felt duty-bound to reciprocate the invitation. His two normal children were younger, but close enough to Elizabeth's age to make a joint outing for all five kids feasible, a rare opportunity for some serious commingling of normal children with the others. Much discussion followed about when, where, how, and—mostly—what. When— the smoke finally cleared, Crockett had agreed to take the whole bunch to a Disney matinee, followed by a little play time at the Big House. I'd do the babysitting (as usual) since Linda planned to be out (also as usual).

"My custody shift ends on Saturdays," he said casually. "Their mother'll pick 'em up at 8:00." So I was finally going to meet the myserious Mira Watson.

Planning such events is easy in concept; actually supervising five kids under 10, two of whom are mildly autistic, is where you really earn your angel's wings. Crockett had the easy side of the bargain, the movie; I was the one assigned the heavy lifting. I did o.k., but by 7:45 my eyes were glued to the clock. I prayed that Mira Watson was not one of those women who were habitually late, and I thanked God when the doorbell rang a bit early, at two minutes to the hour.

"Come in!" I shouted, being too distracted by some incidental crisis to answer the door myself. Our large front door opened slowly, and a slim, almost waif-like figure stepped through it, into the house, into the hall, into my life, forever. She was quite short, no more than five foot one or two. Her hair was thick and shoulder-length, but the hall was unlit and I could not determine the color. It was obvious she had regular features, but I could not make them out. She was bespectacled, as was I.

"Mr. Kelsey?" she called out lightly. "Can I come in?" That voice again, and this time it is for certain that a bit of enchantment did begin.

"Of course," I said. "In fact, I can't tell you what a welcome sight you are. And the name's Walt."

She laughed and moved—or, more accurately, floated—a few feet down the hall. Once again I would like to avoid the superlative, and once again subtle nuances of prose have to yield to the crude elegance of reality. Mira Watson moved with more physical grace than anyone I had ever met in my life. "Oh, I'm just another pretty face," she said, not inaccurately. She was quite attractive in an idiosyncratic way—not perfectly formed mannequin good looks (those I despise) but interesting, intelligent, alert, alive.

As she approached me, without thinking, my right hand came to my temple and whipped off my glasses. (I am vain about my eyes; I don't like to be photographed with glasses on, and I invariably take them off when I am meeting someone I want to impress.) Almost simultaneously, Mira did exactly the same thing. We looked at each other and then away, slightly embarrassed, since it was hard to pretend that the simultaneous mutual gesture implied anything other than what it obviously did.

"So you're Mira Watson," I said stupidly. Duh.

"So I've been told," she agreed politely. "How are you holding up?"

"As well as can be expected. But you didn't arrive a moment too soon."

"I see. I'd better round up the savages and get going. You're wonderful to do this." She was one of those women who could bestow a casual compliment with a natural, unforced sincerity that went directly into the bloodstream. I felt my heart skip.

We gathered up toys, we tied shoes, we buttoned buttons, all the rest. I did not want her simply to say good-bye and leave. I wanted to do something, knew I had to do something—how I would mesh it all with my lifestyle was a problem I would consider later. But try as I might, I could not think what to do, what to say. Besides, the kids were all around. Finally, though, they had all been herded into the back seat of her station wagon, and she was standing in front of the driver's door.

"Thanks again," she smiled, and it was now or never.

"Right," I said. I hoped I didn't look agitated, but I was almost certainly hoping in vain. "Look, I'd like to take you to lunch sometime, if you're ever free." The invitation was made in one gauche, rapid, juvenile breath, understandable enough, since this was the first time in twenty years I'd asked a woman out.

She either didn't notice the speed of delivery or (more likely) pretended not to. "I'd like that," she said, with the usual clear musicality, and a slight, intimate smile. She put her glasses on. "Call me sometime. You've got the number." She got into the car, and disappeared into the night. I was left standing in the dark, with the nicest and most pleasant feeling of anticipation I'd had in ten years.

*

Call her I did, a day or two later, after the probable bedtime of her children. I was delighted to find her in, up, and alert. I re-extended the lunch invitation, and she accepted immediately, for the first Saturday free of child-care responsibilities. We talked, and I learned a few more facts about her. Mira had actually trained well into her mid-twenties in modern dance, and become good enough to tour in one of the national companies. That accounted for the physical grace. As Crockett had told me, she was making a living at that time managing two office buildings for one of the major commercial real estate firms. But she considered that only a beginning; she had considerable ambition. In her laid-back manner, she casually mentioned she was taking classes towards an MBA in finance at one of the night schools, on course to obtain a degree in another two years. Her life was evidently as harried as mine, although she made no complaint as we talked. I asked about the divorce and the relationship with Crockett, a major factor in these situations, and she left me with the impression was that it was friction-less.

And she flirted with me from the outset, skillfully and provocatively. "You're a closer, Mr. Kelsey," Mira said, "I can tell," and I knew without asking more what—or rather whom—she thought I might be closing in the near future. I was married for sixteen years, alone and celibate for a year afterward. For the first time in nearly two decades, I experienced desire for a woman not my wife whom I had some realistic chance of possessing physically. The thought stirred an anticipation of a type I thought had left my life forever. Over the next few days, I found myself thinking about her constantly. (For that matter—the thought occurs to me only as I write these lines—I have thought about her constantly ever since.)

By no means was I abandoning my fortress—quite the contrary. I had (I believed) a settled life. My perception was that she did as well. Neither one of us (I thought) wished to disturb what were effective and efficient post-separation parental relationships. I was done forever (I was sure) with romantic love of that sort. What I hoped was that this mutual realization could lead to a relationship that would be effectively confined to the time and emotional space available, somewhat in the way that settlers in one distant frontier town might visit settlers in another, to conduct essential business, but with no thought of relocation. I had no idea that there was the remotest possibility that these modest overtures ever could or ever would shake the universe.

Ten days later, we met at one of the better local Chinese restaurants. She wore a blouse and jeans, which emphasized her slenderness and the shape of her legs. She told me more about herself. She had been an extremely dedicated dancer, in class and rehearsal nearly twelve hours a day. This accounted for the waif-like profile and the absence of curves; she had exercised them away. For the same reason, Mira also proved to be one of the cheapest lunch dates imaginable; her drink of choice was hot water with a lemon slice on the side, her preferred entrée, a plate of steamed vegetables of which she seldom ate more than a third. The microscopic appetite was another legacy from her dancing days.

"I don't want to be your transition girlfriend," she said.

"Transition girlfriend?" I asked.

"Yes. The girl who transitions you over from marriage to the single life. I don't want to be that person. That girl always gets hurt."

"I don't think I'm even in transition," I said stupidly. "I don't know what you mean."

"That," she said, smiling, "is *exactly* what I mean."

All this was said in the course of attempting to persuade her to see me some Saturday night. "No," she said sweetly, but with finality. "Saturday night is big date night. I like you, Walt, but I'm not ready for that." I had never given the date status of Saturday night much thought, but she obviously had, and what she thought was all that mattered.

But I persisted, finding time from the child-care responsibilities to telephone and for one or two more lunches. Her voice and manner increasingly captivated me. She referred to me frequently as a closer; it was evident in that way and in others that her interest in me was also growing. But she clung stubbornly to the Saturday night rubric, and her view of me as in transition. I could make no headway.

Almost two months passed. I scoured the weekend entertainment sections in the newspaper for something—dance, theatre, whatever—

that would be a sufficiently strong motivator to weaken her resolve. Finally, one Sunday, I found it—a stop on the tour of one of the world-class classical ballet companies, performing at the major municipal theatre in the City. She might have been a modern dancer, but I was sure she'd be interested in classical ballet as well.

"I'd like to take you out Saturday," I said that night.

"Walt—"she began refusing as usual.

"It's the Balanchine pieces," I interrupted. "The American Ballet Theatre. It's only in town for two weeks. It's a tough ticket, but I've got two. For the Saturday matinee."

A long pause. "The ballet?" she said.

"Yes."

"All right," she said at last, "you win, Walter. I suppose it's about time anyway. So—yes. I'll spend the night—I mean, the *evening*—with you." This minor league Freudian slip did the erotic tension building within me no harm whatsoever.

"Fine," I said, exhilarated. "I'll pick you up in the morning, we can see the performance, and have lunch at the theatre. Then dinner afterwards."

"Sure," Mira agreed, and I hung up, well pleased with myself. She had agreed to spend a long day with me, in conversation and close contact, which is exactly the type of day I needed for what I had in mind.

For I had decided to accept the challenge implicit in her continual references to me as a closer. This was one opportunity I was determined would not slip away. Our lives matched, our personalities meshed—she and I as a couple made solid, rational sense. ('Solid, rational sense'—what nonsense that seems to me now. But that was what I thought at the time.) In any case, I was not going to let the chance that Mira represented in my life simply vanish tracelessly without trying. I had thus resolved to do my best to consummate the relationship on that day, to become in reality the closer she thought I was.

To put the same thing in a different, very old-fashioned form, I had decided to seduce Mira Watson that Saturday night—for her own good (I told myself) as well as my own. But it would be more accurate to say I had decided to *try* to seduce her—for I had never been terribly good at that sort of thing.

CHAPTER 3

▼

Grace is the essence of the dance. Be the gesture simple or complex, easy or impossible, the dancer's movement must be graceful, as spontaneous as light, as effortless as air. A dancer exhibits a state of grace, or she is not a dancer at all. The pose of effortlessness is the ultimate illusion.

From the outset, the performance delighted me. I didn't see through the illusion until it was much, much too late. From the beginning to the end, I was always the most gullible member of the audience.

*

Mira had hated the house from the moment she moved into it, a week or so after the sale of the one they owned as community property closed. It was over fifty years old, poorly heated, poorly ventilated, poorly wired, as dark as a cavern, and far too small for a woman with three children. She kept them content for now, with an immense amount of energy, guile, and artifice. But soon, too soon, they would outgrow this residence, this lifestyle, their own mother, if it came to that. So it must not come to that.

She had given her youth up to her art, in an unabashed, headlong pursuit of beauty. During her early 20's, between rehearsal and class, she had sometimes spent as much as 12 hours in exercise or at the bar. She did not regret the complete dedication of her life for an instant. It had given her poise, confidence, a striking presence, and her marvelous physical grace. However slight the tangible benefit, the intangible had been immense.

Later she had focused the same concentrated effort, the same dedication, on the world of business. The segue had been relatively easy; she was bright, a quick study, and no special credentials were needed to exploit the numerous commercial opportunities available in real estate. She was enormously skillful with men, quietly certain (with reason) of her attractiveness, and socially adept while becoming intimate only on her own terms. She accumulated a small, but interesting, amount of capital, which she was bent on expanding, a nest-egg, by the time she met Crockett Watson.

She had not planned on marriage, or three babies, one-two-three, or the divorce, or the aftermath of the divorce. Above all, she had not planned on the special needs of her only daughter. The nest egg disappeared; her children, as much as she loved them, were a severe constraint—and thus she had come to dwell in this desolate house. It was necessary that she move before her children became too much older, and in any event she was determined for her own sake to stay there no longer than was necessary. But she was in her mid-thirties now, times had changed, and opportunity no longer knocked ceaselessly at her door. For the first time, she had to think about getting on with her life in a milieu in which credentials mattered, amongst people who might believe that the time she had spent on dance in her twenties had been squandered.

Even here, her wide range of friends, particularly male friends, did not fail her. She was directed to a job as a commercial manager, responsible for the maintenance and administration of a number of commercial buildings. It was an ideal entry level job for her, requiring little in the way of formal education, but a great deal of intelligence and energy, both of which she possessed in abundance. Now, however, it had become essential that she obtain some formal recognition of her skills, a diploma with her name on it. So she had enrolled in an MBA program at one of the more reputable off-site Universities. Though her schedule had become incredibly complex, and there were times when it seemed her life had veered completely off course, she pursued it with the same doggedness she had once pursued a dancer's art.

A dancer never complains about the difficulty of the choreography. Effortlessness is an illusion. The maintenance of the illusion is the essence of grace.

*

I had no inkling then of any of this. All of which I write here, I learned long afterwards.

*

She hung up the phone with me that night with her own mounting sense of excitement and anticipation. She had liked me from the first moment she laid eyes on me, been drawn to me more at each new meeting. Her perception of me was of a big, clumsy, two left-footed bear of a man, who would have been as out of place on a stage as an iron skillet in a porcelain display. She was completely correct in that. Yet, as she saw it, I did possess my own sort of grace, in word and thought. Putting modesty, false or true, to one side, she was probably more right than wrong about that. In any case, it was a quality that appealed to her immensely. My kindness towards my own bewildered child, towards hers, had touched her at her core. It seemed to her the best of all omens. She had already accepted me as her lover, in the calm, matter-of-fact manner in which women who have no problem attracting men make such decisions. Whether that would occur on Saturday night was something she did not intend to think about until Saturday night.

The house that evening was uncommonly still, as it often was when the children were over at their father's, and dreadfully dark, as it always was. Her hatred of this place, never far from her mind, changed in a nonce from quiescent dislike to an active, frustrated loathing. How had she managed to end up here? And just how dead was this dead end at which she had *arrived? Suddenly the prospect of enduring even one more day there, one more night, seemed intolerable. And yet she knew she must, and without open complaint. All things take time.*

It was not yet time for bed. She still had a considerable amount of coursework to do before she retired. At least there was something interesting to look forward to on Saturday—the ballet, the date, the inevitable romancing. But what excited her most was the growing rapport she felt developing between herself and me. It was too soon to do more than note possibilities, too early to do more than hope, but she sensed there could be something truly meaningful between us.

Exactly how meaningful, then—and later—she had a far, far better idea than did I.

CHAPTER 4

▼

I am not and have never been a sexually confident man. My love life—well, that's a misnomer right off the bat—in my youth consisted of one disaster after another. The same dismal story repeated itself over and over and over again. Some girl would notice me behaving naturally, unselfconsciously, and let me know (in the subtle manner of young women in those days) that she was interested. Then, like clockwork, the full set of inhibitions instilled by my dragon of a mother, by the Irish version of the Roman Catholic Church, by God knows what else, would kick in. Instead of the easy, open personality she'd originally liked, the girl would encounter a twisted, tied-in-knots parody a thousand light years removed from that individual. And—naturally—the brighter and more attractive the girl, the more I wanted her, the more twisted and grotesque would be the counterfeit of my real self that ultimately emerged. The result was one catastrophe after another, debacles that could have been avoided if I had only had the common sense to act like a real, live human being, like the man I truly was. Even now, memories of ludicrous incidents thirty and forty years old will ambush me at unexpected moments and leave me seething with frustration and embarrassment.

Matters improved as I got older, but I live with a fundamental diffidence that was never, and will never, be lost. The notion that an attractive woman might look forward to being touched by me, kissed by me, even bedded by me, does not exist in the universe of my subconscious—and it never will. I suppose there is a positive aspect; I am much more open than many men, and I never take anything for granted; I am grateful even for small favors. Men who believe they are blessed by God with some sort of sexual imperative are in my experience generally annoying, silly dolts—and yet I do envy them the strength of their egos. Women have an unfortunate tendency to rate men on their evaluation of themselves, one of their more exasperating characteristics.

So there it was. At the best of times I would have approached a woman as desirable as Mira with considerable fear and trembling. But these weren't the best of times. What little confidence I had built up during the last years of my bachelorhood had been destroyed by the dreary, semi-celibacy in which I'd lived for the last half decade of my marriage. Mira was fresh, alive and exciting. With her frequent references to me as a closer, she obviously saw me as a man skilled with women; I wanted desperately to justify that opinion. Whatever else, I was *not* going to start this new single life with a failure. It is embarrassing for me now to reveal the fact that at the age of 48 I still felt the need to prove my manhood, but that is obviously the truth, and so here it is, in cold print, revealed for once and for all.

Thus it was that I planned the day with care and meticulous attention to every detail. The day before, I had my cleaning lady come in and go over the condo so that it shone. I brought in firewood and stacked it in the fireplace so that it could be ignited simply with the gas lighter. Though neither Mira nor I drank, I bought a nice bottle of white wine, some good table crackers, and a crab dip—the basic elements of the classic seduction formula. I also obtained a gourmet goose pate, put it inside a nice little wicker basket, and sliced up a fresh baguette—something rich to snack on in the car. (Mira barely ate anything, but I was taking no chances.) Because I'd have to park the car, if we did come back to my place, I cleaned out the garage. The last thing

I did, before I went out the door on Saturday, was to change the sheets on the bed.

Her house surprised me. The neighborhood in which it was located was reasonably upscale, populated by junior members of the faculty of the local college and the younger sort of techie. (All this occurred just prior to the coming of age of dotcom commerce and dotcom fortunes. Values in that neighborhood have risen insanely since.) But the house itself was well beneath her deserving—small and shabby, utterly out of keeping with her personal style. The front yard was the size of a postage stamp, neat, but gray and brown. Obviously she had neither the time nor money to tend to it. I was surprised, but understanding—one of the consequences of the divorce, was my educated guess. I felt a sudden twinge of sadness that a person of her charm and substance had been reduced to such living quarters. It wasn't right.

But then Mira was at the front door, smiling and ready, and there was no more time to dwell on the matter. If there was anything out of sort with the house, it didn't show in the slightest in her manner. She was completely unfazed.

"Nice neighborhood," I said diplomatically, as we got in the car. It was the only truthful compliment I could think of.

Her eyes sparkled. "I won't be there long," she said, understanding me completely.

*

Mira as a personality in those days had a tremendous inner balance, the analog of her dancer's grace. If I have given the impression she was somber, I have been misleading. She was anything but somber. She laughed freely and easily, often with a child's surprised delight. It was always a wonderful thing to hear. But she never lost her equilibrium, her fundamental stability, in either laughter or tears.

The drive to the City from our little suburb is more than an hour, long enough for small talk to become intimate. We talked of our hopes and fears for our children, our former marriages, our recent history. We did not talk about each other. I remembered a question I meant to ask her every time we met, but always forgot.

"What about the name 'Mira'?" I asked. "Where'd it come from?" I had found out at our first lunch that she was a Southern girl, born and raised in Ashton, North Carolina, before she came west. (This gave us something in common, since by an accident of my father's military posting, I happened to be a North Carolina native myself. As a result, I had become a rabid North Carolina basketball fan. I had thought at first this gave us a shared interest. As it happened, she could have cared less.) The only Mira of whom I had ever heard was the actress Mira Sorvino, but this Mira was not Italian and too old to have been named after that celebrity.

"Well, actually, if you must know"—she dropped her voice to a stage whisper—"and if you swear not to tell anyone, it's short for 'Elmira'. An old family name. Or maybe curse."

"Now that I know, I'm going to tell everyone," I said.

She threw back her head and laughed her uninhibited, delighted laugh, and I ran the back of my hand down her sleeve. Throughout the trip, I touched her frequently—sometimes her hand, sometimes the sleeve of her coat or her shoulder. Partly this was the initiation of the campaign, but mostly it was because I wanted to touch her.

Of course she knew what I was about. Women always do. But she did not protest my half-caresses, and in fact reached out once and stroked the back of my hand with her little finger. Her hands were small and delicate, compared with my huge paws. I believe the comparison excited us both; it certainly did my interest no harm. The atmosphere became warm and even more intimate. My hopes for the evening grew exponentially.

Better. The April day was overcast, wet and showery, ideal for my purposes. It was necessary for us to share an umbrella as we moved down the slick streets, huddled together, occasionally my arm around her waist. Once in a while our eyes would meet and I was fairly certain

I could kiss her if I chose. But I did not want to take any risk of doing anything prematurely. A better time would come.

We ate a light lunch (the pate had been a total non-starter; typically she had taken half a bite and pronounced herself stuffed—I had pate sandwiches for lunch the next four days), talked a bit more, and touched—I liked to hope—a bit more unguardedly. After another huddled walk under the umbrella, which again did my dishonorable intentions no harm, we arrived at the theatre. I was not then, and I am not now, a big fan of the ballet. My natural inclination is to entertainment forms with a lot of narrative content—plays, movies, musicals, even opera (it hasn't hung around for 400 years because it's dull). Movement for the sake of movement, the essence of dance, is actually not terribly interesting to me. But watching a dance performance with Mira was eye-opening in the real sense of the word. She saw nuances no one but a professional would have noticed, meanings that would have utterly escaped me, artistic presence in the most ordinary postures and gestures. For an afternoon, I had an insight into what all the fuss was about, eyes that were not my own, vision of a beauty that I would never have seen, let alone appreciated, without her guidance. It would have been one of the most magical afternoons of my life even if the events of the evening had never occurred.

Afterwards, we drove back down the freeway, with her hand sometimes lightly on my knee, towards what I hoped would be a dinner as light as the lunch and then the culmination of the entire exercise. Then all at once, from out of nowhere came what I first took to be the inevitable Crushing Setback.

"Walt, I'm sorry to ask this," Mira suddenly said, "but I have to stop by one of my buildings. We're doing some tenant improvements, and I really have to look in on the electricians. They're hopeless without supervision."

"Sure," I said gamely, with my heart sinking into my shoes. There went the nice, even flow of the day, the smooth progress towards the goal, and—more than likely—the goal itself. But duty called, and I clearly could not say no to it. Any chore being done late on a Saturday afternoon was obviously a fairly important chore.

"It won't be ten minutes," she reassured me, which made my heart sink more. My experiences with Linda, also a dedicated career woman, had taught me that time estimates, particularly short time estimates, meant absolutely nothing. With Linda, ten minutes might mean forty minutes, or two hours, or even four hours. What it almost never meant was ten minutes.

We came to the building she managed, a two-story office condominium, and she hopped out of the car. "I won't be a minute," she said. I nodded despondently. Then she turned. "Want to come along?" I got out of the car myself and shuffled along behind, trying not to mope too obviously.

The office that was being improved was small, a three-room suite. There were two men in blue coveralls in the room, and a third, tall and unnaturally thin, with a pale, blotchy face and thin beard, maybe a little older than Mira, wearing a bulky sweater and jeans.

"*Mira!!*" the thin man exclaimed when he saw her, in a thick Russian accent. "Where have you been? These circuits have to be finished today!! You promised me!! Where have you been?!"

The hour was now near five o'clock on a Saturday afternoon. Obviously someone had gone to considerable lengths to solve whatever problems this man had, for which efforts he showed not a particle of gratitude. It was obvious the two electricians had reached a point at which they'd just as soon wire *him* up as the room. But Mira smiled at him affectionately; she obviously liked him despite his behavior. A quick spasm of jealousy passed through me.

"Gregor," she said gently, "the circuits will get done. Trust me. Now guys," she went on, turning to the workers, "what's the problem here?"

I didn't understand too much of what followed, except that the electricians seem strongly inclined to feel that the major problem, and perhaps the only problem, was Gregor. Mira seemed no more comfortable than most women directing blue-collar workers, but she did what she had to do. Gregor kept trying to interrupt, but all three ignored him. The age of miracles hadn't passed; in about ten minutes, to my amazement and delight, the crisis had apparently resolved. Mira turned to Gregor.

"Gregor, sweetie," she said gently, "this will go a lot faster if you don't worry so much about everything." She turned to leave.

"Mira!" he cried. "You're leaving? How can you leave? The work isn't—"

"Gregor," she interrupted with firmness, "I have a date. And the circuits will get done. Now good-bye. And good night. I'll see you Monday." She spoke with a much kinder tone than I would have used. But at least she was done. She squeezed my arm. We walked back towards my car.

"Thank you for the cooperation, Walt," she said softly. "Now I'm all yours." *All yours*—the phrase went straight to the hollow of my stomach. I wondered if she had intended it to do so.

Dinner was light. While I ate a garnished salad, Mira nibbled on the edges of a dish of steamed cauliflower and told me something about Gregor. He was a Russian émigré, in the country only a few weeks, with a lot of Internet ideas, a lot of ambition, next to no money, and an ego the size of Outer Siberia. My own first impression was that he was a royal horse's ass, but even so he amused her. She liked him, but she could not say why. I listened without really hearing. This was nervous, anticipatory small talk—we were both avoiding the big issue, and we both knew it.

Finally the meal was over and the bill paid. Major crunch time had finally arrived. I braced myself. "Let's go back to my place," I said, in as even a tone as I could muster. Back in the old days, the word would have stuck in my throat all evening long, until the girl had lost all patience with me—and all interest as well.

Mira had been expecting the obvious. "Maybe we should see a movie," she said, a bit too quickly.

"I've got a great VCR and a big screen TV," I answered firmly. "We can watch a movie there."

"All right," she sighed, after a moment.

*

It was after dark when we arrived; anticipating just that eventuality, I'd left the porch light on. Mira stepped through the door and looked around. "Very nice," she said, then unexpectedly lifted her left leg and did an arabesque, a little forget-me-not from her performing days. She was nervous.

The condominium I owned was a two-bedroom unit, with light from two angles and a skylight, spacious and roomy. When I had furnished it a year earlier, however, I had planned only for the short term. The separation then had been of the trial variety, and I had some dim, forlorn hope that it would be over quickly. The upshot was that the family room had not been designed for company. It was dominated by a large recliner chair that faced the television, at right angles to the fireplace. An eight-foot couch was situated at the angle at which the family area shifted into the dining space, thereby completing the definition of the area.

Mira declined my offer of wine—another non-starter—then watched as I started the fire and got the VCR ready. When I turned back, to my surprise and delight, she had seated herself on the edge of the reading chair. I sat down beside her, my arm lightly around her waist, and she put her marvelous, delicate hands around my neck. I started the movie—a romanticized biography of Chopin, as I recall— and we watched in silence for a while.

My next move was the big one, the one I had planned the day around. It was a line I had thought of during one of the fantasy moments that occur from time to time in marriage. I would never have had the courage to use it when I was younger. I lowered my voice to what I hoped was a low, sexy drawl.

"Mind if I ask you a personal question?" I said.

"Sure," she answered nonchalantly.

"How long," I went on, "has it been since a man seduced you?"

She reeled back, startled. "*What?!?*"

"I mean, *really* seduced you," I continued in the same low voice, "for no better reason than he wanted you." She was staring at me, but with an expectant curiosity, her libido engaged, wondering what was coming next. "For no better reason than that you're lovely and desirable, and he wanted you more than he wanted anything."

She turned and faced me. "It's been quite a while," she said. I could see she was excited—very excited, in fact. All this was going as well as my happiest daydreams. "Quite a while since any one has done that to me. Is that why you brought me here? To seduce me? Are you that wicked?"

The word `wicked' signaled that she was doing her own role-playing; knowing that didn't lessen the excitement of its effect. In my early bachelor years, I would have ducked the challenge with a muttered denial. Not this night. "Yes," I said, "I like you a lot, Mira. But I am a man, and I've wanted you since the first moment I laid eyes on you. You're a lovely woman, Mira, with a lovely woman's body. Warm"—I touched her cheek—"soft"—I broadened my hand and caressed her face—"penetrable"—and at this point, I pulled her toward me. She came willingly. Our first kiss was a chipmunk peck, but then her hands on my neck clenched convulsively, and she opened her mouth. We began to neck like teenagers. It was thrilling, superb. Passion had disappeared from my life so slowly, so imperceptibly, that I had forgotten what a wonder it was to be with a woman I cared for and wanted.

She shifted out of my lap and faced me, her knees on mine. "Walt," she breathed, "I like you, too, but I'm not ready for this. Can't we let up tonight? Can't we do this the next time?" In response, I pulled her to me and kissed her again, she responded even more passionately— and I took my final cue that night from that. This was not going to wait till next time.

"No, Mira," I answered, in my best male growl, "I'm going to have you tonight. I'm going to put my hands under your clothes"—I matched the action to the words—"caress you so you tingle in your entire body, until you can't help yourself, until you're completely helpless, and then—then—I am going to take you. Completely. Make you mine," I added. She shuddered as I spoke, as my hands spread out over her upper body, pressed herself hard against me, and opened her mouth even wider. Then she sat up abruptly, pulled my hand out of her blouse, and began to kiss the fingertips of my hand, one by one. It was a wildly exciting thing for her to do, simultaneously an act of stimulation and surrender.

"Your body's going to ready itself for me before I even touch you," I continued, in the same low drawl. "You're already wet and ready—"

"No, I'm not," she breathed. "But you don't believe me, I can tell. Why don't you find out for yourself whether or not I'm telling the truth." And she let go of my hand and looked directly into my eyes.

We were close to finality. I put my hand on the waistband of her pants suit, and shifted downward, and found out for myself. With my right hand I explored her, while my left caressed her hair and face. She closed her eyes and let the breath hiss slowly out of her mouth, all resistance gone. The final moment had finally arrived.

I unbuttoned her pants and blouse, then stood her up. She cooperated passively, completely mine for the moment. It was easy work to undress her and in an instant she stood naked in front of me. She was as flat-chested as I had assumed, but gorgeous, her body magnificent in its slenderness and tone, a proof of the existence of God and His bountiful generosity to the male sex. She was utterly unselfconscious in her nudity. She knew she was beautiful.

"I wouldn't trade places with anyone in the universe this moment," I breathed softly. "And there isn't a man in the world who wouldn't sell his soul to be standing where I am."

I had changed the sheets, but it would have been ridiculous to take her to bed. The room was warm, the rug was thick and soft, the firelight played on her body, and she clearly did not expect to be moved. I turned off the television—the movie was still playing—and tossed one of the pillows from the couch down on the floor. We had exchanged enough personal information previously to know that there were no 'safe sex' issues. Mira had had a tubal ligation after her last pregnancy; I'd had a vasectomy. I hadn't been with a woman except Linda for fifteen years, and her contacts had been infrequent and discrete. So there was no reason why this night we couldn't be purely male and female.

I undressed myself. Mira lay on her back with her eyes half-closed, a breathtaking vision of Venus herself. A half-smile played on her lips. "What are you thinking?" I asked softly.

"That you planned everything," she whispered. "That I have been thoroughly and completely seduced, and now I am going to be thoroughly and completely taken." 'Take', I was to learn, was her preferred sexual word. I recognized this as more sexual theatre; Mira was evidently one of those women for whom the illusion of surrender adds the last, small, perhaps necessary, dash of paprika to the omelet. But recognizing it as theatre didn't make any difference. It still worked.

I had been doing my own theatre up to that point, but a small cloud of doubt and worry had formed in the back of my consciousness, that my body was not quickening in the way that was required. I was on the verge of slipping into the horrible self-consciousness that precedes impotence and frustration. But that timely little speech, made in her wonderfully musical voice, galvanized me. All doubt disappeared. I felt a welcome rush of blood and potency. I knelt beside her, now fully ready, fully male, and unspeakably grateful. I kissed her long and passionately, stroked her, gentled her, extended my body beside hers. For a long, long time, I simply stroked her, looking into her eyes. I could not remember when, if ever, I had seen or experienced anything more beautiful. Finally, she sighed, and shifted slightly.

"Please take me, Walt," she breathed, eyes half-lidded, and this was *not* theatre. "Make me yours. Like you said." This was stuff right out of a romance novel, but the reason such stuff is in romance novels is that it's extremely effective. It certainly was on this occasion. I felt empowered as a man in a way I hadn't felt since I was a teen-ager. There was no sense in delaying the consummation any longer. I pulled her to me, and shifted her body underneath mine. I heard Mira's sharp intake of breath, and then her small, delicate hands were clutching my shoulders.

The finish was as direct and satisfying as everything that had led up to it. Mira reached ecstasy comparatively quickly, expressing herself in a dancer's manner, silently, with a vigor that shook her entire frame from side to side. A few seconds later, I shuddered myself, and our relationship was fully perfected.

It was over.

*

Thus ended the first seduction in my life that I had planned from scratch. I lay on my back in the dark, with Mira's head on my shoulder. I was enormously pleased with the day and the outcome. Everything had gone as I had hoped it would. I had proved to myself what I wanted to prove. I could now look to the future with some assurance that I *had* learned something, that I was not doomed to the same ineffectual diffidence that had plagued me in my youth.

We lay there for a few moments, silent in the darkness. "I have to tell you, Walt," she said, from my shoulder, without stirring, "I was of two minds about this. I was worried that it would happen, and worried that it wouldn't. But now I'm very glad it did." That, too, was music, for this was I had been apprehensive about the aftermath—*do I dare to eat a peach?*—but it was obvious that I was holding a completely contented girl. It was one more magic moment in a day that had consisted of nothing but.

But like all days it had to end.

"I've got to go home," she said after a while. "I didn't bring anything to sleep in. And I have things to do in the morning."

"I know," I answered. She rose and began to gather her clothes. I got up and, running on autopilot, went into my bedroom. I was still dazed and happily woozy, or I would have recollected that my own clothes were also scattered around the family room. I fetched a pair of trousers from my closet, pulled them on, picked up a pair of shoes, and sat down sluggishly on my bed.

Suddenly Mira was in the room, fully dressed. She knelt on the bed, straddling me. She looked me dead in the eye for a long, wonderful moment, and then kissed the right side of my neck, the left side, the center—uncontrollably—my lips, my eyes, my neck again. I began to respond. She paused for breath, then began again.

"*Mira,*" I said, laughing, and she laughed herself, a little self-consciously. She had her purse with her; she had been dressed to leave, waiting for me, when an impulse carried her away. All at once she opened it, reached in, and pulled out her diary. "I've got to make time for you," she said thoughtfully, speaking to herself. "This is a love relationship and it takes precedence over everything else." She began to turn the pages and cross out dates. There was nothing possessive or controlling about this; this was a *love* relationship, as she saw it, and that's what you do with a love relationship. It takes precedence over everything. Quite a simple principle, actually.

It was at this point that the night began to become more than simply an exquisite sexual encounter. I wasn't at all taken aback by this display. I was amazed, even a little envious. She was utterly fearless; the world of self-consciousness and doubt, hesitancy and deliberation, in which I lived, in which everyone else I knew was mired, seemed to be completely alien to her. She leapt off the trapeze without the slightest worry that someone would be there to catch her. The inner sense of balance I'd noticed earlier had not disappeared. Her self, and the acts that she required of that self, were indivisible, like an arrow shot from a bow.

I watched her do her editing, too touched, too honored, to say anything. Then, abruptly, she arose, walked into my closet, and began to sort through my suits in a 'this goes, this stays' manner. This totally spontaneous possessiveness did not offend me in the least; it was every bit as wondrously natural and flattering as the calendar. I laughed lightly. "Mira! Don't you think you're getting a little ahead of yourself?" She blushed a little at that and stepped out of the closet.

"Well, all right," she said, "but you do dress terribly, Walt. I'm only trying to help." I could only smile and laugh again—she was right, I did dress horribly—and she laughed with me. The thought crossed my mind that this was the best day I'd had since the early days of my marriage. I felt enormously grateful to Mira—for her warmth, for her openness, for her fearlessness, for being herself. This day I had come in out of the cold, a cold in which I didn't even know I was living, and she was both the means and the end.

If I'd been sixteen, perhaps I would have made love to her again. But I was 48, and spent. So I contented myself with pulling her against me, kissing her, and mussing her hair. This turned into more kissing and semi-passion, but then soon, all too soon, it was finally time to go.

"Are we going to see each other tomorrow?" I said.

She shook her head from side to side. "I wish. I pick up the kids from Crockett about noon." I was silent for a moment, then, and so was she. The basic reality that governed our lives had reasserted itself with all its mass and gravitational force.

"I'll call you then," I said lamely. "We'll find a time." She nodded and smiled broadly. Then we left, and I drove her home.

*

I did not sleep that night until the wee hours of the morning. I kept replaying the events of the day, alternately congratulating myself and marveling at her spontaneity. I was pleased to the point of being smug. Between my careful planning and Mira's natural and acquired skills we had created a classic romantic experience, right out of Don Juan or Casanova's diaries. Or so I thought.

It did not occur to me even slightly that the reasons for the success were far more profound and significant than I was prepared to acknowledge at that time. The thought never crossed my mind that what had happened had happened because a force had entered my life that night that was far larger and more significant than anything with which I was prepared to cope.

CHAPTER 5

▼

As splendid as was the beginning of my affair with Mira, the basic texture of our lives asserted itself before I had even taken her home. The ultimate bottom line in both our situations was our children. These were the actors that held the center of the stage. Our interest in each other would have to take its place behind that. All this was self-evident to me, and I assumed Mira was essentially in agreement. The subtle flaw implicit in this apparently mature view of the world would be revealed to me soon enough.

Thus it was she had custody of her children all day Sunday, and Monday night was the rehearsal night for the amateur orchestra in which Linda played the clarinet. I was at the Big House that whole evening. The result was that the exultant high spirits of Saturday night could only be vented in two late night phone calls. We did not see each other until Tuesday, three frustrating days after the consummation of Saturday night.

Nonetheless I was moronically giddy the next few days, and Mira experienced her own version of that mood. My friends at work kept asking me what was the reason for the constant idiot's grin; and Mira told me her staff at the buildings could not understand why her focus would fade in and out. I did not help the situation by having a ridiculously large bouquet of flowers delivered to her office on Monday morning. Everyone wondered—or rather suspected—what the reason was, and the identity of the mysterious sender. Evidently the preposterous Gregor pestered her with questions the entire day. These were some of the happiest days of my life.

Tuesday evening, one of my nights off from child care, I visited her at her house. I was genuinely dismayed by the interior. Mira had done her best, but it was too dilapidated and antiquated to be disguised completely. The interior was no better than the exterior, with faded colors and wallpaper, a small dark living room that adjoined an even smaller dining room—a dining space, actually—and a midget kitchen. The furniture, what I could see of it, was tasteful, but worn, good things that had seen better days. She owned no television or stereo system. The only new item in the front room was a small steel safe, about the size of a cigar box, with a digital lock. I assumed she kept her personal papers in it.

But the most basic problem was that the house had only two bedrooms, far too small for a mother and three children of opposite sexes. The children shared a single bedroom, with bunk beds for the boys and a twin for her daughter. It was barely adequate for the children at their present level of maturity, and they would not be at that level for very much longer. Obviously there was a financial problem. What was she going to do when they were older? And how much was a commercial property manager paid, anyway?

These obviously practical thoughts flashed through my mind as I stepped over her threshold. Mira was no fool. She was as fully aware of these realities as I was. But she was absolutely unfazed. She spoke of her present difficulties as if they were rain rolling off the roof, and of her future plans as if they were already present realities. I could detect a slight Southern accent in her lovely voice now that I knew of her upbringing. I wondered whether the laid back attitude was part of that heritage.

I have mentioned it before, but that was what got to me, then and later—her inner balance, a wonderful nonchalance about even the most substantial issues of her life. I marvel at it still. Her daughter Alicia was not quite as disabled as my Nick, but her condition was severe enough to create the fundamental doubts about independence and self-sufficiency, the adequacy of financial resources for a lifetime, anxieties that plague the parents of all mentally-impaired children. I knew these worries well. They had kept me company though many a sleepless night, and way back when had been my drinking companions as well—pretty glum company. I knew for certain Mira was no stranger to them.

However, she was able to keep them at a distance that was impossible for me or for anyone else I knew. I knew she was concerned; she was up to date on every little detail about the Special Ed class, programs that were available in the area, medical advances in the field, and all the rest. But the obsessive anxiety that was the characteristic of the rest of our community was missing from her. She spoke of Alicia's condition as if it were a common cold, or some insignificant character trait her daughter might easily outgrow. It was an attitude I could only admire and envy.

She delighted me that evening, as she always did, the same thrill of excitement as when I had first laid eyes on her. The house might have been run down and unworthy, her clothes might have been ordinary working casual, but it didn't make any difference. Every corpuscle of my being seemed to be pulsating and alive. She glowed herself, with a lightness and vibrancy that leapt like an electric spark between us. Even when I was younger, I had seldom felt like this with anyone, and rarely if ever when it was reciprocated.

We were well-chaperoned that evening. We sat on her couch as the children popped in and out of bed, talking through the frequent interruptions about her and me, everything and nothing, and looking into each other's eyes. Our minds were clear, the mood was apparently untroubled, I was as content as I had been in forever—and yet, though I did not know it, the bright sky was beginning to darken, the small crack in the surface to widen.

I said as much, as we sat there, with the children darting about—that one thing I liked about where we were, where we might be going, was how nicely our lives meshed, how comfortably we could fit it all in, how smoothly and easily it could work. She sat facing me, with her hand against her hair, smiling and listening, saying very little, nodding and keeping her thoughts to herself. I assumed she was in agreement with what I believed, that we were on the same wave length. What was actually happening was that a gulf was widening under my feet, for her private thoughts were actually much, much different than what I assumed.

I have to get this right. If I am giving the impression that Mira was a weak or passive personality, I am not telling this story correctly. She was an extremely strong individual. But she was also as conventionally feminine as any woman I have ever met, by virtue of both upbringing and temperament. It was not in her character to argue with her lover, to reform him to educate him…to attempt to make him wise. Instead, she smiled and listened—and came to her own conclusions and decisions, which she kept to herself for as long as possible.

Finally, with her children in the other room and dozing, we began to kiss; when they were fully asleep, I attempted to make love to her. Another one of my long-term companions in romance, namely secondary impotence, made its unwelcome appearance at that time, and I was unable to do anything. Mira was completely untroubled by the failure, mostly because the circumstances were hardly major league in the first place. I rearranged my clothes and said good night. What was more frustrating to both of us was that it would be ten long days before we could be alone together again.

I phoned her the next night, and the night after, and all the nights in between. Thus, if I may wax metaphorical for a second, did the threads of the new relationship begin to weave themselves into the fabric of my life. The days were given over to the work routine; the evenings to Nick and Elizabeth; and only the late night hours were free for Mira and me. I phoned her regularly between 10 and 11 every night.

Often we talked until past two. I cannot remember now a single word we said or a single subject we discussed. But the memories of those nights I treasure.

What we conspicuously did not discuss was her marital situation. I had met Crockett before I met her. He seemed to be the same, laid back personality that she was (although of far lighter weight; for all her grace, Mira never struck me as anything less than formidable.) She surprised me once by casually mentioning quarrels so serious that the police were called. But the subject passed quickly and I assumed that whatever had happened had been isolated and untypical. My overall impression was that her relationship with Crockett was stable, the basic parenting co-op that everyone in these messy situations hopes to establish.

Finally ten days had passed and the Saturday arrived with mutual freedom. I took her back up to the City, this time to a regional play. Established lovers now, the day had none of the sexual tension of our first long date, and yet it had its own, different importance. To be a 'real' couple, we had to have our ordinary days as well as our special ones, and find satisfaction in each. For the first time, she slept over in my bed. Nothing sexual was possible that night due to the time of the month, but waking with Mira in my arms was delight of a different kind, more pure and perfect than I could have imagined.

What I did not imagine—could not imagine—was that the spring time of our romance—the first flush of excitement and acceptance, the best time, of fondest memories and least regrets—was flying by, was already more than half-gone.

*

The Monday following my first full night with Mira, I received an invitation to speak at a conference of Internet technical types down at Asilomar, on the Monterey peninsula, the following Friday. The subject was pornography on the `Net, a subject on which I was considered to be an expert at the time. Nice timing, I thought.

I am not a career prosecutor. I was actually a lateral hire, joining the district attorney's office about five years before these events. Mired deep in the depths of what was probably a clinical depression (although I did not know that at the time), drinking myself to sleep every night, and totally at sea in just about every area in my life, I had come to the transparent conclusion that I either had to make some drastic change in my life, or I would shortly sink with all hands on deck. Linda was an enormous help back then, in the last strong days of our marriage.

At a Halloween get-together for parents, after I brought the kids back from trick or treating, and had a beer, or two, or five, I was loose enough to express some of this quiet desperation to an old friend, without being too specific as to how badly off I really was. She was a woman of action. A day or two later, I received a call from the District Attorney of our county. I'd known him for some fifteen years, since he was a junior prosecutor and I was doing defense work by appointment. He was interested in knowing whether I'd join the office as a specialist in white-collar crimes, with a particular emphasis on high technology offenses.

In theory, I had an ideal resume for the position. I had an accounting background, and I had spent the previous decade as an entrepreneurial lawyer, involved in start-ups and software companies. One or two of them had gone public, which was what had provided me with the leisure and wherewithal to drink myself to death. I also had a substantial amount of trial experience from my days doing criminal defense for the indigent, unusual in a practitioner with my background. In theory, the only drawback was that my income level would drop substantially.

In practical reality, the job offer was a lifeline. The anxiety of private practice was killing me, and I had become so bored managing its business aspects that it was disintegrating. Linda, who had been reading the handwriting on the wall for some time, was not of two minds; she urged me to take the job. Finally I did. It was perhaps the wisest move I have ever made, the first major step out of the depression in which I was mired. Never mind that I left entrepreneurial law just before the Internet boom, that in theory (again) I would have been rich, rich, rich if I'd just hung in there. In practice, I would have been either too dead drunk or too dead—period—to profit much from it.

The five years that had passed since then had been rich in experience and rehabilitation. I was now a confirmed tea-totaler (my resolution as to that actually strengthening during the break-up), and a fully contributing member of the District Attorney's Office. The ultra-specialized niche of criminal law that I practiced came to be one that interested the public enormously. The result was that I was featured in a small, but steady trickle of publicity that I pretended to find annoying, but which I secretly enjoyed enormously. I had always been more motivated by recognition than money. Occasionally, too, a nice side benefit would appear, such as this Asilomar invite.

I had become an expert on Internet porn simply by providing a two-line quote to a reporter about one of the earliest cases. The quote was picked up by the wire services; after that, someone sought me out for an opinion each time the issue came up again, which was quite often. It's not as tough to become an expert these days as it used to be.

Normally, I would have politely declined, as this particular expert reputation was one I was desperately trying to lose. Not this time; pornography on the 'Net might not interest me at all, but Asilomar in April certainly did. The only question I asked was whether I could bring a guest. The sponsor was floored for a second, but then politely assured me that I could. He then asked me tactfully whether the guest was a woman. I answered that she certainly was, and he said he'd make the necessary arrangements.

I immediately called Mira with the news. She agreed that the commercial offices could undoubtedly spare her for a day, and our plans were set. The change of scene was one to which we both looked forward.

We drove down the next Thursday afternoon. Mira announced that she was tired of sitting in the passenger seat in my car, and that she intended to do the driving this time in her own auto. That was fine by me; I don't have any ego that way. The afternoon was another drizzly April day, but the gray skies provided a superb backdrop to the rich colors of the Peninsula.

We talked as we drove of the past, present and future. About an hour into the journey, the subject of remarriage arose—when and whether either of us would ever commit again. She wasn't fishing. The topic was purely hypothetical, since as a matter of prosaic legal fact I was still technically married. I had not done anything dishonorable—Linda and I were separated for good, finished for good, and she had filed the petition to terminate the marriage. But re-marriage wasn't legally possible no matter how clear the moral water was. Nonetheless, it was a matter to which I had given considerable thought and I gave her the same answer as always.

"Not for me," I said. "I've been married. It was actually a pretty good marriage for a long time. I can't see myself getting that serious about any one—ever again. The kids and I are sort of an extended family, and I don't think it would work to invite even the nicest stranger in." And I touched her hand and smiled. This was not the first time I had made the same point—I'd said pretty much the same thing that Tuesday night, nor the first time I had made the same gesture.

But it was one time too many.

*

The first few times I had described this world view and my plans for the future—or more accurately, my absence of plans—Mira had done her best to disregard them. I often tended to be literary and metaphorical; she had hoped that I was simply expressing my commitment to my children in a hyperbolic manner. Perhaps it was the particular manner of expression on this occasion, perhaps it was simply the cumulative number of expressions.

But the time had arrived when she could no longer ignore the reality, that I was literally serious.

Which meant that this affair, no matter how splendid its beginning, no matter how deep the feeling (and she knew how deep that actually was, even if I did not), was doomed to languish in the sphere of the casual. But this was not something that could ever be confined to the realm of the merely casual. She had known she had more experience in romance than I did, but now she realized how great the gap actually was.

Passion of the type that was possible between us—grand passion—was (she believed) the greatest and most glorious gift imaginable. It could not be compartmentalized, it could not be confined. By its nature it swept away boundaries, divisions, uncertainties. Of course there were competing claims, duties, obligations, serious matters, and of course they were utterly irreconcilable with the force of this feeling, the dimensions of possibility. So you did what you always do when two irreconcilable forces of this dimension and intensity clash—somehow you reconcile them. You don't insist on some artificial compartmentalization of life and feeling. You don't slander the depth of your own emotion.

You don't hide from it behind the walls you've built, alone in your fortress.

I did not notice her gnawing her lower lip. All my idiot emphatic pronouncements about the importance of keeping things in place and what not had hit some critical mass. The realization spun down, unavoidable, like being punched in the solar plexus, that I meant that stuff—that I was dead serious. Mira knew she had a decision to make and what the decision had to be. There was nothing more to say. And yet helplessly, compulsively, she spoke again.

*

"I don't think you're being entirely fair to yourself, Walt," she said lightly. "Your children are very special, mine are, too, but we have to leave some room for ourselves and our own needs. We can't give up our own lives entirely for them. It won't work."

"They're not the ones responsible for this mess," I answered. "Linda and I are. You and Crockett. I don't want them to suffer any of the consequences of this. And if that means I have to do some giving-up of my own—" I shrugged—"so be it. That's what I'll do."

*

You're a good man, Walter, she thought. A very good man.
Too good.

*

Our dialog more or less died out as we proceeded down Highway One. Mira seemed lost in thought, and I became involved in meditations of my own. I had not the slightest idea what I'd done. The evening had drawn on before we arrived at the hotel/inn. I carried our overnight bags up to the room. We changed, and came down for dinner.

The restaurant was truly excellent. I had hoped that cuisine of this quality would tempt even Mira to eat something of substance, but not so. She seemed to have even less appetite than usual (a thing astonishing to say), and a lot less gaiety. I wondered if something was wrong, but she explained that the drive had tired her more than she had expected. I did not entirely believe her; her mood was darker than any I could remember; and it began to affect me as well, to unnerve me.

"Darling, is there anything the matter?" I asked.

"Nothing at all," she answered, with a forced smile that did nothing to reassure me.

I decided not to press the issue; I had known her scarcely a month, which is to say I scarcely knew her at all. She was a human being. Of course she would have her dark moods and moments, like all of us.

Could I expect anything else? And yet I was bothered. I could not shake the feeling that the darkness was related to something I had said or done. I did not associate it with our light talk on the subject of remarriage in the afternoon, for this was stuff that had come up often enough before. I did not realize that the problem was that it had come up one time too often.

After dinner, we went back up to the room. We watched television for a while—Mira hated television, but she obliged me—then turned out the light. I thought we'd make love, but Mira was totally lacking in enthusiasm, and I was unable to do anything. We fondled each other in the dark, I caressed her face and body. Finally, we—or rather I—lapsed into an uneasy, puzzled sleep.

The morning was a different story. Whatever inhibitions I had had vanished with the dawn. All I knew was that I was a man and beside me a willing woman with a slender, exquisite body and the elegance of royalty. I decided to awaken her honeymoon style. I moved her gently off my shoulder, nuzzled her ear, her neck, then kissed her softly. She came to semi-wakefulness, I aroused her fully, and then pulled her to me.

As she felt the penetration, her hands came up and clutched my shoulders convulsively, literally smacking aloud as they did, as if she were a drowning woman and I was salvation. She had been passionate before, but not like this. She came to the end more quickly than the other time, in the same silent, graceful way. My own finish came a bit later. As I bridged my weight, canopying her body, she pressed her face hard against my shoulder. I felt moisture. Immediately all the misgivings of the previous evening returned.

"Mira," I said gently, "darling…my lovely Mira…what's the matter?"

"*Nothing's* the matter," she insisted. "It was just beautiful is all."

"Are you sure?" I whispered softly.

"Yes," she whispered back. "I love the way you take me, Walter. So direct and masculine, but so tenderly." I held her for a long moment, treasuring her, fully aware—for a moment—of how precious she truly was. What I would have done, how I would have reacted, if I had known how long and tortuous the road ahead was going to be, how completely different the ultimate denouement from anything like a fairy-tale ending, I don't know.

We got up, then, and began the day. Mira went for a run, something she found time to do nearly every day. I ordered us some breakfast. After a while, we went over to the assembly hall. This was the last day of what had been a week-long meeting. The conventioneers were all computer network people, software gurus, system operators, and the like. They were a fairly nerdy lot that particular day, but unless they were extremely unlucky, since then they've all become filthy rich. Though the seminar I was in was serious enough, it was also the getaway event. So to add interest and entertainment value, the organizers had broadened the panel. It transpired I was sharing the podium with a fairly well-known ACLU type from the Pacifica Foundation, and a genuine porn star from the San Francisco area.

The morning thus unexpectedly had quite a lot of entertainment value, with a good, lively debate. It worked out particularly well for me. The ACLU type proved to be a typically fussy, ivory-tower liberal, and the porn star—not surprisingly, quite striking and superbly endowed—had the i.q. of a fence post in June. That left the field clear for yours truly, a very sweet situation when there's someone in the audience you want to impress. I managed to be wise and witty, in a charitable, kindly understated way, comfortably in command of all I surveyed. I could see Mira in the back of the hall, laughing with the others, her eyes filled with admiration.

All my misgivings of the night and morning vanished. Her mood, so I supposed, was just one of those things. Everything was going to return to normal. Everything was going to be fine.

*

Not so.

There were a few lively moments on the way home, but for the most part Mira had returned to the dark, pensive mood of the day before. She gently, but firmly, resisted any attempt of mine to tease or cajole her out of it. My worries returned. Something was clearly wrong, and I didn't know what.

It was impossible for us to be together that Friday evening, as I had child care, or later that weekend, as her turn for custody began. We had two brief, impersonal phone conversations that did nothing to allay my misgivings. I was sure I was losing her, but I didn't know why, and she refused to give me any explanation or even to admit that there was anything wrong.

With heart and mouth, I called her about 10:00 Monday evening, the time when we had our customary heart-to-heart chats. But this evening there was no connection, no rapport. I knew I was trying, my impression was that she was trying as well, and yet it seemed as if some invisible barrier had sprung up between us. I did not press her for reasons; I had done that already; but I hung up the phone agitated, in feverish anxiety. I did not fall asleep until 4:00 in the morning.

The next night I was determined to find out what in blazes had happened. "Mira," I said the moment she picked up the receiver, "I know that something's wrong. You can trust me, you know that. I'm not going to hurt you, my darling, and I'm not going to be angry. But please tell me what's bothering you. *Please.*"

After a long moment, the ax fell. "Walt," she said quietly, "I don't think we should see each other any more."

My worst expectation had become concrete. "Why not?" I asked, in an even a tone as I could muster.

"Walt—" she began—I heard a hesitation in her tone and I knew she was choosing word carefully, speaking from the heart—"do you realize how special all this is? How unusual? I've worried you think I let every man—"

"I never thought that," I interrupted truthfully. I'd never thought any such thing.

"Good—because I don't. What we have is very special, Walt. I feel I can talk to you like I can't talk to anyone else, like you'll understand anything I say. And I feel like I'm completely open to you, like you know my thoughts even while I'm thinking them. I haven't met many men who affect me like you do, Walt. Certainly no one recently."

"The feeling's mutual, Mira," I agreed quietly.

"You talk about finding space for each other. But I don't want to be just a *part* of your life," she answered immediately. "Don't you under-stand—we *can't* be just a part of each other—it's not like that for us. It's not like that—" she could not find additional words.

"I don't know what to say," I answered. "You know we both have commitments."

"I know," she answered, "and we have to honor those. But we have to be fair to this one, too. It's too special."

"I don't know what to say," I repeated stupidly.

*

In those earlier conversations, I had spoken truth in large part. Those priorities *were* my priorities; those plans *were* my plans; and, as much as I wanted Mira, wanted to be with her, the nightmare vision of that eternal recurrence, my mother's life collapsing at age 10, my soon-to-be ex-wife's at the same age, Elizabeth's, Nicholas and his problems—these *were* the major basis of my unshakeable commit-ments.

But side-by-side with the large part was the small part, and maybe it wasn't all that small. Maybe it was even the larger part. It had to do with shattered confidence. Romeo, if he meets Juliet in his late 40's, will think a lot of thoughts. But mostly he won't believe it's really happening. There will have been too many false starts, too many misjudgments, too much disappointment for him to have the energy, the resolution to pledge his entire being on his own sense of destiny. He will be too unsure of himself, too hobbled by self-doubt and uncertainty. Perhaps that is the price that must be paid for maturity and wisdom.

Perhaps it is too high a price.

I had known her only a short time, but I understood entirely what Mira meant as she spoke to me that night. I had my own sense of what she might mean to me, how important we might be to each other. But I was not ready to stand my world on its end for her, disrupt the universe if need be. I was too shaky, too unsure of myself. I lacked the confidence, the resolution, to do that—in a phrase, I did not trust myself enough to make the colossal leap of faith necessary.

Or perhaps all this is just a gussied up way of saying I lacked the guts. I don't know. I hope not.

*

"You *are* important to me, Mira—more important than anything—except those kids. And what I have to do for them," I answered.

"I understand, Walt," she said quietly, "and I respect you for that. But compartments and space and that sort of thing won't work for us. Don't you see?"

"*Mira,*" I said, because I *did* see, and argument was failing.

"It's going to hurt now," she said, then gulped. "Walt, it's not that I don't—I mean, I do—" *love you,* I believe she was going to say—"but I will not settle for less than what we owe each other. It won't work. It's going to hurt a lot more later. So I think it's best this end right now."

The thought crossed my mind that Mira was as decisive, as true to herself, in finality, as she had been in commencement. She was never the weepy type, but suddenly I knew that her eyes were bright with tears, and the vision was unendurable. I could not continue with this.

"Whatever you say," I said despondently. "We're still going to be friends?"

"*Of course* we're going to be friends," she said warmly. The thought that I would never hear the rich musicality of her voice directed towards me, to me, for me personally, never be mine again, stuck like a dagger in my heart. "But maybe not for a little while. For just a little while."

"All right," I said. There was a long, long silence.

"I guess this is it, then." She was on the verge of tears. "Good-bye, Walter Royer Kelsey," she said softly.

"Good bye, Elmira Watson," I said. I pronounced the 'Mira' part with a deliberately long 'I'. I heard her musical laugh—well, better that than tears—and then the line was dead.

She was gone.

*

So many things are apparent to me now that weren't then. What had happened in plain terms was that, in the short time I had known her, the happiness of Mira Watson had come to matter a great deal to me. She possessed a remarkable personal beauty that both charmed and fascinated me. It was a rare and delicate quality of spirit that I regarded as precious beyond estimation. Of course there was a strong sexual element in this feeling—she was also a wonderfully attractive woman— but in this case the sexual pull was where the caring ended, not where it began. I wanted her, and in that wanting, I wanted her to be happy.

What all that meant was that, in the prosaic, non-magical, non-transforming actual meaning of the word, I had come to love Mira whole-heartedly. That was the reality. Denying that reality didn't alter that reality. Denial didn't make me care any less about her well-being; it didn't make my well-being one iota less dependent on hers. All denial did was leave her and her marvelous self open and vulnerable to all those others who might not prize her as highly as I did—and thus, inevitably, make me vulnerable as well. Like it or not, our life tracks had been tied together.

But I did not see these things then in the same clear light I do now. Back then I was a demoralized man, trying to keep a shattered life from collapsing altogether. I was through with love—so I thought. The last thing in the world I had ever expected was feelings of the magnitude that Mira had engendered. I was not prepared to admit that that had happened, let alone cope with that fact. I was not ready to change the world for her.

Such was my mistake, and such was the essence of its simplicity— for my world *had* changed by my meeting her and knowing her. It was useless and silly not to accept that fact as a fact. When the configuration of the universe has been rearranged, it is stupid and even dangerous to insist that it has not. But that's what I did.

Ending with Mira was the decision of an idiot, the largest, stupidest, and silliest mistake of my entire life. But by itself it was not fatal. There would be plenty of opportunities in the days and years ahead to rectify the error. The Destiny that I didn't think existed exhibited an incredible amount of patience and determination with us. A long, long time would pass before the final lines of the story would be written.

CHAPTER 6

▼

The grace of the dancer is illusion itself. The performer's craft is most in evidence when least perceived. What is difficult seems simple; what is extraordinary becomes commonplace. What is impossible actually seems to exist.

*

These are the most difficult parts of the story for me to tell, for after this I lost contact with Mira for large periods of time. Later I would learn a great deal of the large outline of what happened, but little or nothing of the fine details. As it happens, what she did on the day after she broke it off is one of the details I do know. It proved to be an eventful day quite apart from the events of the night before. It was one of the things she filled me in on—much later, as we spoke, wandering among the ruins.

What she had done was much harder on her than I had any idea at the time. The next day was one of those on which the complexity of her life was an enormously useful distraction. The children, used to thinking of her as an elemental part of their emotional landscape, like the sky or a mountain range, noticed nothing. Her tenants were in their usual state of perpetual crisis. If anyone noticed she was not entirely her usual self, no one said anything.

A new tenant was scheduled to occupy the entire second and third floors of one of her buildings. A shipping firm, it had required both an elaborate PBX installation and a state-of-the-art computer network. The two networks were interdependent; the two independent contractors were supposed to have consulted with each other and developed a joint plan of attack. As is so often the case, what was supposed to happen and what actually did happen were two entirely different things. Two sets of workmen, each with their own directions and priorities, both sets of directions and priorities developed entirely independent of the other, and—inevitably—each completely and irreconcilably inconsistent with the other, had arrived at the office suite at 9:00 a.m., whereupon all hell had broken loose. She felt a bit guilty; her voice mail contained several messages on the subject, all received on Friday at a time when the only thing on her mind had been how good it was going to feel to wake up the next morning in my arms.

But on this day she welcomed the distraction. These were situations in which she excelled. She hadn't the slightest idea where the technical solution might lie, but she had a good idea where the human one lay. First she got the two sides talking to her, then, after a while, talking to each other. Soon someone had an idea, and someone else had an improvement on it. The knot began to untie itself.

It was a good project for Mira, requiring a decent exercise of her skills and keeping her mind off unpleasant recent events.

*

I was not having that great a day myself, but nonetheless better than hers. Although I'd had a premonition of what was coming, the abruptness of it was still a shock. But—in the mindset I had at that time—I regarded it as one of those consequences that I had to accept if I was going to accomplish what I had to. And I found a perverse reason for optimism in the whole chain of events—if I had found one Mira in so short a period of time after the separation, surely I could find another, one a little more on my wavelength about life styles. Also—I have to

reveal a blunt truth here—the fact that it had been sexually consum-
mated, and at a fairly high level at that, I saw as another plus. A vitality
had returned to my life, something that I thought had disappeared forever; once regained, it would never be lost again.

Yet despite all those upbeat rationalizations, I sat in my office for
most of the day, numb and brooding, getting next to nothing done. I
had at that time only a shadowy access to Mira's larger wisdom. I had
only an inkling, only the slightest glimmering of a realization, of how
much I'd truly lost.

*

*In the midst of the mediation, she was interrupted by the inevitable
Monday morning phone call from Gregor Volkov. I say inevitable because
a weekend seldom passed without some issue or other jumping up, This
time it was security; evidently, one of the janitors had left the back door to
the building unlocked, or so Volkov thought. The fact that nothing had
been disturbed in no way reassured him. All that meant was that the
intruders had been sophisticated and sinister enough to cover their tracks.*

*She had to have lunch, and get the workmen—a common plan having
finally been agreed upon—launched. But a little after two, she made her
way over to the other site to settle down Volkov.*

*Mira had an interesting relationship with Gregor Volkov. I had seen
some hint of its complexity during the excursion on that first Saturday
night. The dislike I had taken to Gregor Volkov at their one meeting was
not unusual; it was typical. Initial reactions to Volkov were restricted to
one-half of the bell-shaped curve. Some people loathed him at first sight,
some people disliked him, others became completely exasperated, and the
rest of them were merely mightily annoyed. No one liked him.*

*The one rule-proving exception to the rule was Mira herself. She was
fully aware of all of the negative qualities readily apparent to the rest of the
world—arrogance, stubbornness, a degree of suspiciousness that stopped
only one station short of paranoiaville (if indeed it did stop there), and,*

above all, a profound self-absorption as near as makes no difference to complete egomania.

And yet she liked him. His offices were always lively. There was always a buzz of something important happening or about to happen. From the outset, she had found him fascinating. I would have been appalled if I'd known she had let Gregor squat in the office for over three months before he signed the lease and began paying rent. He'd been penniless, imploring, and belligerent when he first appeared in the rental office; the combination had been oddly moving and ultimately impossible to resist. The risk to her job had not been negligible, but she was fully aware of how difficult she would be to replace. Anyway, the job was going to be as temporary as the house.

Gratitude was not a major quality in the personality make-up of Gregor Volkov. A different personality might have kept a low profile, stayed out of harm's way, made her job as easy as possible. Not Volkov; he called on her constantly, querulous and demanding, even before he began paying actual rent. Once he did get some money together and sign a formal lease, the calls became incessant. However, the meeting that occurred on that Morning After was unusually significant, even fateful. Most of what follows is reconstructed from what Mira told me directly, a little from my own experience of the way these things usually go.

*

Since Gregor Volkov was also one of the most volatile personalities she had ever met, Mira was not surprised to find that the monumental crisis of the morning had either been completely solved or (more likely) completely forgotten. When she arrived, he was standing in front of a whiteboard, engaged in a heated argument with the two other members of Echelon, the small company he had formed. There was a block diagram on the whiteboard, some sort of rudimentary software architecture, that much she knew from glimpses she'd had of the premises of other tenants. But that was about all that was clear to her, as this heated argument was conducted in Russian, the everyday language of Echelon.

"Mira!" he exclaimed, when he finally noticed her. "You're finally here! Where have you been?!"

"I had more urgent problems to deal with, Gregor," she said. "Whatever happened here happened over the weekend. There really isn't much that could be done this morning. And I'm not so sure that anything did happen."

"What! You mean you haven't called the police?!" His face bore a look of pure horror.

Mira sighed. As usual with Gregor, the possibility of error on his part, despite the fact that he was the stranger in the strange land, had not even crossed his mind. This was the reason that he'd been feuding with all the neighboring tenants and half her staff within a month of moving in—even though he was not paying rent at the time.

"The police would think we were both idiots, Gregor. There's nothing missing. There's nothing disturbed." Before he could interrupt, she pressed on. "What makes you think the building was open?"

He told her. His normal morning routine had been interrupted by a Usenet posting on a software newsgroup that panicked him into thinking a rival start-up might be beating Echelon to market. He'd raced out to buy a copy of a technical journal. As he returned, he was shocked to see the back-door open.

"Gregor," she explained patiently, "occupancy in this building begins at about 6:00 in the morning. The security service opens the door at that time because it has to. It's code—fire and earthquake safety. It happens every morning. The building wasn't open over the weekend."

She knew him too well to believe that this explanation would satisfy him, and she was entirely right. His eyes opened wide. "What!! You mean, security is compromised every morning between six and eight? Mira, I had no idea! Oh my God, we have been vulnerable this whole time! Who knows how much we have been compromised?! How could you do this to me?"

Today was not the right day for this nonsense. "Gregor," she snapped, "you have not been compromised in the slightest. No one has seen anything. No one has stolen anything. Be sensible. The valley is loaded with start-ups just like yours. There's no reason why any one is especially interested in Echelon."

Gregor looked at her with an expression that was an equal mixture of exasperation and amazement. "Mira, you don't know what you are saying, You have no idea, you literally have no idea, what we are doing, how important it is, how valuable it is, how many competitors—" His expression suddenly changed. His voice softened. "Look, perhaps you would like it if I told you of these things over dinner. I would love you to know why it is I am so nervous about these things."

The dinner invitation, too, was a Monday morning ritual, or Tuesday ritual, or every-time-she-had-any-kind-of-contact-with-Gregor-Volkov ritual. She had been gently declining them for nearly four months now. She was about to decline this one as well, when the thought struck her—why not? Her friend Nancy would cover for the kids for a couple of hours; they had a reciprocal arrangement covering this sort of situation. This was not an evening in which she could be content with the satisfactions of motherhood. A little time with a naive—an extremely naive—admirer would be a welcome tonic. Perhaps a necessary tonic.

"All right," she said, and had to laugh, because his jaw literally dropped open. The notion that she might accept had obviously never occurred to him. "I'll meet you about six. I can't stay too long. I have custody of my children tonight, and I have homework for my class. But I'd like to hear about what you're doing."

Gregor Volkov looked like a man who had just discovered that the age of miracles had not passed after all. "Mira! So finally you relent! I promise you, you will not regret this! When I tell you what we intend, what we have done—"

"Now, Gregor," she teased, "aren't you afraid of compromising your project? After all, you hardly know me." Before he could answer, she moved off.

"I'll see you at six," she called over her shoulder.

*

A dinner date as planned by Gregor Volkov took place at a working man's bar, sawdust on the floor, one step up from Burger King if that. It was pretty much what she had expected. She felt fortunate to find a chicken Caesar salad on the menu; she was able to nibble away at that—

—while Gregor Volkov talked…and talked…and talked—about himself, his company, his product, himself, his life in Odessa and then Moscow, his product, himself, and finally himself. In the nearly two hour monologue, he did not ask one question about her, not even about so elementary an item as her marital status. It was the easiest socializing Mira had ever done—all she had to do was smile and nod her head from time to time.

It was all about the Internet and Internet security in particular. She knew what the Internet was in general, of course. She had too many tenants and there was too much buzz not to know. But this was 1995, she did not at that time have Internet access of her own, and the extent of her knowledge was a vague impression that some vast computer interconnectivity existed out there somewhere, doing something. From what she could glean from Gregor, he and his friends were working on something to do with an Internet security device, a black box that could function as what he called a `firewall' and do all sorts of marvelous things as well. Gregor and his friends had named the gizmo the Firebird. Mira could not at that time have told the difference between a computer byte and a shark bite, but she had developed over the years a keen general business sense. Besides which, there was something in the relentless egoism of Gregor Volkov that she found oddly attractive.

"How big is the market for this thing?" she asked, when he paused for breath and she was finally able to get a word in edgewise.

"Infinite, Mira, infinite! Every sysop—every local area network man-
ager—not to mention wide area networks—and of course intranet and
ISP companies—all of them—"

"No, no, no," she interrupted. "How big in dollars?"

"Hundreds of millions! Billions! Billions of billions! Around the world!"

She felt a tremor of excitement. She thought of her house, how much she
hated it, how much she wanted out. "Gregor, how are the three of you
going to be able to exploit a market of that size? I mean, I'm sure you're all
marvelous technologists, geniuses and what not, but you're going to need
marketing people, sales people, competent and experienced and able to work
internationally. How are you going to do that?"

"We will get venture capital, of course," he shrugged, almost contemptu-
ously. "Once they see what our firewall can do, they will come to us. Beg-
ging to invest with us, pleading to be shareholders."

The delusional innocence of this was so awesome in its grandeur, that
she was touched despite the infantile arrogance. She knew little of comput-
ers, but a great deal about performing arts, enough to be aware that his
chances of making any effective presentation to the venture capitalists she
knew (more than a few) were non-existent. The thought of the crushing
disappointments that lay ahead of him, just over the horizon, made her
suddenly tender.

"It's not that easy, Gregor," she said gently. "The VC's I know are pretty
tough—"

"You know venture capitalists, Mira?" He sounded as if she had just
admitted knowing Martians.

"Well, of course I do. As tenants, and friends—I've even dated some of
them—and I—"

"Then you can help!" he boomed. "You will tell your friends of us! Once
they know of the Firebird, they will invest for certain!"

This of course was exactly what she had intended to propose, but she had
not expected to be co-opted so swiftly and so directly. Somehow her role had
been defined without her participation. There was the small matter of com-
pensation to discuss, finder's fees and the like. But Gregor's face was alive

with enthusiasm and determination, fixed on the distant goal, strangely transformed from its usual homeliness—and fixing the price seemed in some way pedestrian and ignoble. Besides, this was the aspect of his personality she found endearing, this naïve, openly self-centered enthusiasm, completely unlike any of the sophisticates she knew.

"All right, Gregor," she smiled, "I will help. And I'll give you a hand with your presentation as well. Because something tells me you really <u>need</u> a hand."

"Wonderful!" he exulted. "Perfect!" Then he lowered his voice and his expression took on a sly, vulpine look. "Hey, what do you say, we go to bed and really seal the deal, huh?"

Mira laughed aloud, her delighted, uninhibited bell-like laugh. It was good to know that some things never change.

"No, thank you," she said. "I think the deal is sealed enough, Mr. Volkov."

The vulpine expression didn't change. "Some other time, huh?" he said, undeterred.

A few moments later, it was time for Mira to return to her children and her real life. She disengaged herself from Gregor, and made her way to the exit. She was no sooner out the door than thoughts of Walter crowded in on her. They were as numerous as the day and night before, but something fundamental had changed. Whatever the losses in the recent past, the future for a change held promise of a little excitement and some genuine hope.

*

I knew nothing of this event, as I have reconstructed it above, at the time it happened. Even if I had it wouldn't have changed anything.

But I believe I shuddered at the time this happened, alone in my condominium, as if someone had stepped on my grave. It doesn't seem possible that the moment passed unmarked.

CHAPTER 7

▼

I am not a man in particularly good touch with himself. It may sound odd in these excessively self-conscious times to hear a man declare that he often doesn't know whether he's happy or sad, content or uneasy, at peace or at war, but it is the fact. I'm hardly unique in this way. Many more persons than you'd ever suppose lose themselves in the hurly-burly of everyday events and seldom if ever bother to take their own inner temperature. I'm one of them. After my marriage fell apart, friends and foe alike would ask me how I was doing. It took me a long time to realize what the only truthful answer was.

`I don't know'. Because usually I didn't.

I genuinely didn't know how I was doing, what I was feeling, where I was going, unless I gave conscious thought to the matter, which I seldom did. When the mild osteoarthritis I have flares up, what I experience is an overall, generalized achiness. It takes an effort of will for me to identify the particular joint that is actually bothering me. The same thing holds true for other types of pain in my life.

Mira left me in the last week of April in 19—. Of course I missed her, and I knew that I missed her. But the affair had been of brief duration, and I expected the missing to be similarly brief. Also, I hoped— not unreasonably, I suppose—that having found one supremely desirable woman so easily that another might turn up just as easily. But early spring turned to late spring, late spring became early summer, and I remained mired in gloom. The days of long twilight just before and after the summer solstice are usually my favorite days of all. But not that year. My frame of mind remained dark, my spirits low. I didn't pay too much attention. I accepted that state of mind as a given, and slogged on day to day, caught up in my daily routine. I didn't give the matter enough thought to consider the causes, or what might have been wrong with my life.

There were other factors as well. May was the first anniversary of the marital separation, the date when I had moved out and over to the condominium. A year had passed, but Linda was still working through problems of her own. It occurred to me she might be clinically depressed (as I could see that I had been), and I said as much out loud. But she had no interest in counseling. She began taking trips nearly every weekend, gone always one night and sometimes both. I didn't know whether she was with a man, or some woman's group (she had adopted a considerable amount of feminist rhetoric), or even some religious organization. I didn't much care. Elizabeth was baffled and hurt by the emotional vacancy. Nicholas was protected to some extent by his condition, but still vulnerable in his own way.

The result was even greater demands on my time and energy. I did not moralize about this with Linda. I didn't have the right. Five years earlier, I had been the deserter. My desertion did not take the form of week-end trips or divorce, but the isolation of the bottle, night after night of the brooding, solitary drinking of a middle-aged Irish melancholic. Linda had been the strong one then, baffled and worried about me, but doing her best to cope. Now her turn had come to hit the mid-life wall. The crunch in her case may have taken the form of anger and separation, rather than depression and alcohol, but the process was the same, and I had no difficulty in recognizing it for what it was. What it meant is that my turn to cope had come.

So there was nothing to be done. I shouldered the burden and soldiered on. Mira's successor, to the extent there could be one—my hopes in that area were, of course, complete idiocy—was another item that would have to wait.

Memories of Mira recurred to me frequently, almost constantly, hardly surprising under the circumstances. What was surprising was the type of memory. As I am a man of normal virility (actually, like most normal men, I believe I am way, way above normal) and I don't enjoy extended celibacy any more than any other, I would have expected my memories to be mostly the hot-hot-hot stuff, as Mira at her most passionate was a triple-x rated woman and then some. Of course these thoughts did occur, on all sorts of unexpected occasions, leaving me sweaty and distracted.

The surprising element was that most of what returned out of the blue was not at all sexual. The vast majority were memories of her voice, its music, its clarity. I was involved in an extended trial in the early part of the summer, involving nine defendants charged with theft and receiving stolen property. The proceeding, with so many defense lawyers engaged in what was essentially an indefensible case, inevitably became hostile and fractious, with committee-think ruling the day and the judge too often disposed to make silly rulings based on the sheer weight of numbers. Since I have never been one to suffer fools lightly, the proceeding became a day-to-day, moment-to-moment challenge to my limited reserves of patience. More than once, as I was on the verge of jeopardizing my career by telling everyone around me what I *really* thought, I would hear Mira's voice, balanced, amused, with all its poise and loveliness, counseling calmness, reminding me that this, too, would pass. It was advice I usually needed and always took.

I did not consider what, if anything, this might mean. Like the other events of my life, I accepted it as a phenomenon without concerning myself too much about the causes.

*

In July, Linda announced that she would be traveling to Tibet for the entire month of October. This naturally exhausted her travel budget for the year. As that left the kids without any summer trip, I sprang into action. I had intended for some years to visit Disney World at Orlando (the Anaheim version was closer, but too familiar), and now an occasion had arisen in which the trip was not only desirable, but almost necessary. I scheduled us for ten days there over two weekends in late August.

It was perhaps the best trip I ever took in my life, the one bright spot in that long, dull summer. We saw all the sights and did all the deeds. The two children were too different in maturity to keep together—all Nick wanted to do was ride on the paddleboat, the whole livelong day. Elizabeth, of course, wanted to do other things. I solved the problem by handing to my eleven-year old daughter her gate pass and, with it, her first taste of adult freedom. For a day she could go anywhere and do anything (I had absolute confidence in her good sense about strangers and like temptations) and that is exactly what she did. Nick and I rode the paddleboat on one of the most endless days of my life. Each time around, he shouted with delight at the same sights, as if he had never seen them before. I stayed at the back of the boat, attempting to read some useless paperback, but mostly thinking over what was past and what was to come.

At that time, my expectation was that I would never see Mira again. Directly after the break, I hadn't let my mind wander down that path too often, as the immediate effect was searing pain. (Whatever my other lunacies, I was never in any doubt that I wanted her.) That day, though, the memories were somewhat wistful, bittersweet, the sort that belong with a long-lost love rather something that had happened only a few months before. It all seemed far, far away, with the Florida sun, Nick delighted and laughing, and the silly book lying open, face down, unread on my lap. Very soon, I decided, Mira Watson would be only a distant, pleasant memory. But even then, with the big paddle spraying droplets, my lovely boy in his own personal heaven on a perfect summer day, even then, I could not be altogether resigned and wistful. The thought hurt.

*

The greeting committee that welcomed me back from Orlando consisted of an overflowing mailbox, and one hundred and three voice mail messages. I opened my mail casually as I reviewed the voicemails. The thirty-seventh made me sit bolt upright.

"Hey there, Walt," sounded the voice I had heard so often in various daydreams. "This is Mira. I hope you've had a nice summer. Could you call me, please? I have a little problem with Crockett I hoped you could help me with."

My pulse rate speeded and the day suddenly took on a fresher, brighter cast. The review of the accumulated voice messages ended that very moment. I returned her call at once. It had been a small, standing joke between Mira and me that I almost never found her in—she was always in transit between buildings or face-to-face with some tenant—but on this rare occasion, she actually answered her own phone.

"Walter!" she exclaimed mildly, with that voice like a matin bell in a small chapel, and her obvious pleasure at hearing from me was the purest tonic to my soul.

"Mira," I answered, trying to sound as pleased as she was and succeeding easily. "I hadn't expected to hear from you. What a pleasure."

"Thank you, Walt," she breathed. "I'm afraid I need a favor. I'm having some problems in family court. With Crockett."

"Crockett?!" I said. The reason she'd called truly surprised me. "My impression was that you guys were getting along great."

"Impressions aren't always correct," she said, with the usual light musicality. If she was feeling pressure, it certainly wasn't evident in her manner. "I need a little help."

"Family court is not exactly my bag, darling," I answered. "Family law is about the only kind of law I haven't done. So I don't know what help I can be. But I'll do what I can."

"Thank you, Walt," she said again, and this time the relief and gratitude in her voice was evident. I wondered what kind of problem she had. We made a date for lunch the next day. I replaced the receiver with my heart singing. I tried to recover the mindset of conscientious civil servant—to be absolutely honest, I found that particular mindset hard to achieve at the best of times—and get back to the voicemail review, but just then it wasn't possible. I left my office and paced up and down the hall for a few moments, working off my exhilaration.

One of the paralegals looked up. "That's the first time I've heard you whistle all summer," she smiled.

*

We met the next day at a little restaurant, a sports bar actually, directly adjacent to one of the buildings Mira managed. We had been there one or two times during our brief affair. It was a good place for us, one at which ordinary human beings like me could get decently fed, and people like Mira could meditate on the inner beauty of baby carrots. On this particular day, she had arrived and was seated before I got there. Mira was one of the most feminine women I have ever met, but not in any conventional way, and one of the conventional mannerisms that she refreshingly lacked was any tendency to be fashionably late. She was always either on time or early.

"What's up?" I asked, after we'd exchanged greetings and caught up on children and family news. A large accordion file sat to her left.

"It's Crockett," she said, "and the family court." She pulled a legal pleading out of the file, and a rough draft of something, and passed the documents over. I scanned them, quickly at first, then more slowly, and with increasing amazement.

Callous neglect...reckless disregard...systematic indifference—it was the worst kind of family court garbage, hyperbolic and ridiculous, with repetitive and preposterously overstated allegations of parental incompetence. The particular pea at the bottom of this enormous stack of mattresses was apparently some problem with the timing of a visit at the camp for disabled children Alicia had attended that summer. I glanced at the heading of the petition. It had been prepared on behalf of Crockett Watson, all right, by an attorney notorious for his misogyny and contentiousness—the worst type of family court practitioner. That is really saying something, since it would place him at the absolute bottom of the barrel both as a lawyer and as a human being.

"Crockett did this?" I said stupidly. "Why?" *Casual, laidback Crockett?* It didn't seem possible.

"Crockett files petitions like this any time he can," she answered calmly. "Every few weeks." And she handed over the accordion file.

If I had been amazed before, now I was dumbfounded. The file contained similar petitions and responses filed over the last three years—every two months or so, sometimes even monthly. They were all venomous—the one I had initially read was hardly the worst—and they all seemed to be based on the same sort of trivial causes, incidents that in an intact family wouldn't be worth a second mention. But the most staggering surprise was the caption on the responses—*Mira Watson/In Pro Per.* The slight, graceful woman sitting across the table from me, a mere wisp of a girl, had been standing up to this the barrage all on her own, without any support or legal assistance, for three years or longer.

"I don't understand," I said finally, stupidly, looking up at her.

"Crockett wants the kids," she answered simply. "Particularly his sons. Or rather his mother does. It's kind of complicated."

"Tell me more," I prodded.

"Crockett's dad left when he was very little. I don't know the exact reason, but having met Suzanne, I have a pretty good guess why." She laughed. "He always felt deserted by his father—and he's determined that the same thing won't happen to his own children. So he brings these petitions all the time."

"O.k. He wants the kids. Commendable. But what's the point in beating up you? They need a mother as well as a father."

She shook her head. "Walt, the process isn't entirely rational. Crockett's mother—that's Suzanne—absolutely dominates him. She's rich and old and he's her only son. He's never really gotten out from under her thumb. He's a soccer coach in his mid thirties. It isn't very much. Everyone knows that. He knows that. Crockett has a lot more to him, but he's never really had a chance. Or maybe never given himself a chance. He thinks he loves her, and I suppose he does, but he's also afraid of her and maybe he hates her as well. But he can't very well say that out loud. So he takes it out on me. I think at some level he feels that if he saves his children from me he'll be saving himself from his mother."

I tried to digest all this. *Good ol', laidback Crockett.* I hadn't guessed and I never would have. The whole process was so sad and futile; its uselessness was possibly the most significant of the insights I had gleaned from my own childhood. It is not possible to win an intimate war; this truth I know from prolonged, direct, painful observation. The gains won on one battlefield one day are surrendered on a different part of the emotional turf the next or the day after. 'What comes around, goes around' is not a saying that is often true in the larger world, but it is absolutely the fact in family wars. Crockett didn't realize that.

Nor is it possible for one parent to alienate the affections of a child from the other. Only the parent him—or her—self can accomplish that feat. My chronically insecure mother, perpetually and neurotically worried that she would be cheated out of her just due by all the people who would otherwise have loved her, continually belittled and undercut my father in my presence during my entire childhood. But each ferocious tantrum only increased my protective affection for my father, while also increasing my fearful wariness of her. This utterly predict-able outcome naturally made her all the more insecure, which moti-vated her to do even more undercutting, and so on and so forth, throughout the whole of her married life. She could not or would not acknowledge the obvious fact, that she was damaging herself, not my father, that the process was working in reverse. Crockett was appar-ently no more willing to appreciate the actual consequences of his behavior than my poor mother had been.

What a complete, senseless farce, visited upon the Watson children courtesy of the immaturity of one spouse and the American justice sys-tem. I glanced again at the responses—*Mira Watson/In Propria Per-sona*.

"You've been answering these yourself?" I asked, stupidly again. Great mental alertness was not my claim to fame that day.

"For about a year and a half," she said casually. "I ran out of lawyer money a long time ago."

"*Mira*." I shook my head. "I'm astounded."

"Why?"

"Only that I had no idea. We went together, we were lovers, I thought I knew everything going on in your life." I spread my hands. "I had no idea," I repeated.

"I had no choice," she answered simply. I shook my head again. The fact that she was representing herself was not the reason I was aston-ished. I had been involved in litigation off and on for better than twenty years. I had seen the uncertainty of outcome grind away at the stamina of the strongest personalities. The relentless procedural pres-sure, the experience of being denounced repeatedly and personally by apparently rational and mature people, the ceaseless anxiety—the pro-cess can unnerve and eventually destroy even the strongest personali-ties.

And this happens even when all that is at issue is money, and maybe a little personal prestige—small potatoes compared to what was involved here. Of all types of litigation, family court litigation is absolutely the worst, with no close second. There is no insurance coverage. There are no recognized standards that mean anything. There are no final outcomes, since any order made by the court can be amended at any time in the future if circumstances change. The most serious charges and countercharges are flung about with reckless abandon, and no one can predict which one will make an impression on the judge, which one won't. And the stakes? Infinite, when children are the issue—not only their lives, but *their* children's lives, and their children's children. (Another lesson from my own life.) The most stressful situation in law I could imagine is to have to defend against a war of attrition mounted in that arena by a dedicated opponent with superior resources and a determination to win at all costs.

Yet this apparently was the situation Mira had been in, and with which she'd been coping all on her own. We had become intimate in April, spent days and nights together, opened our souls—I am not the most observant man in the world (obviously), but neither am I deaf and dumb; I would have expected to get some drift of this side of her life; but I hadn't had the slightest clue that she was involved all alone in this kind of intractable, unwinnable fight. Her poise and graciousness had been absolutely unscarred by any of this.

My initial amazement faded, replaced by what I can only describe as pure admiration. Previously I had prized her beauty; her charm and grace were a complete delight to me; I had noted and valued her alertness and intelligence; these alone were enough to produce a high regard for her. But to all these attitudes was now added genuine, unalloyed, unstinting respect. Hemingway, male chauvinist pig that he was, would never have dreamt that his definition of courage, `grace under pressure', might apply to a middle-aged mother of three, slogging her way day by day, month by month, through a preposterous and unfair custody battle in family court. But that would have been Hemmingway's mistake, because Mira Watson, with her poise and her pro per responses, was the living embodiment of grace under pressure. I could only be awed and humbled by her.

I told her then and there how much my respect for her had grown in that moment. She was pleased by the sentiment, but shrugged it off with her usual nonchalance. I asked her what help she needed from me. Not much, it seemed; she simply wanted her material reviewed by a professional. All the prior decisions had gone her way (Crockett and his fool of a lawyer hadn't considered the obvious fact that the constant petitioning would damage their credibility), but that made her concerned that the court would consider giving way to Crockett simply on the basis that no one should win them all. Courageous or not, she was only human, and my sense was that she had become a bit intimidated from the constant demands.

It was easy to be reassuring. Mira was a dancer, not a writer. Her work was literate but not professional, but that was actually helpful to her in the present circumstances. She stated her case in simple, ordinary language, without any of the hysteria and exaggeration that is the trademark of the typical family court litigant. Her responses must have been a breath of fresh air to the clerks and judges in that beleaguered court, who try to make order out of the constant chaos. Thus I could truthfully say to her that her stuff was more than adequate, was quite good, in fact, and that the best advice I could give her was to continue doing just what she had been doing.

Her gratitude and relief at hearing these obvious facts embarrassed me slightly, since I really hadn't done that much. She also wanted some background on the judge who had been assigned to her case. It was possible to be reassuring about that as well, because her luck was in. The Watson case was before an experienced and decent man, one without any baggage or issues of his own of which I was aware. She could count on a fair hearing, and she could be reasonably confident of the right decision.

"Thank you, Walter," she said, with evident relief. It was like thanking the weatherman for predicting sunshine, and I said as much. I wondered if she had any other problems that she hadn't mentioned.

"No, Walt, everything's fine. Even the family court isn't much different than it was. I just wanted a reality check. Which you've given me, thank you."

"Are you sure?" I asked. "How did the finance class turn out?"

"I did quite well. I may be looking for another job. A better job."

"Do you have your resume out right now?"

"No." She paused, as if she were coming to a decision. "Actually, I've been working with a start-up. It's pretty exciting, actually. A little black box that does all sort of wonderful, Internet-ty things. I've been helping write the business plan, and working with their presentation skills. I'm trying to line up some venture capitalists I know."

"That's wonderful," I said, "if it works. Maybe you really won't be in the house long." We both laughed. I leaned forward and took her hand. "Mira, that's a pretty rough arena. I've been there. Take care of yourself. Because those guys are all on a macho trip. They'll cut your heart out just to prove how tough they are, because they really aren't tough at all, and they know it. Do you have your own deal in place?"

"Oh, Walter," she laughed, "how naïve do you think I am? Of course I do. It was the first thing."

"Good," I said.

Our eyes met then, suddenly, unexpectedly, awkwardly. As lost to myself as I usually was during those years, in that instant I knew—could not avoid knowing—how much I wanted her, needed her, missed her—and I knew, I knew for certain, what could be, what was still possible. The words, the phrases came to mind, trembled on my lips.

Do you have anything planned for this afternoon? I wanted to say.

No, I knew she would answer, not because it was true, because it was what she wanted the truth to be.

Then come away with me some place. I've made a royal jackass of myself, a complete idiot. I don't want to go on being a fool any longer, and I knew she would take my hand and leave with me. It was a certainty.

But I said nothing of this aloud, for I had already reasoned my way far enough towards certain disastrous conclusions to be inhibited. The moment lingered an instant longer, then we both smiled quick, shy embarrassed smiles, then immediately looked elsewhere. Then the moment passed. We walked out to the parking lot.

*

A British historian once remarked that basic art of history is obtaining the perspective of people for whom the events under consideration, now far in the past and unchangeable, were once far in the future, unknown and infinitely alterable—no easy trick. It's tough enough in your own life. From where I stand now, everything that happened between me and Mira seems foreordained, the cog of one gear catching the next in a neat, inevitable clockwork progression. But that is not so. Right until the last moment, events were soft, malleable, completely indeterminable. Everything could so easily have turned out differently. I know that to be a fact, even if I have no sense of its force.

But there are days that are more important than others, when the eternally restless flood of events, capable of surging in any direction, suddenly roars into one particular channel. That day was one of them. This was the day when I put it all together, all of the little errors, the small misunderstandings, and molded them all into one monumental, disastrous delusion.

Mira and I had enjoyed (I decided as I drove away) a short, marvelous affair, terrifically sexual and alive. But as delightful as it had been, it was essentially a distraction from the settled structure of my life, the angle of repose into which I believed my life had settled. If Mira had been settled in a similar fashion—as I had thought she was when I pursued her—the relationship would have been ideal. But now I knew her life was anything but settled. She had genuine needs for both financial and domestic stability—needs (I further decided) I couldn't possibly supply. She needed a man with a full life to give her—not someone already shackled to his own unbreakable commitments.

I had no interest in remarriage, but (I decided) remarriage for her was not only desirable, but essential. And that she could remarry, on her own terms, I had no doubt. Mira was of the chooser class, not beggar, three children notwithstanding. She was lovely, graceful, accomplished, and that day I had become aware of her full stature as a human being. She would be a tremendous catch for any man who had the means and resources to handle her.

Added to all this sound good thinking was just a dollop of the basic diffidence that I have always lived with as regards attractive women. I now had a clear perception of the astonishing reserves of poise and courage her laidback nonchalance concealed. I was too old to believe in pedestals and unapproachable goddesses; I had, after all, held her in my arms and taken her to my bed. But I did wonder if my sense of the rightness between us was a self-serving illusion of my own, if she might not be better matched with a man with more sense of himself than the stumbling wanderer named Walter Kelsey.

So for all those reasons the man she needed—my mature consideration concluded—was not me. Wanting her was an act of pure selfishness on my part. I was not the right man for her. Our lives, our fundamental needs, were too different. She needed and deserved a man who could give all of himself to her—a husband, not a part-time lover. I did not possess the freedom of action to be that for her. For me to woo her, to occupy the center stage in her life, while the clock ticked, while the petitions arrived, would be unfair in the most fundamental sense of the word, a waste of the fleeting time that was critical to her. Simple decency required that I withdraw, be content with memories and friendship—and that's what I decided to do. This is what I did do.

This was clear thinking, this was sound, informed judgment. The only small details omitted from the equation were the quickening of my pulse when I thought of her, the eagerness in her voice when she caught sight of me, the brightening of her glance, her warmth in my arms, the unstinting admiration I felt for her, the importance of her welfare and happiness to me. It ignored the fact that I was the man she sought out when she needed reassurance and support. The one tiny factor overlooked was the entirety of the human feeling between us, the rapport, the intangible sense of rightness, the wild cries of both our souls.

All that my mature deliberations omitted, in short, was everything that truly mattered.

So it was with the best of intentions and all the honor in the world that I kept silent as our lunch ended and steered my ship directly into the iceberg. In my experience the most pernicious delusions are not illogical, but rigidly logical, ultralogical in fact. They are not demented flights of fancy. They are flights of demented rationality, in which all the infinitely shaded colors of the spectrum of human experience, all the infinite variety of sizes and shapes of human reality, are refracted through some monochromatic lens, to stark shades of black and white and absurd, unnaturally perfect, Euclidean figures. The result is neat, perfectly formed, white and black recognizable shapes that fit comfortably into neat, perfectly formed, white and black conventional patterns. All the messy complexity that makes thinking difficult and life interesting is thereby neatly eliminated.

The rational delusions are the worst, because their superficial plausibility allows them to masquerade as sound thinking. It is in this manner that the deepest and most pernicious folly disguises itself as adult wisdom. At least so it was with me, on the day I turned my back on everything I really wanted.

CHAPTER 8

▼

Mira had not called me with any conscious ulterior motive or seductive scheme. She'd called me because she needed help, which happened to be simple reassurance. But, as events developed that day, I had read her thoughts precisely—not all that difficult, since they had exactly matched mine. When our eyes met, what she had indeed been seized with was the hope that in one supremely romantic gesture, straight out of a paperback bodice ripper, I would simply call off the remainder of my day and hers, take her by the hand, lead her somewhere, and make her my own in the most emphatic and traditional way possible. Then all the doubt and uncertainty would vanish into the sea as if it had never been, and there would just be she and I, at a new beginning that would be the only beginning. At that moment, it all seemed as simple to her as it did to me.

But the moment passed, as they all did, the prisoner of hesitation and too much thinking, nothing happened, and whatever her disappointment, she moved on. Mira never shared my fully rationalized nonsense about us—but she did understand my reasons, and accepted them, as much as she might privately disagree. To that extent, she was conventionally feminine, conventionally Southern. To that extent, perhaps she was victim to her own delusions.

＊

The job that Mira had mentioned to me at our lunch was, of course, the one with Gregor Volkov. It wasn't actually a job—more a time-to-time consultancy. But it was beginning to occupy an increasing amount of her time, her attention, and—most important—her hopes. Having learned that she had some genuine connections, and at least a glimmering of a notion as to how to launch a company both legally and financially, Volkov began to call on her constantly. They were calls she was more than happy to take. She had gleaned enough from Gregor and his cohorts to know that the technology, and particularly its economic potential, was genuine. If Echelon and its product, the Firebird, succeeded, as it easily could, and she were even a small part of it, her financial problems would be history. The dreadful house would be only a distant, laughable memory, and she would have the resources to cope with Crockett, without asking help from people before whom she always wanted to keep her head high and her spirit bright.

I didn't know the details of these developments in her life, but the people who did gave Mira all the obvious advice—not to count her chickens before the eggs hatched, or to cross the bridge before she came to it, all of the other bromides, and of course she would have known these things even if no one had said anything. But it is one thing to know these bright prospects should be put firmly out of mind, and quite another to actually accomplish that feat, particularly when there is constant communication, constant demands, constant excited news, the real possibility of instant success—and all the other avenues out of the swamp seem so dreary and far-off. So Mira did her best to continue with her prosaic day-to-day plans while banishing Echelon from her thoughts. But she no more succeeded than most people in that situation do.

Thoughts of Echelon intruded into her daydreams, dominated them. If it made even a fraction of the revenues that the conservative forecasts she had developed with Gregor indicated, it could be a two hundred, three hundred, million dollar company in six months, a year, a twinkling of an eye. Gregor and his friends would be filthy, unimaginably rich, as well they deserved to be. But if she got even a tiny sliver, a minuscule fraction, she'd have everything she needed.

I know the feeling. I've been there, in the 80's, when I usually accepted stock in lieu of fees when I did a start-up and rode the wave with my clients, up or down. You do your best to ignore the prospects, because there are so many rivers to cross, so much time to travel, because things like this don't happen to people like you. It may all be witches' money, the stuff of moonscape, gone at the first light of daybreak. Only a fool would change his life or his plans on the whims of this kind of fortune, and very few do. I didn't, and Mira didn't. Yet the possibility is never far from mind. Try though you will, you cannot put it entirely to one side and go about your business— because you also know that this isn't mere fantasy, that such things do happen to people, and maybe one of them is you, and you cannot stop yourself thinking about what could so easily be, and how sweet it would be if it all came to pass.

I used to warn the creators of these start-ups and those others who shared in the dream, about clinging too closely to it. There is a story told about the way monkeys are caught on the island of Ceylon. The monkey catcher sets a trap, wide enough for the monkey's open hand, but too small for its closed fist. He puts a candy or sweet fruit at the center. The monkey comes bounding out of the tree in pursuit of the treat. He finds it easy enough to get his tiny hand into the trap and grasp the sweet—but impossible to pull out the treat in his closed fist. The monkey catcher closes in; all the monkey has to do to keep his freedom is let go of the candy and flee. But he won't do that. As he struggles with the trap, trying to find some way to escape with the candy, the Ceylonese monkey catcher catches him, and he finds himself spending the rest of his life in a cage. It's a story that should be true even if it isn't.

To Mira, what was at stake was not a trivial sweetmeat, but financial security for herself and her children, particularly Alicia. I don't know the exact sequence of the events in her life at about this time, the precise date on which this or that happened. But I do know that it was about this time when her fingers began to close around the bait in the trap.

*

I also know that she helped put the financial projections together; was the major author of the text and organization of the Echelon business plan; and, most importantly, was able to put Volkov into contact with the financial community. I don't want to overstate this—Mira did not have the stature to give Volkov's company credibility. But the people she'd met socially, and professionally did think enough of her to return her calls. So she was able to see to it that Gregor Volkov got his audience.

This, or rather these—Mira set up two presentations—turned out to be disasters. In particular, they were personal disasters for Volkov himself. They did confirm that the product Firebird was as exciting as she had been led to believe. An experienced interpreter of audiences, Mira could sense the excitement of the venture capitalists, no matter how well they thought it concealed, in nuances of body language, the questions asked and unasked, the rhythm of the meeting itself. There was huge potential here, mind-boggling in its scale—both meetings were alive with the sense of it.

But an investment of this type is not made in the product alone, but in the product and the people both. It was here that both meetings failed unequivocally. Volkov was impossible—he talked when he should have listened, interrupting sensible questions to make impassioned, irrelevant answers. He mistook the ordinary, professional, prudence of investment managers for moral cowardice, and was insulted by it. He managed to be both snarling and timid at the same time, like a cringing, growling dog. What became apparent to all early on is that he hadn't the slightest idea how the American financial and business culture worked. I have my own problems with that culture, and can make my own case against it. But that's an outsider's privilege, which I am these days. The prosaic truth is, that if you want to work within that culture and succeed there, you are going to have to understand it and adapt to its norms. That's a fairly mun-

dane, obvious fact of life, but one with which Gregor Volkov refused to come to terms.

So Mira took on still another chore for Echelon, the turning of a sow's ear into a silk purse. She had been ill at ease writing the business plan for Echelon, but in educating its president on presentation skills, she was in her element. There was no way she could transform Volkov into a Park Avenue gent, but she could at least tutor him to the point where his eccentricities became colorful, rather than outrageous.

The natural consequence was that she began spending more and more time with Gregor.

✳

I was not then, nor have I ever been, jealous of the other men in Mira's life. Back when I was in my first year in law school, in the late 60's, I had a relationship with a girl infinitely more sophisticated than I (which was not a hard thing to be). She had had many lovers, and all of them tons more skillful than I was—or so I thought or—to be absolutely accurate—so I obsessed. Jealousy in this modern era is nearly always rooted in personal doubt. In that respect my case was typical. I underwent the tortures of the damned the next two years, with gnawing uncertainty about my comparative sexual adequacy commingled with unbridled lust, some long stretches of real physical frustration, and an agonizing sense of belittlement, almost entirely self-inflicted. When the smoke cleared, shortly after graduation, whatever tendency I had to jealousy had been burned away in the furnace. I have never been jealous since. A woman's romantic past is simply one more element in the compound of the present, literally a fact of her life, and making judgments about it is as absurd as judging sunrises.

What I hoped for for Mira, at that time and during the years that followed, was that she would find a suitable man and remarry. It seemed to me a virtual certainty that that's what would eventually happen. I expected that some ordinary day I'd receive a card with an announcement. Or maybe there'd be a phone call, and I'd hear that wonderful voice with a tincture of pure happiness in it, not simply the delight a woman feels in the prospect of marriage, but the relief of the sailor home from the sea—the stormy sea—with the awful house permanently behind her, Crockett defanged forever, and some basic emotional and financial security. That day would have been a bad day for me—not being jealous is not the same thing as not having regrets. My memories of her presence, her voice and body, would bestir themselves in active longing, and that day and the few following would be difficult. But I would have been happy for her, happy that she had found port, I would have come to the wedding, bringing with me a nice congratulatory gift, and rejoiced for her at the same time I agonized over what might have been.

She did date often, that I know, and she was never without admirers. But very few of the dating relationships came to anything at all, not even romantically. There is a forest-and-trees aspect to be mentioned here. Quite apart from all the high falutin' errors and misjudgments I made about her and me, there were a few of the nuts-and-bolts, common-as-dishwater variety. She was the mother of three children under 10, one of whom was significantly disabled. Those circumstances in her life didn't make the slightest difference to me, since they happened to match circumstances in my own. But they were more than sufficient to send most ordinary suitors scurrying to the hills.

The thought never crossed my mind that anyone who had the freedom to take her to himself would not do so. There is another, more prosaic reason for that. I loved her, and in all the essential ways, with the pure innocence of a first love. I could not imagine it was possible that anyone could come to know her well and not love her.

Come to think of it, I still can't.

*

Mira had not told me the truth at the lunch we shared. She did not have a deal in place with Gregor and Echelon. It was a white enough lie, not at all important to the real business of the lunch, and probably moti-

vated by minor-league personal vanity more than anything else. At the same time she was asking for my help in the arena with Crockett, she did not wish to appear in need of other help. Mira didn't like appearing helpless and dependent any more than most modern women.

Irony of ironies. She didn't really need my input in family court, and I didn't have anything important to say. I didn't know that much about it. But I would have had plenty to say about Echelon, beyond the basic clichés that I did offer, because that was territory with which I was thoroughly familiar. I'd have told her that talk of stock participation is fast and loose before a company is funded. The stock really doesn't mean anything and the idea that it ever will is shrouded in a haze of unreality. Everyone thinks about it privately and obsessively, every one talks about it, but no one really believes in the reality of it in their heart of hearts. So people make all sorts of cheerful, handshake agreements and come to informal understandings, without worrying too much about it, since none of it seems to matter too much. We human beings are here-and-now creatures, and we are always mired in the present, no matter how hard we struggle to clamber out of that swamp.

But everything changes instantly when—if—the funding arrives, as quickly as light floods a dark room. The processes that were fluid and easy harden and calcify with the speed of thought. The engineers scramble back to their desks to find out what exactly was in that contract they signed so nonchalantly a few months before. All sorts of firefights break out—'you said 10,000 extra shares if I finished the beta before February 1ˢᵗ', 'no, I didn't,' 'yes, you did'. At the same time, the new investors, who are parting with hard money for the equity they own, are looking with a jeweler's eye at all the stock promises that have previously been made, and damning as God's own fool the chief executive officer who made them. This comes at a time when even the most confident CEO is anxious to make the very best impression possible.

If Mira had asked me, I'd have told her that being in a situation in which she was providing open-ended services—which she was—with no fixed agreement as to what she'd receive in return—which it also was, or rather, was not—was absolutely the worst possible place to be, an invitation to be fucked royally, and not in the happy bedroom sense. What she would have done if she'd heard me, I don't know. My sense is that Echelon had already become too big a part of her daydreams, the one shining sword which could at a stroke cut through all the knots in her life and free her from them. I think the monkey's hand was already in the trap. Even so, I wish I'd had the chance to tell her those things. Sensing is not the same thing as knowing. Perhaps it would have made a difference.

As it was, Mira continued the way she had been, doing whatever was necessary, refining the financials, editing the business plan, coaching Gregor, an absolutely essential outsider, but the adjective was `essential', the noun was `outsider'. She began to see more and more of Gregor socially, as her time became squeezed between family, school, work, and Echelon. It was not as if there were that many alternatives after I'd removed myself.

Also, slowly, her feelings toward Gregor evolved—from condescending charity, to curiosity, to fascination. The impermeability of his egocentricity fascinated her; she had never met a man so obsessed, so driven, so caught up in his own goals and ambitions. Behavior of that type, over a limited period of time and in a restricted context, can masquerade as alpha-male traits, which are almost always appealing to women (although they don't run around broadcasting that fact). Her handling of men had always been a source of strength and pride to Mira; she had always been confident of, and had always received, at the least, a measured responsiveness, a basic quid pro quo, in response to her own efforts. Now she was spending time with someone whose demands were limitless and drive relentless. In different circumstances, without Echelon rising like a Bavarian castle from the mist in the back of her mind, she might have been repelled; instead, she found herself drawn closer, fascinated.

So she went on, day by day, doing whatever had to be done, and for her own due, trusting in the kindness of friends. That was the one last bit of advice I might have given her, if I'd known. The kindness of friends is much more complicated and far more uncertain than the kindness of strangers.

CHAPTER 9

▼

According to the high school theology I learned from the good brothers of Holy Cross, despair is the one unforgivable sin. The reason is that the sinner abandons hope, and without hope there can be no forgiveness. Perhaps this is just another example of one-dimensional logic, as the God who could conjure up the notion of an unforgivable sin, afflict some poor sucker with it, and then pack him off to an eternity in hell as a consequence of not asking forgiveness, would seem to the general sensibility of most of us to be in considerable need of forgiveness Himself. Since God also created the same general sensibility that decries Him, the result is a typically theological vicious circle of a type in which I long ago lost interest.

But I remain interested in the masquerades that despair, or—to be precise—its twin brother, depression, uses. I have had a considerable amount of 'been there, done that' experience with them. Its trademark gimmick is that the victim does not believe that there is anything really wrong with him, but instead that he has finally perceived and accepted reality, as bleak and dreary as that might be. Those that disagree he sees as cock-eyed optimists unable to accept the grim truth of the futility of it all. The stray thought that maybe he is the one in need of the reality adjustment is rejected as patently absurd. So perhaps the notion of an unforgivable sin is lousy theology, but it makes for pretty good psychology. That I know for certain.

There were miracles happening all over my life back then. I have already described the major one and my idiot rejection of it. But that was not the only example. Slowly, but not imperceptibly (had I been in a perceiving mode, that is), the problems in my life that I regarded as intractable began to solve themselves. The force of renewal, of springtime, the one that drives the green fuse through the flower, has no truck with depression, no interest in forgiveness, and perhaps knows God a little better than the theologians would care to admit.

These positive developments are not sideshows to my story. They are integral to understanding the main event—for they are the story of how I gradually regained my freedom of action without knowing that I had done so.

*

Nick celebrated his seventh birthday that summer, the day before we left for Orlando. 'Pervasive Development Disorder' is a grab bag label that means everything and nothing. What it translated into in Nick's case was a laundry-list of neurological quirks and oddities that collectively had the effect of disabling him. A lot of the behaviors were autistic in nature, although he is not autistic. Nor is he retarded— that's almost a fighting word with me. He is exceptionally bright and alert, fully aware of his environment, both physically and emotionally. The problem occurs in the processing after the input. The doctors don't know exactly what goes wrong, let alone why—the medical solution for Nick's problems lies a couple of centuries in the future—but his difficulties are obvious from the first moment you meet him.

He walks on his toes. He talks like a child half his years. He has the attention span of a mayfly. During the first eighteen months of his life, his mother and I were genuinely worried that he might be so severely disabled that he'd end up institutionalized for most of his life. He displayed no personality or affect until he was over one. He did not walk until he was past two, or speak recognizable words until he was well over three.

But he did walk, and he did speak—finally—and, by the time he was seven, the once blank little infant had become a delightful little boy. Like all children, his maturation was not linear, but jumped from one plateau to the next. The difference with Nick was that the movements were not the typical hop and skip, but huge quantum leaps that seemed to come from nowhere at exactly the moment when we were all ready to assume that nothing more would ever happen, that he'd gone about as far as he could go. It is one of the fixed articles of what faith I do have that nature intended Nick to be far more disabled than he is, completely and irremediably autistic; that if the doctors and teachers who work with him had any notion of the full extent of the handicaps he lives with, their mouths would drop open in amazement; that the considerable progress he has made is due largely to his own will and determination. It is odd, I know, to talk about a neurologically-impaired six-year old boy, burdened by a range of bizarre and inexplicable behaviors, with admiration, with respect, as if he were a hero, simply for the ordinary adjustments he has made to life. But I believe in the deepest, stillest waters of my soul that my son is a hero, that what adjustments he's made required astonishing effort, and I talk of him with admiration and respect because in fact I admire and respect him.

Three weeks after we got back from Disneyworld, about the same time Mira contacted me, Nick began a new program at a new school. Although he had only turned seven that August, he was already in his fifth year of public education. All but one of the teachers he'd had had been concerned and dedicated, worth a thousand lawyers and ten thousand professional athletes. The only bad year had been the one that ended that June, just a few weeks after things had ended between Mira and myself.

With a normal child, a parent writes off a bad year as a bad year and moves on to the next. There is no worry that the journey to maturity won't resume. But with a child like Nick, there is always the question of whether the year was bad because he had reached a final limit beyond which he was not educable. For sure, this was the opinion of his teacher that year, who without question had reached a final limit beyond which *she* wasn't educable. (She was not my favorite person, to put it mildly.)

It had made for a long summer, of doubt and uncertainty. On the one hand, Nick's horizons seemed to expand the moment he was free from the disapproving eye of Ms. Dismal, or so it seemed to my fond parental eye. But there were still the obsessions, the incessantly repeated verbal formulations, the insistence on riding the paddleboat and only the paddleboat. As much as I wished I could damn his former teacher to the hell she deserved, I could not escape the nagging possibility that she might be right.

The beginning of that school year was thus a beginning like no other. There was not only the question of what could be done, but whether anything could be done. I met Nick at his school that first day with as much anxiety as I have ever had about anything in my life. The physical plant of the school was dismal, the corridors dark and unwaxed, the playground going to seed. But Nick's new classmates seemed cheerful and disciplined, and his new teacher—Lucia—competent and ready for anything. So we did have some hope.

Within three weeks, the verdict was in. Perhaps it was the teacher. Perhaps it was all those endless trips on the paddleboat around the waterway at Disney World. Perhaps it was some subliminal message Nick had received during the last disastrous school year. Most likely it was that his receptive brain had reached a critical mass of input that allowed him to make another great leap forward, as had happened before. But whatever the reasons, the discontinuous scraps and shreds of his personality began to knit themselves together into a coherent whole, an event unprecedented in his life. He dressed himself, more or less. He got more food into his mouth than he did on the floor. He responded to questions, or at least he tried to; and sometimes, when he was asked a follow-up question, he'd respond to that as well. I don't wish to exaggerate; he was not suddenly transformed into an age-normal child. That didn't happen, and it's never going to happen. These miracles I describe were secular miracles, wonders within the realm of possibility. But he was moving again, at a time when we wondered whether he was capable of any further movement.

The progress did not end with the first few weeks. Nick remained at the Children's Development Center for the next three years. He thrived during the entire period. He learned to count, and to do simple sums. He learned the alphabet. During the last year, he learned to read or at least to decode words—and once he did learn, he made amazing progress. Theretofore, my expectation had been that Nick would have to live with either myself or Linda, and what would become of him after we were both gone had been the type of 2:00 a.m. thought that froze the marrow of my bones. Now I could see him coping with a group home setting, with only modest supervision and financial support. Finding the financial support was another huge problem, but of a different order and in a different universe. One problem at a time; sufficient unto the day is the evil thereof.

Translation: now I could see a future for Nick, whereas previously I could see none. The difference was simply that between everything and nothing.

*

At about the same time that Nick began the school year, I opened up my first personal Internet account. (I had been a user at the office for some time.) It was shortly after that I discovered the interesting phenomenon of Internet dating.

The world of the divorced and single parents was a strange, new one for me. My parents were married for forty-one years, until my mother's death. No one in my family, none of my brothers and sisters, none of the brothers and sisters of *their* husbands and wives, were divorced. All my close friends had been family men. What to do and how to function in this wilderness, common knowledge in so many sad lives, were absolute mysteries to me. The primary issue, when my job and parental responsibilities took up so much time, was how to meet people—more precisely, how to meet women. Mira had been something of an anomaly, the mother of another child in the special-ed class. Life usually didn't work things out so neatly.

I quickly discovered how large the new universe was, how commonplace were the problems I faced. Becoming aware that I was socially marooned was a nice start, but not at all helpful in getting me off the island. For years, even while I was married, I had scanned the `personals' ads out of idle curiosity, noting sympathetically the occasional flash of literacy or personal sparkle. Now I read them in earnest, and occasionally—very occasionally—answered one. Nothing happened, other than a few mostly guarded phone calls, and one or two lively replies. Only once did any of these embryonic romantic relationships get as far as a face-to-face meeting, at which I discovered a woman with an otherwise fascinating personality who had, unfortunately, been deceiving herself about the true condition of her body—verging on obesity—for a considerable period of time.

But quite apart from the results, the whole process made me queasy. By the nature of the game, I had to reveal enough of myself to induce a total stranger—one whom I was assessing on the basis of some fifty-word self-description—to call me back. It was like shooting an arrow into the air with more than a faint possibility that the arrow would descend back out of the sky straight into my forehead. Not a good situation.

It was in this context and to deal with these frustrations that I began to explore Internet dating. Both professionally and personally, I had been aware of the `Net' and its potential for commercial and personal exchanges for some time. But the benefit that e-mail and anonymous servers could provide socially marooned persons like myself had not been immediately obvious to me. Aided by those devices, it was possible to carry on a guarded correspondence with some interesting individual, until such time as a sufficient rapport had developed to make disclosure of true identity and a flesh-and-blood meeting natural and comfortable. These features greatly enhanced the safety aspects of the situation. The unacceptable 'pig in a poke' aspect of personal ads was thus almost entirely eliminated.

The result was—I was delighted at first to discover—that large numbers of competent, interesting women felt comfortable enough with the process to make their availability known through it. Doctors, lawyers, any number of technical people, musicians, writers, even a fairly well-known minor novelist, used the various matching services with reasonable confidence that they were not endangering themselves.

And so I waded into this ocean, not without some trepidation despite all these reassuring factors. The women I contacted were always mothers with children. There were a large number of women in their late thirties and early forties, childless, and with the biological clock ticking loudly in their ears—'single girls', as I called them, not unkindly—who tempted me, as they would have tempted any man, with a combination of looks, intelligence, and need. But I did not feel that it was fair to waste their time. It was also my intuition that only a woman with children herself would be able to understand the priorities and limitations of my own life. Children are the ultimate end stop to the ego; in a sense too fundamental to be articulated verbally, they define where one personality ends and another begins; and it is difficult if not impossible to share that understanding with a childless person, someone who has never experienced the relentless selfishness of an infant's demand.

What I was searching for was what I thought I had found in Mira— someone with a settled life, no special problems or regrets, wanting (but not needing) a man to round out her life. Naively, I thought it would be easy to find a woman interested in this sort of intimate, sexy friendship. The women I was interested in were all mothers and all in their late thirties and early forties. (Some of the married men around me wonder why I am not interested in younger women, with glowing skin, glorious bodies, unencumbered lives. Because they have nothing to say to me is the reason. This invariably produces a locker room response to the effect that talk has nothing to do with the real object at hand. Dead wrong—it has everything to do with it, as even the most Neanderthal among them would admit if he weren't making jokes.) I thought it would be a fairly easy matter to find an attractive woman comparable to my own age, with her own version of my practical outlook—my female counterpart, in other words—and establish some understanding.

That's what I expected. That's not what happened. I quickly discovered that the myth of romantic love is as potent among middle-aged women as it is among teen-age girls and maybe more so. Life lessons and realistic expectations could matter less. When I was a boy, the notion that women are the more practical and down-to-earth of the two sexes, men the dreamers and fantasists, was accepted as an axiom of human nature. Perhaps it is, but for my part, I have in my life encountered an enormous number of women—otherwise talented, sophisticated, intelligent—who in their heart of hearts believed that despite all odds the day would at last come when every last wish they had ever wished would be granted, with the mechanism of fulfillment being the arrival of the Prince in one form or another. Successful womanizers succeed because they are manipulative enough to disguise themselves as princes for as long as is necessary.

More. I also discovered that the dating game was infinitely more, not less, complex among us middle-aged folk than it is among the young. It is not that any two people at any age are ever as smooth and contourless as to match exactly the yin and yang prototypes of the ancient Chinese symbol. But in youthful personalities there are definitely fewer edges, fewer twists. There certainly was in mine. As life goes on, each new experience—with lovers, spouses, children, the

world at large—alters the shape, makes and leaves its mark on the bor-
der. The processes of discovery and accommodation thus become far
more involved and complicated. To push the jigsaw metaphor to the
limit, and probably beyond (my apologies), the shapes that had to be
fit together in my middle age were no longer two simple curves, but
twisting and idiosyncratic shorelines, with countless bays, coves, penin-
sulas, and promontories. It was as if the coasts of Ireland and Madagascar had to be somehow united seamlessly.

So what seemed in theory to be an easy process, in practice turned
out to be anything but easy. I didn't want to form another household;
I had no use for a second wife; I didn't want to be anyone's prince, and
I didn't want to disguise myself as one. I didn't meet many women
who matched me on those points—and when I did meet someone
interesting who did match, some sort of baggage, some personal trait or
requirement, almost always showed up as well, that made any sort of
long or medium-term relationship impossible.

Even so, despite all the impediments, during the fall and winter of
199-, I did meet a number of interesting women, fascinating women,
memorable women. All of them were intelligent, and the majority
quite attractive. The cyber introductions led to meetings for coffee, for
lunch, for dinner, to movies or plays, to long discussions, and every
once in a while, when God was smiling in His heaven and all right
with my world, to bed. None of these incidents I would dismiss as
casual or meaningless; had the structure of my life been different in one
fundamental respect, things might have turned out entirely differently.

For underlying all the problems with the search for princes, the fact
that Ireland and Madagascar lie in entirely different oceans and are
impossible to join, all the other practical difficulties, lay an even more
basic difficulty. My problem wasn't the myth of romantic love. My
problem was with its reality. I could not give my heart to any of the
charming women I met because I had none to give. None of them had
a voice that made wind chimes sound like unoiled door hinges. None
of them moved with the grace of God's youngest angel. None of them

gave herself to me with an uninhibited freedom and eagerness. I could go on and on and on in this vein, but you get the idea. The point can be summarized, completely and definitely, in six words.

None of them was Mira Watson.

*

I kept in periodic contact with Mira throughout that fall, that winter and the following spring. She prevailed against Crockett's petition—the one she'd called me about—fairly easily, as I knew she would. But that one was followed about eight weeks later by another, based on some equally trivial incident. She won again, another followed, and then another, as regularly as clockwork. A routine developed; after she received the new filing, she would draft a response, and then send it over to me for comment before she filed it. She always called first; we had lunch once more, just after Christmas. Her calls were always the star moments of my day. The lunches, one and all, remain golden memories.

She really didn't need much in the way of help. The direct and somewhat naïve way in which she stated her case was, to my way of thinking, much more effective than a glib, smoothed-out professional presentation would have been. Nonetheless, I did add a word or phrase here and there, as well as making some serious suggestions about formatting. It was obvious to me that Crockett and his counsel didn't actually expect to prevail on any of the applications. What they hoped to do was wear Mira down, exhaust her, until she finally gave up the battle out of sheer weariness and frustration. The bastards were conducting a war of attrition, a strategy that is too often successful in family court, a place of endless twilight and confusion, where the truth has no consequences and neither does falsity.

I hoped with my subtle changes to signal to the opposition that the plan wouldn't work, that Mira was not without friends and resources of her own. It was at first a forlorn hope, as alertness to subtle changes in style was not exactly the trademark of Crockett's lawyer. But over time I detected or thought I detected some reaction from the opposition, some recognition that Mira was no longer alone. It pleased me to believe that my contributions meant something.

The astonishing poise she continued to exhibit in the face of all this excremental flak did not cause me to do anything as sensible as rethink all of my noble poses. Quite the contrary—it reinforced my conviction that I was not the right man for her. The mundane caring I had to offer, stolen moments shared in a two bedroom condominium, work, children, the treadmill monotony of everyday routine, seemed to me ridiculously inadequate to the degree of personal elegance she possessed. Alone of the women I had met, she actually was deserving of the sort of life-changing romantic coup for which they all longed. I had thus become prisoner of my own romantic illusions, the inverse of the feminine version I observed with such detached sympathy. I would find this a very funny joke, if I found anything to joke about in the whole delusive mess. Other people's illusions are like other people's pain, a lot easier to handle than your own.

Thank God (I thought) changes were happening in her life, good ones—or so it seemed to me at the time. From time to time, Mira gave me guarded news about the start-up she had mentioned to me at the first lunch. The business plan she had mentioned was completed, the round of presentations of venture capitalists begun. She was deliberately sketchy with details—evidently, this particular founders' group was maniacal about security—and characteristically off-hand about its potential. But I could sense her growing excitement beneath the studied nonchalance, and I hoped and prayed for her. In a different age and different time, becoming involved in an embryonic business would have meant she had taken on one more hair-raising risk in a life-style that already contained too many. But at this time and particularly in our unique place, participation in the ground floor of the right kind of high technology enterprise was the best thing that could happen to anyone.

There was a man in the mix as well, a looming romantic interest, I could sense that, too, despite her discretion. If she was sketchy about details concerning the business, she was even more vague about the man. My assumption that he existed was based on the scraps and shreds of facts—mentions of late hours, business dinners, and so on. For that matter, I said nothing at all about the women I was dating, or in some cases bedding. What had once passed between us was in theory ancient history—but it never became history in practice. We never became two old friends who could discuss these things as if they didn't matter, as if they concerned two mutual acquaintances in which we had no interest, but whom we wished well.

So the days passed, summer into fall, fall into winter. I had a brief affair with a vascular surgeon, a fascinating, but ultimately incompatible woman. (Or perhaps it was simply another instance of the fundamental problem, that she was not Mira; I will never be entirely sure.) The holiday season came; Mira sent me a charming Christmas card, with her children dressed as elves in front of her Christmas tree. About five weeks later, Crockett filed another petition, even more vicious than the usual bilge, complaining about the hours Mira was spending moonlighting on the start-up. I provided some unusually stiffish language in response. Mira told me later that the family court judge had expressed his impatience with the continual repetitive petitions in harsh, unmistakable terms—which were about time.

But after that, the news flow stopped. Whether Crockett had given up (which seemed improbable), or she had given up on the new venture (also improbable), or the new man so fully satisfied her that she had quite forgotten me (entirely probable, but too painful to contemplate seriously for any length of time), I didn't know. I worried a bit—why be coy, a lot. The springtime within which most start-ups can blossom is a brief one at best, a moment that vanishes in a breath of wind. Almost always, they either bloom quickly or die. Mira did not have time to waste on barren ground.

I had another affair, even briefer, with another interesting woman who wasn't Mira. Winter became spring.

*

It was not until the first week of April that I once again heard the musicality of that exquisitely modulated voice on my telephone receiver. Early one Tuesday morning, a week short of the first anniversary of the start of our affair, the phone rang and there she was.

"Hello, Walter," she said. "I hope you're still friends with someone who calls you as seldom as I do."

"Mira," I said, taking enormous pleasure in the simple pronunciation of her name, "don't be silly. It's only a little after ten, and my day is already made. You know that."

"I've missed you, too, Walt," she said, an innocuous statement that will haunt me always, because at that time she meant it—she did miss me—and not merely as a friend. "But things have been frantic. Absolutely frantic."

"Crockett?"

"Oh, no. He's been quiet for a while. I think I owe you for that," she continued. "I can't tell you how grateful to you I am."

"Don't be," I answered. Her tendency to be grateful disproportionately for small favors always bothered me. "I didn't do all that much. It was mostly you. But what's up, if it isn't that?"

"The start-up," she answered immediately. "It's been frantic. We did presentation after presentation, and every one had something else to say, some comment or advice, and then we'd re-write and re-write—
"

"The usual drill," I said. "NATO—No Action, Talk Only. What my college girlfriends used to say about me." She laughed my favorite laugh, the peel of delighted surprise; she'd evidently never heard the phrase before. "When they're not going to fund you, they give you advice instead. Which is worth about what you pay for it."

"That's what we found out," she said. "But—Walt—"and now she made no attempt to disguise her excitement—"it's happened. Two days ago. $6,000,000 dollars for thirty percent of the company—and a quick close—in just four weeks. I'd told you about it, and so I wanted you to know. And to thank you."

"*Mira,*" I said, "I haven't done anything. There's nothing to thank me for. But I'm glad it's worked out." I paused. "Can you tell me more about it?"

"No," she laughed, a bit embarrassed this time. "They're a pretty secretive bunch."

"I'm not asking for details, just an overview." The need for confidentiality is one thing; this sounded slightly over the top.

"I know, it's ridiculous," she answered. "But I've made commitments about this. I know they're kind of silly commitments. But for now I'm going to honor them. Even with you."

"You are all right, though? You've got a place in all this?" I didn't give a damn about the business. Its only reason for existence as far as I was concerned was as a mechanism for securing her future.

"I'll be fine, Walt," she answered. "Everything will be all right. This is wonderful news." I let her leave it at that, we exchanged news about Nick and Alicia, made a lunch date, and a little while later she hung up.

Something in the tenor of the conversation bothered me, though at the time I could not say exactly what. Only a long time later did the cause emerge—a slight thing, really—a grammatical nuance—the use of the future tense. *I'll be fine, everything will be all right,* she'd said. She did not in fact have her deal in place. She was embarrassed as before to tell me that fact out right; she was hoping—I believe—that I would infer it, and do what was necessary.

I am writing about the woman who I prized above all others. I am not describing a goddess. Mira had her fair share of human weakness, perhaps more. In particular, she was too conventionally feminine ever to be comfortable demanding forthrightly what was rightfully hers, particularly from a man with whom she was romantically involved. She would trust—hope—wish—instead that demands would not be necessary, that the right thing would be done spontaneously, out of pure generosity of spirit, rather than from any sense of obligation—in the manner of a Prince. It's a traditional woman's failing, not being able to get tough with her man, expecting more of him than he deserves or good sense indicates. Perhaps it is the oldest. Certainly it is the most dangerous.

But all this came later. At that time, it did not occur to me that Mira was anxious. It did not occur to me that she had phoned me for a reason, either to stiffen her resolve or—better—to ask me to look into the matter myself. This was obviously not the politically correct approach to the problem, but it was her approach, to appeal to me, her one reliable protector, and I have certainly done much more out of common courtesy for women for whom I had little or no romantic feeling. She could have said more. She should have said more. But she did say enough. Something bothered me—but I did not press the point.

Nor did the most obvious fact of all occur to me, one that required no interpretation, only a calendar. Slightly over a year had elapsed since the day our affair began, on which Mira had declared with cheerful confidence that she would not be in her dreadful house much longer. But a year had come and gone, and she was still in her house. Her children still slept in one ridiculously overcrowded bedroom when they stayed with her; it was still as disgracefully decrepit and run-down. In fact, nothing of importance in her life had changed in any respect, except that she was another year older and—as the song goes—deeper in debt.

CHAPTER 10

▼

A psychologist, whose name I can't, but should, remember, once observed that the predators of either sex are totally transparent to members of their own gender, at the same time they are opaque to their victims of the opposite sex. School girls see straight through the hip-swaying, eyelids-lowered antics of the Jezebels, while university professors stare, fascinated and helpless. Garage mechanics shake their heads watching a Don Juan seduce one alert, well-educated professional woman after another with the same glib, transparently insincere romantic patter. But this objective view of the predator, completely available to those standing to one side, cold, clear-eyed, sober, is completely masked to the prey—for the predator's target is the core sense of self, the naked, beating heart in all its vulnerability. Brain stuff, wisdom and learning, has nothing to say to which it will listen. Thus neither intelligence nor experience confers immunity—and so it happens that even the strongest and wisest members of one gender may fall victim to obvious, even rather silly, wiles of the other.

I think the psychologist was correct. I believe his insight describes a fundamental truth.

*

Mira and Gregor Volkov became lovers some time shortly before Echelon received its first funding. How it came about, how the one-time consultancy was transformed into a romance, is an old, very familiar story. The basic cause was the oldest one of all, simple propinquity. Mira did not begin to have the range of choice in men that I imagined and hoped she did. As time went on, and she spent more and more of her free time at Echelon or in the company of Gregor Volkov or on working on Echelon projects, the range narrowed considerably. Between school, work, family, and moonlighting, her free time evaporated, steam boiling out of a kettle. Finally, the range narrowed to one, for her interest in Echelon and her social life coincided in the person of Gregor Volkov. The evolution was thus simple and natural, perhaps inevitable.

Also, he was charming in those days. He owed Mira an incalculable debt, and at that time he knew it, or appeared to. There was nothing substantive he could do. So his expressions of gratitude took the form of extravagantly theatrical gestures and declarations, simultaneously comic and endearing. They cost him nothing, but that didn't matter, for he had nothing to give. There are few women who would not have been touched and amused by them—and Mira was already disposed to find them touching and amusing.

For there was more than simple propinquity or charming words at work. Echelon had come to represent Mira's main hope for the future, and Gregory Volkov was for all practical purposes Echelon. His engineer friends were gifted, one even at the genius level, but they were technologists only. None of them had any interest in business or the driving personal ambition necessary to build an empire. Volkov did. Without him, there would be no Echelon, and without Echelon, there would be no new house, no end to Crockett, no transformation of her life.

Echelon represented salvation to Mira, and from there it was an easy, natural, psychological leap, actually more of a small hop, to attribute to

Gregor Volkov the virtues of a savior—kindness, generosity, magnanimity, the works. In reality, he was no one's savior but his own; not only did he not possess those virtues, but he was contemptuous of those who did. He was a shallow, relentless, determined egoist, completely self-centered, disinterested in the well-being of any other human being but himself.

This sounds like I'm demonizing Volkov, but I don't mean to. He deserves the credit for creating Echelon; it would not have come into existence had he been anyone other than who he was. He was not malicious; at the outset, he did not mean to do her harm. He was certainly not the demonic type of Don Juan the psychologist I quoted had in mind, a flamboyant sexual predator, misogynist posing as seducer, seeking to destroy her to complete the ritual of conquest. What he was, was an almost entirely goal-directed man, to the exclusion of any interest in any one or anything that lay outside the direction of the goal. The delight of Mira's body was not something he deliberately sought, but simply a perk, a fringe benefit that could be enjoyed along the journey. (My hands jerk off the paper as I write these words; I smooth my hair; I arise and pace stiffly about the room. Right this moment the posture of neutrality is not an easy one to maintain.)

But he did stiff Mira about the stock, and after a while he did it purposefully. Again I will try to put this in the most objective light possible. Gregor Volkov was not particularly greedy. He was just, even generous, to the techies he worked with, who would not have been sophisticated enough to argue if he had undercut them. He rewarded others who befriended him. But he did not give Mira her due. Why? The reason, in my opinion, had nothing to do with avarice, and everything to do with his insecurity. (It is only my opinion, but this is turf I know very well.)

The investor reaction to the first presentation that Gregor had done scared the bejeezus out of him. The investors had loved the product, but hated him. They had even hinted that a deal might be possible if he left the company and the engineers stayed. Volkov was no better than a mediocre technologist; his cachet was his organizational energy, his drive to succeed. If these qualities were of no value, he was useless—and that possibility terrified him.

Mira's business sense and business know-how were invaluable to him. But his need for that sort of help was the one thing above all else he wanted to conceal. Someone with a bit more sophistication might have realized that American businessmen and investors don't give a damn who is responsible for a solution so long as a solution is obtained, and that Mira's delicacy and charm would be a definite plus in any corporate equation. But Volkov was a Russian peasant—I have become tired of objectivity—and he approached the problem with a Russian peasant's cunning. The safest course as he saw it was concealment.

To go to his lawyers and direct that a contract be drawn up, or stock be issued, or a stock option granted to Mira, would have been to acknowledge overtly the one fact he wished most kept secret. If it had been a different service she had performed, a different favor she had done, doing her justice would have been no problem for him. But she had done him the unforgivable favor of helping him in the one area where most he needed help. That was a favor that would never ever be acknowledged, let alone recompensed. I will do him one last reluctant charity. I believe he probably thought a time would come when his position would be safe, when he could take care of her as she truly deserved. But that time never came, or when it did, was so chaotically entangled with the romantic threads that nothing ever happened.

If Mira had insisted forcibly on her rights, if she had stamped her foot and demanded her due, Volkov would have had to swallow his pride and give it to her. He needed her and her skills badly. But direct confrontational force was never Mira's style, her design for living—she wouldn't have been who she was if it were. What she did instead was allow herself, or persuade herself, to fall in love with him. Contracts and eye-to-eye negotiation she found uncomfortable. Love was what she believed in.

Mira imagined that their needs coincided in other ways. He was alone and friendless in a strange land. She was a woman with a huge number of social contacts and a ready-made family. It was (she thought) a good fit. She invited him over, on the major holidays and also for working sessions. It did not go as well as she might have hoped. But it did not go badly.

Volkov got on moderately well with her sons, and even expressed some guarded affection. Alicia was a different matter. Her appearance gave no clue to her disability; it was only when she spoke, and the delay in speech became apparent, that her condition became obvious. Volkov was clearly unnerved by this. That initial reaction bothered Mira to some extent, but it did not deter her. Many of her friends had to adjust to Alicia. She anticipated that Volkov would be one of them, and privately hoped that his increasing engagement with Alicia and the boys might lead him to take an interest in their financial well-being.

I wrote earlier that I am not describing a saint, but a woman, and so I am. There are few, if any, intimate relationships between adult men and women in which the comparison between what is offered to what is needed, that is, the basic formula for determining what is possible, does not play a part. Only school children and adulterers think otherwise. That practicality certainly was a component of my own relationship with Mira, and it was a big element of hers with Volkov. Occasionally, some born-again cynic comes along and points that practical fact out in some witty parallel aphorism a la Oscar Wilde, as if he had proven by algebra that love means nothing. But all he does is demonstrate his own naiveté. The world is not otherwise than it is, human beings are no different than they should be, and surprise at the discovery of commonplace truths is both trite and absurd.

But what Mira didn't comprehend was the actual character of Volkov. I wrote above I was almost done with charity towards him. Now I am completely finished. The description of him above as self-centered was a supreme euphemism. What he was, was narcissistic, with a capital `N'— not only that, but passive aggressive to boot. It was true he lacked malice, but only true because he lacked as well all of the other emotive reactions that link one human being to another. He was completely confined to his own ego, utterly unable to relate to any other human being in any empathetic manner.

All these personality traits were open and apparent to anyone on five minutes' acquaintance. The only type of person who could possibly have been deceived would be a member of the opposite sex, for the reasons the psychologist I quoted stated—and not just any woman, but one whose life was verging towards desperation, who could sense the cliff edge nearby, even if it were not visible to the rest of the world, and who was thus motivated to blind herself to all of the insurmountable difficulties the man's personality presented.

And that woman was Mira, at that time and in those circumstances.

*

Mira had handled the affairs of Echelon with a basic, native shrewdness that she did not display towards her own. She had hoped for the best in Gregor in those first presentations, but she did not expect any too much. The woeful performance he actually provided had justified her expectations, not her hopes. She had not set up appointments with any of her A-list investor sources, but those a little further down the list—in some cases, venture capitalists, in others, wealthy individuals, `angels' in the lingo, borrowed from Broadway jargon, most of whom were either problems or problematic themselves. It was a long shot, she knew, that any of them would come aboard, but not impossible, and there was no downside—none of the groups and individuals had enough stature in the investment community to poison his reputation if he mucked it up, which he did. Her foresight thus proved to be genuine wisdom.

Mira kept this aspect of the initial presentations to herself. Had Volkov known she had A-list contacts, in his impatience and conceit he would have demanded to meet them first, and that would have been a disaster. As it happened, things worked out perfectly. The scale of the fiascoes was sufficiently great that even Gregor Volkov realized he had a problem, and all the avenues to more serious investment money remained open. Over the next few months, she worked patiently with him, smoothing the rough edges of his personality (which were everywhere), teaching him at least the rudiments of business tact, trying to lighten him up. The goal was to prevent his inherent aggressiveness (a good thing) from becoming belligerence (a bad thing), his natural efficiency, an immature impatience. It was not one of those goals that could ever be completely realized, but every step in that direction was one more important step.

The reasons for this were the other events in the Echelon saga—for progress in the technological development of the company did not stand still while Gregor was learning to ape the behavior of the man in the gray flannel suit.

Echelon exhibited the Firebird at COMDEX in the fall, the big computer trade show at which anyone who is anyone shows up, and some four months later at the Interop Convention, a more specialized exhibit for businesses directly involved in internet communications and security. It was a wowser at both places, with the booth crowded with interested parties and potential customers. The Firebird was slick, efficient, practical, and cheap. Similar products were coming onto the market, but nothing with its bang for the buck. Somehow Gregor and Mira managed to scrape together enough capital to build three units for beta site testing, and the result was more raves.

All of this was proof enough to Mira that Echelon was possibly her dream come true. She redoubled her efforts with Gregor, putting him through several videotaped sessions, suggesting shticks for responses to difficult questions. Although Gregor was an irredeemable sow's ear, and a complete transformation to silk purse an impossibility, he did acquire at least the patina of sophistication. Time was flying; the moment for the product had arrived, the market niche was yawning open, and someone else would fill it if Echelon did not. She could wait no longer. With heart in mouth, she contacted the top name on her A-list, Mark Stewart, a junior partner in one of the major venture capital firms. She had known him way back when, as a tenant in one of her buildings with his own modest fund. He checked out the bona fides of the product, more as a favor to Mira than with any real belief in it, and was astonished to discover there was a fair amount of industry buzz about it among the ultra-insiders, to the extent that bringing the company on board would be a triumph for him. With rising excitement, he got back to Mira and scheduled a meeting.

Everything had changed in a year. The Firebird, touted only by its inventors in the first presentations, now had some real momentum. The Internet had expanded exponentially, so had the number of local area networks, and so, accordingly, had the market. Mira had sanded off the roughest edges of Gregor Volkov's arrogance and belligerence. What had come across as a brutal coarseness now fit into the category of the eccentricities of genius. Throughout the room the sound of opportunity knocking echoed, but also the sound of hoof beats—Mira's friend and his partners had done their homework, learned enough to know, that if they did not act, and quickly, that someone else would. Echelon's time had arrived.

Thus the deal came together, and—as is typical when the time arrives—with blinding speed. The light turned on, and it was as if the darkness had never been. It would not be accurate to say that Mira was responsible for the success—the quality of the engineering, the size of the emerging market, all the substantive factors, weigh far more than personality. But it is true that Echelon avoided failure because of her—she provided guidance and, more important, hope, at precisely the point and in the degree that Volkov and the others needed when they needed it. If it had not been for her, Echelon might have been just one more casualty of time and naiveté, an urn filled with ashes, frustration, and recriminations.

But now the company was launched, and on firm ground. Echelon was no longer the stuff of dreams or sandcastle fantasy. The theme song was no longer 'I can't give you anything but love. The time had come for substance and performance, not theatrical gestures.

It was exactly then, however, that Mira learned exactly how harsh and merciless was the world that she and Echelon had joined.

*

Mira had thought, reasonably enough, that the right time to take up the matter of what she was owed with Gregor was immediately after the investors had made their commitment. He was bursting with gratitude as well as what she took to be affection. The future seemed limitless. She asked for a number of shares equal to about two percent of what Gregor and the other founders owned, or one percent of the total. They were to be common shares, like the founders. If the company thrived, she would do well, anywhere from between two to ten million dollars. But if it failed she would get nothing. She would take her chances with them. These were not disproportionate demands. Gregor agreed to them immediately.

But what she had not counted on was the new dynamic of the situation. Suddenly the shares, less valuable than wall paper the week before, were priceless. The investors, who had paid hard money for their shares, begrudged any issuance to anyone. The portfolio managers were hard, flinty-eyed men. As far as they were concerned, day one for Echelon was the day of their investment. Whatever Mira might have done for the company before then didn't count—she hadn't done anything for *them*. Mark Stewart was a junior partner, of little consequence and less use. When it came down to cases, he kept his mouth shut and looked after his own interest.

Gregor Volkov was catapulted into this new universe with equal suddenness. As soon as a handshake agreement was reached, the investment group began meeting with him as the CEO. He was introduced into a world he could hardly imagine, of elegant violence and hushed, sophisticated threat, of accounting and reporting responsibilities of which he had dreamt. He had thought he'd be a free agent; he quickly learnt he'd be anything but. The lessons in poise and posture he'd learned from Mira had at least gone deep enough to mask his anxiety and uncertainty. But he realized quickly enough how negatively his new partners would view the payment of a finder's fee, how weak and naïve they would perceive him to be if he insisted upon it—and he came quickly to dread the appearance of weakness and naiveté.

Mira for her part waited patiently for action, and none came. After a time, she brought the matter up again, delicately, and was put off again, also delicately. Finally she pressed again, harder—and Gregor Volkov exploded, into a passive-aggressive tantrum.

It was all *her* fault. He had been embarrassed, humiliated, and he blamed *her*. No one paid finder's fees or gave stock for past services. Why *hadn't she told him that? He had embarrassed himself in even bringing the matter up. The deal should have been in place before they ever sought out venture capitalists. He relied on her for this sort of counsel, but she had let him down. Mira was his adviser; she should have warned him; but instead she had allowed him to steer straight into the iceberg when she knew, she must have known, what a fool the investment manager would think him to be. He had tried for her, he had done his best, but the only result was that he, Gregor Volkov, had been made to play the fool before people whose respect he needed and craved—and it was all her fault.*

She pressed him then, hard. What was she going to get?—and he finally told her: Nothing. Not a share. There was nothing he could do. He had done his best, begged, pleaded, but this was priceless stock now, and he could not point to any value she was going to add to the company from this point on. All he had done was damage his own credibility—for which he blamed her. History meant nothing to these people. Why hadn't she known this? Why hadn't she told him? How could she send him to these people with her silly requests with no forewarning?

(As always in the case of the truly manipulative types, there was a small kernel of truth in Volkov's whine of self-justifying complaint. She really should have taken care of herself earlier. I had told her as much. But the whole was a monstrous lie. Of course he could have secured her stock for her. All it would have taken was some insistence, some banging on the table—the stock was not that much that he would have encountered any entrenched opposition. The only consequence he would have experienced was a few sidelong glances and a small dent to his pride. But he was unwilling to sacrifice even that much.

He could also—perish the thought—have compensated her out of his own stock holding. After the investment shares had been accounted for, he owned about 35% of the company, with the other founders holding another 20%, and the investors the rest. The shares Mira had earned wouldn't have made any difference to him; there was more than enough left to make him rich beyond the meaning of the word—and without her, none of those shares would have been worth anything. But neither then nor

later did he ever consider such a deed. He was always willing to do her jus-
tice, so long as it cost him nothing. Any act that would lessen the power,
glory, or personal estate of Gregor Volkov was not within the realm of his
contemplation).

Mira Watson was not a fool, then or ever. Her first instinct was to leave
immediately, and that was the right instinct. But he begged her to stay. He
swore he had no choice. He needed her, wanted her—without her, he
would be nothing. Somehow he would make this up to her, he promised.
One day it would all be made right—if only she would stay.

So her life came down to harder choices than she had ever imagined she
would face. She may have deceived herself in large part, but her affection
for Volkov was real enough—it is impossible to associate with anyone on a
long, difficult problematic project, without moments occurring of shared
intimacy, private jokes, a sense of us-against-the-world togetherness devel-
oping. There was that, plus the sexual bond; Mira was the type of woman
could not give a man her body without giving him her heart as well. Pride
was involved; she could not believe that any man who she thought she loved
would treat her so callously, so indifferently, if he had any real choice. He
relentlessly exploited that small kernel of truth—her deal really should have
been in place, and her responsibility for it. Perhaps it was her fault—after
all, I told her as much. She was at least partially to blame.

Finally, and hardly the least significant, there was the monkey's hand
clutched around the bait—Echelon itself, an opportunity that blind luck
had brought her, the solution to all her problems, that might not recur in a
thousand thousand lifetimes. If she stayed, she at least had some hope that
she would get what she earned. To walk out was to write off all she had
done, all she had sacrificed, as wasted effort.

In this way the tapestry unrolled, in a manner she could not have envi-
sioned when she began in all innocence, the Law of Unintended Conse-
quences exhibited in all its glory. The bottom line is that…she stayed. She
chose to wait, and hope he would make things right one day soon—and in
deciding in this way, she closed the trap tight behind her. The only action
in which her better instinct showed itself was that one phone call she made

to me, and that odd use of the future tense describing arrangements that should have been history. It was a subtle message, too subtle for the real world—and yet I did hear the strangeness in her words, pondered its significance, and, as was typical in those years, did nothing. I believe that the possibility of betrayal had already become too painful a subject for her discuss aloud, so horrible and unthinkable a prospect that it could only be hinted at.

For by that time she had staked much more on the success of Echelon than mere time and money.

*

I had also noticed that the flow of monthly petitions from Crockett about the children had ceased. I assumed that the reason was that Crockett and his pig of a lawyer had finally given up the struggle. I was mistaken. The petitions had been filed as relentlessly as ever. What had changed is that Mira had become reluctant to show them to me. The reason was that they now contained some genuine causes for complaint.

Mira was a superb mother, then and later. But every working woman will understand her situation. Family pulls one way, job pulls the other— two massive gravitational forces, relentless, implacable, contorting the normal lines of life into all sorts of twisted and unnatural curves. Such is the lot of the typical single mother. But start-ups aren't typical—if a normal employed mom feels the gravitational force of the job pulling on her like the distant moon, Mira was living right next door to a black hole, a dark pit of absolute demand that vacuumed everything nearby into its depths. There were no five o'clock whistles at Echelon. There were no coffee breaks. There was no paid vacation or scheduled holidays. There were no job descriptions. There was only the constant pressure to do, to perform, to accomplish an infinite amount of work in a finite and constantly decreasing amount of time, which is what the basic start-up dream of making something out of nothing amounts to.

Everyone else at Echelon worked without stopping. For the techies, that was no problem—their vocation was their avocation. They both had cots at the offices; if intravenous feedings could have been arranged, they would never have left their work stations. All Gregor Volkov cared about was the empire he hoped to build. If Mira hoped to keep up with them, if she hoped to participate in the world they were creating, she knew that she had to match that degree of dedication. The fact that she was the only one of the group with other responsibilities didn't matter. Gravity is conscienceless.

She had not realized when she began how open-ended the process actually was. Each concession, small or large, was to be the last concession. But then a new crisis would arise, a new demand on her time. Volkov, whose ego was probably more infantile than any of her children, neither knew nor cared about the other demands on her time. His only concern was his own needs, and his constant whine was that they were not met speedily enough.

So the first cracks appeared—a forgotten appointment here, a late arrival there. Crockett's petitions took due note of every oversight. The worst came two nights before the first Echelon trade show. Either the babysitter overlooked her message or she never left one, Mira could not be sure (although she was next to certain it was the former). The result was the children were left unattended for nearly three hours. Nothing happened; her sons were then over nine, old enough to be unsupervised for a short period of time in their own home, and to see to it that Alicia did not get into any trouble. But it did not look good in cold print, particularly in connection with all the other recent mishaps. Mira began to sense a coldness in the family court now that she had not encountered before, a change in the direction of the wind. She had been anxious about the constant petitions before, in the way that anyone can be worried about the range of possibility, but in her rational mind knew there was no need to worry. Now that same rational mind told her that circumstances had changed—that there was good reason for worry and fear. All she could do was hope that the Echelon process would come to some definite end—at which point she could return herself and her children to something resembling the lifestyle that had so recently been hers. Only a short year had elapsed, but it seemed to Mira as if several centuries had passed.

Graduate school, of course, had disappeared almost at the start, a luxurious expenditure of time she could no longer afford. Her relations with her family had suffered subtle, but real damage. As year two began, all she had in exchange was the promise of the chief executive officer of the newly capitalized Echelon Corporation, that a day would come when he would make everything right.

The hopes and dreams of Mira Watson had thus come to depend almost exclusively on the good will and honorable intentions of Gregor Volkov.

CHAPTER 11

▼

I hung up the phone that day full of melancholy, with the wistful longing that was the usual aftermath of a contact with Mira—wanting her, frustrated that I could not have her, too blindly convinced of the correctness of my own short-sighted rationalizations to fight back against the fate that had supposedly arranged matters that way. The woman I was seeing—I have forgotten who—would wonder why I was so distracted and out of myself that Friday or Saturday night. But whatever my own frustrations, I was truly happy for Mira, that her luck with money matters had finally turned.

I was not in the least envious of her. Almost the worst sin anyone can commit, a compound of two of the deadliest sins, envy and greed, is to be jealous of someone else's good luck. One of the works I sang in my college choir (I have a more than passable bass voice, a point of vanity) was Carl Orff's *Carmina Burana,* a collection of medieval chansons, drinking songs of the university students back then. *O Fortuna Imperatrice!*—Luck, the empress of the universe—goes the verse of the first, set to a magnificent fanfare and a massed chorus. When I was nineteen, I believed the sentiment was true, maybe because of the magnificence of the fanfare, maybe because when you're nineteen you can believe that luck does indeed rule and that all of yours will be good. Luck, the Empress—why not?

But it isn't so. Luck comes in too many shapes and sizes, plays too many parts, to be cast in any one role. Sometimes it does indeed beckon imperially from a throne—but other times, perhaps more often, it plays a bit part, scurrying around the back alleys of a life, tugging at the sleeve of the top-hatted main events, begging for a moment's attention as they stride down the avenue. Most often it wears disguises. Many of those who think they have colossal amounts of it actually don't have much. Many of those who think they don't have any at all have more of it than they could possibly imagine.

I have met a boatload of people in the last few years who commiserate with me about Nick. They have got it dead wrong. They've read the tea leaves backwards or are looking in the wrong cup. The entrance of Nick into my life was the most marvelous break I ever got in my time on earth. I've learned more from Nick about human nature, about myself, about the complexity of this moral existence, about the paltriness of linear achievement and trophy-hunting, than I could have from a library of philosophers or a cathedral of bishops. I do have worries, but they are for Nick and his future—the extent to which he is and will be vulnerable to the cruelty and indifference of the larger world. For me personally, knowing Nick, parenting him, has been a pure, undiluted blessing.

Many of the same people who offer me comfort about Nick are openly envious of my luck with money. That has been more than good, that has been extraordinary. But if there is such a thing as irrelevant luck, my good fortune there qualifies. Of course it is much better to have money than not—who's kidding whom—but my attitude towards money has always been binary. I either have enough of it or not enough. I have been fortunate enough to have enough during most of my adult life. That's all that needs be said about that. Money has never been a way of keeping score or a measure of success or—worst of all—an indicium of moral worth. Beyond a certain point of living well and with reasonable security, goals which most middle-class Americans in these extraordinary times are able to achieve, there isn't much you can do with money, except squander it in one way or another.

So my good will for Mira was genuine. I hoped the money would work out, and I hoped—and believed—that the man that came with it would work out as well. That man, his identity then unknown to me, I did envy. That man I considered to be one of the luckiest men on the planet.

*

Elizabeth, the older of my two children, had been my primary concern at the time of the separation. Elizabeth had none of Nick's disabilities. She was an exceptionally bright girl, quick, verbal, thoughtful, and with a social intelligence quotient as typically high as bright girls' usually are. Nick's problems are birth problems, only marginally connected to the decisions I made about my own life. But Elizabeth could be hurt, and hurt badly, by what Linda and I did to one another.

I have sometimes wondered whether she was aware of the breakup even before Linda announced it. Elizabeth did and does have that kind of precocity. When we found a suitable condominium for my move-out, we took her and her brother out to see it. She pretended great enthusiasm—it had a swimming pool, and a number of the owners kept cats, which she loves. It would be a wonderful place to spend weekends. But I sensed that she knew that something was up, something that was not too cool—a caution, a distinct wariness that provided a sepia undertone to all the surface acceptance.

Linda's and my dissolution began as a trial separation. I moved over to the condominium, but I saw the kids every day. I did not raise the subject of the change in our life style—but on those rare occasions when Elizabeth brought it up or when it came up naturally, I would point out that her life hadn't changed at all. I had always been an early riser and usually gone to work before she was up and about. She was not used to my presence in the mornings anyway—and I was still available, as I always had been, during the evenings.

These were truthful enough statements, but self-serving, and she saw right through them. Elizabeth became watchful, openly wary, in those years, waiting for the other shoe to drop. She knew other kids from broken homes—children whose parents didn't speak to each other, children who had to be delivered from one parental residence to the other by neutral third parties because the one-time lovers could no longer stand the sight of each other. She waited and wondered, and worried, whether her mother's relationship and mine would deteriorate to that state of warfare.

Continual anxiety of this type will leave its mark on anyone. Elizabeth had always been a private child, in many ways a remarkably private child. Even in happier days, before she had started kindergarten, when her horizons were completely unclouded, I would occasionally come across her sitting on the floor of her room, cross-legged lotus style, thinking deep thoughts she would refuse to share with me.

But these had been domestic moments. Now she became brooding and markedly more introverted at school and elsewhere, places where not long before she had been gregarious and outgoing. At the parent-teacher conferences, we learned she spent much of her free time in the library, reading all manner of books, and kept to herself far more than she had previously. I don't want to make this appear too melodramatic—the change in Elizabeth's behavior was not all that striking, she had always had her private side, she was still friendly and popular with the other girls, and there are worse things in life than being a little bookish. (In fact, she reminded me of myself at that age.) But there was cause for concern.

The other shoe finally did drop for Elizabeth, but not in the manner or to the degree that she expected. On July 4th, some eighteen months after I had moved out, Linda finally told me that she wanted to divorce formally. This came as a blow, but not a shock. She also informed me that she'd told Elizabeth a few weeks earlier about her decision. This was one of the few occasions when I became really angry with Linda, for Elizabeth had said nothing about this and I knew (knowing her) that she had been thinking about it—thinking about it a lot. As it happened, she was at some day camp outing for the Fourth at an amusement park. It was my turn to pick her up. She chattered happily as she got into the car. As I drove her back towards the Big House, I mentioned that her mother had decided on divorce and that I knew Elizabeth was aware of this. At once she became very quiet.

"Does that worry you at all?" I asked gently, in the silent car.

"Kinda," she answered after a while—a very surprising answer, as Elizabeth usually denied having any worry about anything.

"What are you worried about?" I asked, gently again.

"Well," she said, "if you and Mom get divorced, maybe you'll move back to North Carolina, you like North Carolina basketball so much." So it happens—even children with unusual insight and precocity need reassurance on the damndest things in the damndest ways. The exploits of the North Carolina Tarheels, in myth and reality, do provide me with a nice winter's entertainment, a diversion from the more serious things in my life. But no way, no how, not in the last millennium, or this one, or the next 500, would a college basketball team ever have that sort of priority in my life.

But I took her worry seriously. In the same tone she asked the question, I answered that she and Nick were the most important human beings on earth to me, that I would not be leaving, then or ever. Then, seizing the opening—because Elizabeth did not give up that many openings—I reminded her that the worse thing that she'd thought could happen, divorce, now actually had happened and that her life hadn't changed and that it wasn't going to change—not any more than it had. She nodded in agreement with this, but this was real life, not television or the movies, and we were a long way from knotty problems resolved in a half hour, by the giving of some patently obvious advice with which the central character agrees instantly.

It seemed like only one more incident among others. Elizabeth still did a lot of brooding, but it pleased me to think that the wariness, the anxiety was gone or at least greatly diminished. I would have forgotten all about it, but as it turned out a bottom was touched that day. It became a milestone. About eighteen months later, I was driving over to a girl's basketball practice for the junior high team she was on. We were talking about everything and nothing, certainly not any of the central issues in our lives. Perhaps it was the basketball practice that sprung something loose in her subconscious. As she got out of the car, she suddenly turned to me.

"You were right, Dad," she said casually.

"When, honey?" I answered, completely surprised. Elizabeth admitting out loud I'm right about anything is blue moon stuff. "About what?"

"That day in the car—when you told me you'd never move. Right about my life. Nothing has changed. I've still got my mom and dad."

"When you get to be thirteen," I said, deflecting the emotion, "you might not think that's quite as good a deal as you do now." The light response was the only one possible. If I'd launched into heavy duty sentimentality, she'd never have opened up to me again. She laughed at the joke and ran off to be with her friends, and all was well.

I don't mean that Elizabeth lived happily ever after, or that she became a perfect kid. This is not a fairy tale. But the adolescent troubles she did have were the standard ones, the pecking order stuff that adolescent girls seem to delight in inflicting on each other, without cease and without regret. She did avoid the major pitfalls—drugs, alcohol, premature sex—and ended up taking the academic high road as well. There is not one day in her life that I have not been proud of her.

Another knot in my life had thus untied itself. My relationship with Elizabeth, like all family relationships, was a continuum; landmarks were hard to come by; watershed days did not announce themselves. Little by little I was succeeding in all I had planned to do when the separation was visited upon me. I was regaining some right to a life of my own—not that that mattered to me at all.

*

Elizabeth has never met Mira. These were the years in which Mira, or anyone with whom I was involved, would have had to remain in the half-light. She accepted that fact; she had similar issues of her own. The success I finally achieved with my daughter was not easily come by, and in the blink of an eye, the raising of an eyebrow, it could all have turned out differently. Mira knew that; she possessed the same insight. But considerably greater wisdom lay beneath it.

The day on which I watched my daughter skip happily away from my car to join her friends occurred only a few weeks after the lunch in which Mira told me of the funding of the company which—I now know—was Echelon. Looking back, it was a day on which my personal options began to return, on which I regained the right to make some choices of my own. Stretching another metaphor to the breaking point and beyond, sunshine could now (cautiously) begin to reappear in all the dark corners of my life. But I was too close to the event to have that perspective. It is doubtless a good thing to succeed at your life's goals. But it is much, much better to have at least some minimal, foggy awareness that you have done so.

Still, I doubt that greater awareness would have produced any different result at that moment in time. Mira had made her choice and was in love, or thought she was. Despite the disappointment she had hinted at so subtly at that lunch, she remained committed to the man and confident (at least at the conscious level) of the outcome. All past lovers, no matter how strong the pull might be, were welcome to remain friends. For the time being, as far as I was concerned, she was out of reach.

*

The speed of time is relative to the degree of familiarity. Start a new job, move to a strange city, and events will move slowly, as slowly as the routines are novel and the streets lead to odd, unique places. As the procedures become customary and the roads common and ordinary, time steps up its own pace.

The marital separation had taken me to a strange new country, one no one I knew had visited. At the outset, I didn't know what to think, let alone what to do. The process of finding my own place, moving out, setting up a relationship with the kids, and all the rest were new and alarming. It had been years since I had been involved in the dating scene and of course I had never been there as a divorced man. The only feature of separated life I was spared was the legal wrangling, thanks to Linda's basic decency, and our mutual good sense.

Time moved slowly then, often with glacial slowness. But as it passed, I found myself becoming accustomed to the face of this new life. Two years had gone by since I moved out, a year since I met Mira, and I found myself looking forward for the first time in a long time. During that whole period, I had lived in my condominium as if it were a motel, sleeping there, eating there, but devoting most of my waking attention to the Big House and Nick and Elizabeth. Now I began to devote some thought energy into transforming it into my own home, and found—to my considerable surprise that I enjoyed the effort.

These were the years of the great boom of the late 90's, if it may be called that—'years of ridiculously inflated stock prices' may be a slightly more accurate description. The small community of orchards and farm workers that I grew up in had now become one of the watch towers of the world. All around me, people were making fortunes, or thought they were. Home prices shot up, including my condominium and Mira's hovel. Anyone who owned a parcel of real property was delighted and speculated about whether they could sell and retire in

Montana. Those who didn't own a home speculated about moving to Montana and not retiring. It was a time of entrepreneurs and charlatans, miracles and mirages, complexly intertwined and commingled—no one was entirely sure who was who and which was which, particularly since the largest miracles had more than a little mirage in them. History has yet to come to any final judgment about the matter, and maybe never will. The moving finger has moved on.

As a card-carrying member of the civil service, I was a cynical spectator to most of this. The 80's had been my entrepreneurial time. I had cashed in my chips on my two major successes shortly after I joined the District Attorney's Office, and I had no wish to climb back onto that roller coaster again. For some people, the natural born optimists among us, it is a giddy and exhilarating ride. But for me, anything but optimistic by nature, it had been a time of uncertainty, nauseating anxiety, one that had undermined my marriage and my life—despite the fact that, when the smoke cleared, I had actually done spectacularly well financially. I had no wish whatever to renew that life, however much money might be available.

As it happened, however, events that had occurred in the antediluvian times of my entrepreneurial practice, items that I thought had been permanently consigned to the dustbin of history, turned out to have a surprising significance in the present. Back in the early 80's, I had been involved with a start-up that had hoped to provide financial services via a personal computer and an electronic bulletin board. It was promising technology, but in those days not that many people owned personal computers, modems were expensive and difficult -to-operate peripherals, and the Internet was still the province of military scientists and academic geeks. The bottom line was that it went nowhere. It was a shame because the founder was a quality guy, someone I really liked, albeit a bit too futuristic for his own good. I took some stock in lieu of fees, wrote off the rest, and forgot about the venture as the years wore on.

The founder, however, proved to be an individual of enormous tenacity in addition to his other virtues. Somehow he stuck it out, throughout the 80's, treading water financially, improving his technology, and building networks throughout the financial community. After I joined the district attorney's office, I lost touch with him. But one day about six months after the second anniversary of the separation, I was surprised to have a letter from him forwarded to me that had originally been addressed to the Big House. When I opened it, I was delighted to discover a check, for payment of legal fees that had been rendered more than twelve years earlier. It was fairly considerable delight, for the amount was just under $25,000, money that I never expected I'd see in my life.

It didn't change much. Half of it went to Linda as community property (I was scrupulous about such matters, which was one of the reasons we avoided the tar pits of family court) and my half went towards a couple of improvements that I had had in mind for the condo. What it portended was what was truly significant. My old friend and client might have been a stand-up guy, but he wasn't a saint, and I wasn't one of the objects of his charity. He didn't have to pay me a dime; the statute of limitations had run years before, and I'd forgotten about it anyway. What was for sure going on is that someone was cleaning up the balance sheet of my old client, paying all the old debts and settling all the old accounts, in preparation either for an acquisition or a public offering—and that meant that my ancient stock holding in the company, the 2,000 shares of common stock which I'd always thought that some day I'd use as wallpaper, might actually be worth something.

There was nothing in the letter to make me suspect that anything was imminent. But I was sufficiently motivated to stop by my safety-deposit box one Saturday and make certain that the share certificate was still there.

It was.

*

It always came back to her voice.

I could live day to day easily enough, by no means unhappily, but without ambition, without any special direction, without any personal ambition. I used the internet dating services. I met women. I liked many of them. I slept with some. These are without exception pleasant memories.

But little by little, sooner or later, her voice would recall itself to me. It would begin as the memory of a whisper, then a modest yen, finally a longing, an irresistible craving—not touch, or see, or bed, but simply to *hear*. Mira should, I knew, be relegated to a map of the past, an island where I had once passed some exceptionally pleasant days before resuming the journey. But, I reasoned, I had done that relegation; the active affair was firmly consigned to history; she was an object of my concern and protection—so what was the harm in phoning her every so often to touch base? Thus did my heart rationalize its deepest needs, without my having to come to any conscious awareness of what that need implied.

I would be as tense as a school-boy when I placed these calls, every six or eight weeks, stomach knotted, heart in mouth, as the phone rang. Mira was as difficult to reach as ever, as the pace of rental activity and tenants' needs picked up with the boom. Usually I left a message. Then there would be another rising curve of tension, as the phone rang over the next afternoon or morning, rising faster with each disappointment that the caller wasn't her. But finally she would be there—and all the nervousness would dissipate in an instant. We'd make relaxed small talk for a few moments—children, current events—and then, my aural thirst slaked, the hunger appeased, I would ring off, until the next time. I never asked directly about the other man, of course, or the larger, more momentous happenings in her life. I have been there myself; discussing prospects and possibilities makes everyone a bit uncomfortable, almost superstitious, like baseball players who don't mention a no-hitter while the game is in progress.

So we didn't talk of anything that was meaningful. But that wasn't the point. It was simply to hear—reciting the multiplication tables would have done as well—and thereby restore the rotation of my soul to its proper axis.

*

So I heard her often. But I only actually saw Mira once that entire year, and then not until nearly ten months had passed since our last lunch. The winter holidays had come and gone, and spring was nigh. I made one of those calls, simply to hear her, or, more accurately, to feel her presence again. A huge, spectacular movie about two young people on a doomed ship was out and doing great guns at the box office. It was loved, or hated, or both, but impossible to disregard. Being the father of a thirteen year old girl, I had already seen it twice. I don't remember the direction our small talk took to bring the topic up, but it did. I was not surprised, given all the demands on Mira's time, that she hadn't seen the film, but nonetheless I was disappointed for her. She was as visual a person as I was aural, and would have enjoyed it on the basis of spectacle alone. But it did have a very romantic plot, and I knew her well enough to know that that, too, would appeal to her. In day-to-day life she liked to pretend that she was the original Hard-Hearted Hannah, but it wasn't so.

"You really should see it on the big screen," I said. "It's not the sort of picture that's going to translate very well to tape."

"I don't even own a television," she said, and laughed.

"Look," I said, "this is just too much, you'd like it so much. I'll take you, if you like. One of these Saturday nights." Up to then, I'd just been talking—but as I said these words, a window opened up into my soul, a rare occurrence in those days. A visceral excitement took hold in the pit of my stomach and journeyed down to the tips of my toes.

The suggestion, and perhaps the mood, caught her by surprise, and she became quiet and thoughtful. "It doesn't have to be a romantic evening," I said in my quiet voice. I did not want the matter to remain a thought only. The possibility of seeing her again socially had suddenly galvanized me.

"It can't be romantic, Walt," she said, reflecting, thinking. "Something's sorta going on. As you know."

"I will be on best behavior," I said. "I promise," and I meant it.

"All right," she answered after a moment. "I'm free next Saturday night. One of my friends"—meaning her lover, I understood her code—"will be out of town. At a business conference."

"Done," I said, ecstatic. I pressed her to let me take her to dinner, but she was having none of it—another one of those arcane dating rules of hers, I suppose. A movie was a pleasant evening with an old friend. Dinner was romantic and thus strictly forbidden.

I made my own feeble excuses to the woman I was seeing about my unavailability for our normal Saturday night get-together and picked Mira up on the appointed night at her decrepit little house about 6:30. Just over three years had then passed since the first time I saw it, and she was still living there, nothing changed. But I gave it as little thought as ever—her life, I believed, was on the move. It takes time to start up a company, have its stock inure value, and then cash it out. In the meantime, hope renders everything endurable and makes patience easy.

Mira did not wait for me to come up the doorstep, but came out to meet me—another dating rule would be my guess—Casual Dates Are Not Allowed Indoors. But as she did so, all the rules, dating and otherwise, vanished. Every nuance, every minuscule speck of beauty and splendor lying in majestic dormancy in the setting coalesced into one flash of pure, unified feeling. A year, more or less, had gone by since I had seen her. The April evening, just a week or two after the switch to daylight time, was spectacular, spring everywhere, in the soft twilight, the green of the street trees, the songs of the birds and insects, music of renewal, diminishing in the dusk. As it happened, the sun was setting in the west behind her as she came up to me. It backlit her, tinged her chestnut hair slightly red, touched her face with a candlelight glow— she seemed to be the live, incandescent spirit of the spring evening, its ultimate embodiment, as if all that was warm and alive in the night and the air was emanating from some deep glow within her. I could live in that moment for the rest of eternity and never complain. She was not at all dolled up, dressed down in fact, and yet I had never seen her love- lier. I have never seen anyone lovelier. Destiny was once again doing its damndest.

I could see the magic of the occasion had caught her as well. "*Walter*," she said with her 100-watt smile, extending the syllables, tak- ing pleasure in the mere pronunciation of my name. She slid into the passenger seat, squeezed my hand—I knew for sure that this was *not* one of the dating rules—and we started off.

We had a wonderful time. I bought popcorn, of course with no but- ter, and Mira even amazed me by eating two kernels. Late in the film, she went to the ladies room and, when she returned, commented wryly on how much mascara was running there. I was too diplomatic to point out that her own was running as well.

When I brought her home, I did walk her to her door. After that squeeze, we had adhered strictly to the agreed decorum—no touching, no hand-holding, just two old friends supposedly renewing their acquaintanceship. She opened the door and turned to me.

"Good night, Walt," she said. "I had a great time."

"Likewise," I answered, and bent to give her a decorous peck of a good-night kiss. What happened then was right out of the movies— not the recent ones, but the ones made back in the 30's and 40's. I administered my peck; she pecked back; I kissed her reflexively a bit harder; she kissed me back harder still, and put her hands on my rib cage; and then—simultaneously—as she stepped up into my arms, I swept her up against me. Then I was kissing her mouth, neck, shoul- der, stroking the softness of her arms and back, melting into the aroma of her hair, the sweetness of her breath. Her hands found their way up my back, over my shoulders, she opened her mouth, she stood on tip toe and pressed herself into my chest. I noticed something odd about her body, something different, but the world was swirling about my ears, too much was happening too fast and with too little warning, to ponder the matter.

Mira drew back from me, looked into my eyes, then pressed her face into my chest.

"Walt," I heard her say, muffled, but still a wonder to hear, "Oh, Walter, Walter." I smoothed her hair, over and over, an absolute delight and wondered what I could do, what I should do. At that moment, I wanted her more than I ever did, or ever will, want anyone.

She pulled back from me and looked straight up into my eyes. It was a look I remembered well, from our very first evening, her *take me* look. I do not believe that a woman has ever lived who did it better. I understood her completely, what she was offering me, what at that moment she was hoping I would do. I broke off the eye contact and looked out over the night, trying to weigh everything, balance all, put the matter into complete perspective. All this time, I continued to stroke her hair. Then I met her eyes again.

"How important is—this—to you?" I finally asked. By 'this' I meant 'this person'. She in turn understood me completely.

"Very, very important," she said softly. She held my eye for another second or two, then broke off. I held her another long, long moment. Then I released her, and stopped back. We had come to a mutual decision. She believed what she'd said. Her instincts, her body, knew better, but she made herself believe. We were so alike in some ways.

"If that's the case, I'd better go," I said.

"Yes," she said, but I could see—feel—her own keen disappointment in that outcome. I knew my own. I stepped back another step.

"I didn't mean this to happen," I said randomly.

"I know," Mira answered forlornly. "We always had great chemistry. Sometimes it's frustrating."

I, for sure, had no disagreement with that.

*

The phone rang in the middle of the next morning, as I sat amidst Sunday papers and bitter second thoughts. Her voice sounded in my ear.

"Hi, Walt."

"Mira," I answered.

"I just wanted—" she hesitated, finding words—"to thank you—for last night. I didn't mean the movie—I meant—you know."

"I do indeed," I said.

"I always respected your nobility," she went on. "I don't know what got into me last night."

"Right this second," I replied, "I'm very much regretting what *didn't* get into you last night," which sent her into peels of the surprised, delighted laughter that always gladdened my soul.

"It was for the best, Walt," she said, when she'd quieted down. "We—you—did the right thing last night."

"Just tell me one thing, my daaaarlin'"—I drew the word out, Bogart-style, joking because I meant to be ultra-serious—"tell me that you love this guy. That it's a good thing for you."

"Yes," she said, surprised, nonplused. "Yes—I mean"—she hesitated for just a split second too long—"yes, I do love him. And it is a very, very good thing."

"You're sure?" I repeated, because the hesitation bothered me.

"Yes," she repeated with more emphasis, "yes. Which is why last night was a good thing. And you must know, if it weren't for that, Walt, there's no one I'd rather—"

"Oh, for God's sake, Mira, don't go *there*, unless you want me to kill myself," which produced another gale of laughter. We moved off to other topics, deliberately small, unimportant stuff, and after a while she rang off. But the initial hesitation in her answer stayed with me.

*

And if I had followed the promptings of my heart—and body—as I held her in my arms on her doorstep? Or listened to the whispers of my inner ear, when I asked her the important questions? I don't know the answers to any of these questions. I don't know what would have happened.

Destiny persisted with extraordinary zeal with Mira and me. It was a very determined fellow. But its patience was not unlimited, and its patience was running out. On that night and the morning after, I squandered completely what still another terrific chance. Another opportunity had knocked hard on my door, and—like all of the others, before and after—been rudely dismissed. They would not be—they could not be—unlimited.

What would have happened exactly if I'd pressed on, I don't know. What I do know for certain is that everything would have been different. I would have found out then and there why her body seemed changed to me, what she had done to herself, and why. She would have had to leave the realm of wishful thinking and consider the actual direction her life was taking. The orderly illusions with which we were both living, convincing in part because they were so orderly, so methodical, so commonplace, would have been kicked into whirring, skithering chaos.

Everything would have been different—that is the only fact of which I am sure.

But that would be enough. That would be fine.

CHAPTER 12

▼

The funding of a start-up company, particularly by an established venture capital company, is not simply a matter of a transfer of funds, a number with a few zeros subtracted from one bank account and added to another. It is not even a matter of dreams coming true, a few lucky individuals living happily ever after.

What it is, is an act of utter transformation. The universe in which the participants have been living is totally rearranged, top to bottom. The good news is that everything is completely different. The bad news is that EVERYTHING is completely different.

*

For a few days after the funding, Mira went on as if nothing had changed. The lack of any solid commitment about stock at that time bothered her, but it was more irksome than a large-scale worry. I have already recounted the full story of that dismal episode. But in those first glorious days of afterglow and optimism, Gregor Volkov was hysterically effusive in his gratitude; she was the most popular person in history in the eyes of the other founders; she was confident that it would all be resolved appropriately. Yet everything had changed, and the effects of the change began to be felt before a week had passed.

The first item on the agenda of the new investors was fleshing out the skeleton that was Echelon. The company consisted of two genius inventors, one red-ass promoter, and a part-time adviser. To become a substantial business—the type that would appear credible first to the industry and later to the public—it needed a sales department, a marketing department, financial personnel, administrative help. The word spread about the new company and its needs throughout the whole MBA-driven world of venture capital, as dense and closely connected as crabgrass. It was the ideal set-up—a newly funded company, solvent enough to be without risk, but small enough to offer the quantities of founder stock and stock options that could make a multi-millionaire out of the deserving twenty-something business school grad with the speed and ease that each considered his natural right.

Endless meetings and interviews took place, during which Gregor Volkov was lionized (if not canonized) by aggressive position-seekers intent on making an impression. Mira had no degree, no deal, no cachet—she was a facilities manager, not an entrepreneur, or so it was said behind her back. There was no reason for her to be included in these meetings after the funding, and she was not. In an astonishingly short period, she went from being the ultimate insider to being one more outsider.

The company began to take on flesh. New faces were everywhere. Before, Volkov had needed her and her resources, and there were no other volunteer providers. Now, suddenly, he and Echelon were swamped with willing advisers, young, hungry professionals on the make, all eager to hitch a ride on the new star. As a matter of political necessity, to make room for themselves, they were quick to disparage Mira and the advice she had given. In fact, acknowledging that the company had any history at all before the date of funding was messy and inconvenient—it undercut their sense of themselves as risk-taking adventurers, never mind that the perils of entrepreneurship in this case were nicely cushioned by the guarantee of a paycheck every other week.

The pace became frantic. Volkov's time became non-existent. He asked Mira to take care of some of the minor personal errands he no longer had time to handle. This seemed a matter of small import, the errands being the sorts of favors couples routinely do for one another. But the acceptance of these trivial burdens was symbolic of something much more substantial. A month earlier, she had been Volkov's mentor, to whom he looked up for advice and guidance. Now she had become his personal assistant, reporting to him.

Everything, everyone had been transformed by the emergence of Echelon from misty possibility into sunlit reality. But for Mira, it had been a reverse metamorphoses. In a few short weeks, she had gone from guardian angel and guiding spirit to proxy status as the boss's girlfriend—from butterfly to caterpillar.

✳

There is no such thing as unselfish love. Blind love? Yes. Bewildered love? Of course. Uncertain love? That is what this story is all about. But unselfish love? There is no such thing. Set your cap on some one, and you want them to want you. Freedom of choice—meaning the possibility of some other choice besides you—is not only unacceptable, but intolerable.

The difference does not lie in the ends, but in the means by which the elimination of all the other alternatives may be accomplished. There are two completely different methods. The first is to give—affection, reassurance, time, money, whatever is necessary—freely, openly, without stint or inhibition, without negotiation, without bargaining, asking nothing and receiving nothing in return, except hope. It is a terrifying, heroic way to love, because it implies and requires complete acceptance of the freedom of that other person and absolute trust in his or her judgment, that he or she will recognize the value of the gift, will prize it in accordance with its worth, and will have the wisdom and energy to return it in kind.

The second method is the reverse—to withhold—to gain somehow a position of advantage, in which her self-esteem, her self-respect, even identity itself, will come to depend on her lover's regard for her, perhaps symbolized in a particular token—a ring, the recollection of a date, a stock *option. The trick then is to withhold the token and with it the regard, keep it just barely out of reach, and keep on with the game while she leaps and jumps for it, each time with the belief that this time the leap will turn out successfully. There is built-in reinforcement with this method, because with each new try, with each new defeat, her need to regain the sense of self that has been expended, squandered, lost, becomes more urgent, more compelling. Often she will refuse to acknowledge the belittlement, blind herself to it, give it the name `love' long after it has been transformed into a mute, sullen fury, because open awareness of the game, the mechanism, the mockery, is too humiliating, too crushing, to face openly.*

The basic substance of the first method is empowerment and trust. The basic substance of the second is disempowerment and contempt. This latter is the dynamic of pimp-and-whore, visible in all its purity in those debased relationships, but observable in more subtle variations everywhere and all the time. It is the coward's method, but it does have the advantage of being safe and easy. The basic mechanism is <u>not</u> giving, which is an easy enough thing to do, with just the slightest nod to the form, the outward appearances, of affection, so as not to give away the game too readily. Very few human beings who have been trapped into investing their one and only self in this deception will easily find the inner resources to free themselves from the coils of humiliation, anger, and self-contempt that tighten relentlessly around them. Some people never escape.

*

Mira adapted to the sudden change with her usual nonchalant aplomb, masking her own frustration and insecurity with the poise I had come to admire. Gregor seemed satisfied with the relationship—it did not occur to her that he had sensed that his new backers were alert with any sign of instability on his part, that a change of any kind in his domestic arrangements would have been extremely unwise—and so she bided her time, adjusted to the new situation and did the girlfriendy things for Gregor that he requested.

He had been living in a run-down, one bedroom apartment for nearly two years. Now, as an American success story, he wanted some of the trappings of American success. Specifically, for starters, he wanted a house of his own, ornate, plush, with all the latest gizmos and electronic gadgets, a trophy house. Mira's tentative suggestion that they might live together he brushed aside with a good-natured contempt that much later she would come to realize was not good natured at all. He wanted his own place; he did not want to share the space with any one—and particularly not with three young children part-time.

But she did know real estate, and so he asked her to find a place for him. While Volkov ran around to meetings with board members and trade shows, Mira started scouting out possible residences for him. Despite the demeaning aspect of seeking out a residence she would not share, it should have been an enjoyable task, for it involved daydreams and plans for her own house, her own homemaking. But it turned out to be anything but enjoyable.

Volkov had been surrounded for a few weeks by expert toadies and sycophants, and the recipient of all manner of flattery, large and small, broad and subtle—not that any particular subtlety was necessary. He liked Mira well enough, but he did not like at all the fact that he owed her. Narcissists resent the people who do them favors; they have to feel grateful and they don't like that feeling. Of course that unpleasant situation can't be the result of any shortcoming of theirs. The memory of all she had done was too fresh and green to be deniable just then, even by him, but that didn't stop him from begrudging her the debt. The process of home showing was the perfect vehicle for a passive-aggressive vent.

His time had become invaluable—why had she importuned him to see <u>this</u> place? It was obviously unsuitable, too small, too large, too close, too far, lacking in some fundamental amenity that Volkov suddenly announced he required. Surely she knew these things. Surely the defects were obvious. Why was his time being wasted, squandered? In this manner, over and over, Mira found herself on the defensive—what were major favors being done for <u>him</u> were transformed into favors done for <u>her</u>.

Mira was not unaware of this unfairness, but it seemed petty enough, and there was the still-unresolved issue of the stock—the monkey's hand around the candy. In the custom of women always and everywhere, she apologized for and rationalized the misbehavior of her man. Also in the time-honored custom, try as she might, her apologies and rationalizations were not, could not be, fully heart felt. Anger and resentment lingered, emotional debts that would one day have to be paid if anything were to be possible. Since they were highly unlikely to be acknowledged, let alone paid, nothing was possible. Mira and Volkov were committed to the wrong road. They had never really been on any other.

If it were all that easy, of course the curtain would be drawn and the stage struck right off that bat. But it isn't that easy. We deal here with full-bodied personalities, not caricatures, and thus patterns that were not easily discernible, that are obscured by the sheer quantity of behavior. So there were moments of humor, insight, tenderness, and great physical passion (a fact that hurts to acknowledge, words that hurt to write). But the basic beat had been established, a bass line of resentment and withholding, and that beat would go on, even though punctuated by occasional snatches of melody and the cadences of real harmony.

Ultimately Mira did find him a suitable residence, a five bedroom ranch house in a plush new gated development, he grumbled and complained, but closed on it fairly swiftly, since it was obvious she couldn't do any better for him. It then fell to her to decorate the residence, normally a job that was a pleasure-and-a-half. But the beat did go on—her suggestions were either ridiculously inappropriate or so patently obvious that no decision was required. His time was being wasted, all right, then, if it can't be any better than that, then that will have to do. Nothing she did was ever exactly right; at its best it was not entirely wrong, and always, always an imposition of some sort on him.

Her own need to find a suitable home for her children was becoming desperate. Volkov knew of this. It was her basic hope that the search for a home for him would raise his consciousness about her major pressing problem, and the basic decency to discharge a fraction of the moral debt he owed her by providing a little help. Her fondest wish was that he would suggest they move in with him. But short of that, he might at least lend her the money necessary to find something decent for all of them.

He did nothing. Volkov gave no indication that his consciousness had been raised a jot. His interest in homes was confined to his own. By this time, Mira knew better than to raise the issue directly. The only result would be a mess or recriminations and resentment—'why do you make me feel guilty?' With the hindsight that always has 20-20 vision, it is obvious now that the time had come then for her to write the whole involvement off as a lost cause. But the issue of the stock was still in play. He was still promising to do what he could, and her other alternatives had become largely non-existent. She was fully enmeshed in a web that was largely her own making.

Behavior of Volkov's typical pattern produces emotions that are from the outset fatally mixed. Mira, being good-natured and accustomed to accommodate and be accommodated, naturally wondered what <u>she</u> might be doing wrong, what might be wrong with her. But Mira, also being realistic and not being a cream-puff, also knew instinctively that she had done nothing wrong. The result was a fierce resentment that she could not bring herself to acknowledge consciously—for to do that would force her to admit how much else was wrong, what colossal mistakes she had made, and what a fool she had been made of in return. This was not a path that her pride would allow her to take—and so another concession to Volkov was made, and her pride became that much more stubborn, and the screw turned still more tightly.

*

Mira continued to cope with her wondrous grace with all the circumstances that conspired relentlessly against her. Her expectations continued to be that she would ultimately receive what she knew she was rightfully due. She recognized that as her best chance. But Elmira Watson had never been a passive person. She was fully aware of what might not happen—and, even if events had worked out as they should have, she would have been nettled that the success was primarily the work of others. Quietly, without making any big fuss about it, she began working on a business plan for her own Internet business...

She called the business Gifter's Anonymous. The basic idea came from what she'd observed of the day-to-day business culture in the facilities she managed. The follow-up to any important meeting with a customer—sales conference, planning meeting, what not—was almost always the presentation of a token gift of some sort. The gift had to be inexpensive enough to be acceptable, clever enough to provide commentary, tasteful enough to inspire gratitude. The hopeless task of finding this non-pareil item invariably fell upon some luckless secretary or administrative assistant.

Mira's idea was to provide an Internet site where that secretary could go to obtain the right gift. It would have a database in which other gifts had been catalogued, and links to various merchants who could produce the inexpensive monogrammed tie pins, the personalized pastry, and so on that made up the usual gift. The site would also be accessible with 800 numbers. It would be staffed with friendly personable women, and would have a distinctly feminine, personal character. As the women who used the site became comfortable with it, Mira hoped that they would come back for more conventional gift shopping—birthdays, weddings, anniversaries, Christmas. The database would expand naturally.

Years later, when it didn't make any difference, I took a look at the plan she ultimately produced. There is no question it was influenced by the Internet dazzle of the times, and it did lack the ultimate bottom-line oomph of a proprietary product like the Firebird. But it was well-considered, and actually quite a bit more thoughtful than most of the schemes that were bruited about back then. The document itself was superb. The care and effort she put into its production were apparent throughout.

Mira worked on it casually whenever she had a spare moment. She did not work with the urgency, the determination, the force, that Volkov showed with Echelon. That drive, the by-product of his self-absorption, was undeniably his one great gift.

*

The tidal wave of dot com frenzy that was to engulf our community was now well on its way towards cresting. Investors were not funding start-ups any longer for their long-term potential or their sound business practices. They didn't even pretend that they were. Building companies for realistic futures was stuff for your stodgy old Aunt Mathilda. The sizzle had completely replaced the steak—in fact, in those rare cases in which a business actually had profitable operations, it was often condemned. It shouldn't be making money; it should be `staking out its claim in cyberspace' (never mind that cyberspace by definition is infinite and you can't claim it) or `expanding its virtual market' or doing whatever it was the blue suede shoe guys said was the right thing to do. The used car salesmen had taken over the world.

Volkov and Mira were catapulted into this world. The pace was frenzied. Social life and business life inevitably became entangled, for there was no time for either one to be lived separately. She was his hostess on occasions staged at his own home; she was his date on functions that occurred elsewhere. Her own scarce time began to disappear altogether.

She did not want to lose any more ground with the family court. She had one extremely uncomfortable near miss. She was to accompany Volkov to some celebratory dinner for the successful IPO of another start-up funded by the venture group behind Echelon. There would be a host of movers and shakers there, investment bankers, major technologists, industry gurus. The dinner took place on one of the Friday nights on which Mira had custody of the children. She arranged for a baby-sitter. The girl was late, and Mira had to leave before she had arrived. As a matter of routine, Mira phoned as soon as it was convenient from the banquet floor. To her shock, she discovered that the babysitter had never turned up at all. She immediately made arrangements to return back to her small home. One of the limo drivers was happy enough to do her a favor and take her back.

Volkov was totally without understanding. How could she leave him at the party? Didn't she know how embarrassing that was for him? Didn't she realize how critical this time was, how important it was to him? How could she desert him? Surely three children of that age could tend for themselves.

Worse. Alicia in all innocence told her father what had happened, and Mira found herself in family court explaining the situation to the judge four weeks later. Baby-sitters do fall through, it happens to everyone, and she had reacted quickly and effectively when it happened to her. No California family court was going to make any change in fundamental custody arrangements over such an incident. But she could feel the weather changing. She did not have any longer the automatic approbation of the judge. There had been too many small incidents in which Crockett was partly justified. She received a lecture a bit longer than it had to be, an admonition a bit harsher than necessary, and left with the clear (and undoubtedly correct) impression that the ice had thinned to nearly the breaking point.

Volkov remained unsympathetic. Though he showed more regard for her sons, he was still more indifferent than affectionate towards her children. In particular, he was still rattled by Alicia. This took the form of uneasy, even caustic jokes and comments, many of which set her teeth on edge. She still hoped and trusted it would change—many people who were unsettled by Alicia's autistic behaviors came to treasure her for her innocence and the pure joy in living she possessed. But so far Volkov was not among them.

Mira was not completely lost to herself. At some point, she sensed a need to clear some space for herself and think things through. She had been scheduled to accompany Volkov on a business trip out of town, but canceled and stayed home instead. It was during that week that I made the invite to the movie. I am certain when she accepted, that it was not from any conscious romantic motive—and yet, and yet...her coming into my arms was as much a thinking-out as anything else she did that week. Her body was speaking, and it possessed greater insight than either of us did at that point. Up to that point in time, that corporeal wisdom was always available to

Mira, one of her strengths. But by that time, she was no longer completely in touch with herself.

Her body—the body that I sensed that evening had changed, but not how. There is a story there as well.

*

The money rush had inevitably produced a woman rush as well—trophy women, to be precise. Radiant young things, with flowing tresses and drop-dead figures, who in different times have been on stage or trying out their luck on casting couches, were showing up instead on the arms of one-time geeks and pear-shaped venture capitalists. Such is the nature of the world.

This phenomenon did not go unnoticed by Volkov. He had achieved the archetypal American success story—it seemed to him only right that he should have the archetypal American girl friend, a Marilyn Monroe clone, noisy in bed and quiet everywhere else. Everywhere he looked, there were men even older than he with girls of that quality. But he was stuck with a small, boyishly-figured middle aged mother of three.

I don't like people who make a big deal out of the bodies of persons of the other gender. Within limits of reasonability, it's part of the whole package and you take it or leave it along with everything else. But Mira's physique becomes part of the story at this point, and so I have to say something about it, as ungentlemanly as that may be.

Mira Watson was the prototypical hard body. During her time with the modern dance company, she had sometimes rehearsed as long as 12 hours a day. All that physical exertion had served to reduce her bodily fat to the bare feminine minimum. Considered as that body type, she was a remarkably beautiful woman even in her early forties. When I met her, she was still in superb shape. There was a marvelous slenderness to her, with flat, tough muscles, and nothing doughy anywhere. Like most contemporary women, she preferred trousers to skirts, but unlike most women, she looked terrific in both. She would have stopped traffic in a mini-skirt. Her legs were a proof of the existence of God.

But there was a trade-off for that slender toughness. The body fat that is an essential element of voluptuous figures had been exercised out of existence. Mira had little feminine upper body definition, and her breasts were barely protuberant. She stopped just short of being flat-chested. But you didn't have to be a connoisseur of women's bodies—I certainly am not—to understand immediately that billowy curves were not, and could not be, part of this particular package.

Mira actually did quite well at the semi-social events and gatherings that followed the Echelon financing. I am hardly the only man who found her voice and bearing enchanting. Whatever her private turmoil, she never lost her superb inner balance in a pubic setting. Her performer's training never failed her; her poise and graciousness, in situations that were often crass and absurd, were striking. Nor did the contrast between those qualities and Gregor Volkov's boorishness and vulgarity go unnoticed. So she had her share, and then some, of whispered asides, quiet propositions, lunch next Monday or a week-end skiing. She encountered plenty of men there who realized her worth.

Volkov was not one of them. Like most narcissists, he was obsessed with outward appearances. All he could see was that she was about two decades older than most of the trophy types and would finish dead last in a swimsuit competition. By those standards, the middle-aged mother of three with whom he was linked was humiliatingly inadequate. He was not slow to make these opinions known. Mostly this took the form of half-humorous asides, mock comparisons of Mira to the woman at the next table, the kind of kidding that's supposed to be funny, but isn't, and leaves the target no way to respond without appearing unable to take a joke—another prize technique of the masters of passive aggressiveness.

Mira was as vulnerable as any other woman to the `perfect body' syndrome. I can expound all I like about the perfection of her physique on its own terms, and I happen to be right. But, like every other woman in this society, she was more acutely aware of what she wasn't than what she was.

`I wish I were a little rounder for you', she'd said to me early on, a little shyly, really a question, not a statement. It was easy to reassure her that it didn't make a damn bit of difference to me, because it didn't. Yet her figure was an issue with her, and a point of vulnerability in relation to a man to whom it did matter. It mattered a lot to Gregor Volkov, and for that reason it came to matter a great deal more to her than it should.

I don't know when exactly she had the surgery—I did not talk to her often enough to know. It was not something she would ever have told me about, because—even though I didn't have the right—I would have been infuriated. Part of that would have been based on a crude notion that she was a perfect specimen of her type and there was no reason to change anything. But what would truly have enraged me is the notion that there existed someone, anyone, who would not instantly recognize and appreciate her worth. The fact that it was the central man in her life who insisted on a change so trivial, so pointless, so stupid, would have incensed me.

*

Echelon was doing well, really well. The Firebird was the hit of several trade-shows and a considerable buzz began through the industry. Gregor Volkov swelled with self-importance. Talk began of a public offering. The offices of Echelon began to fill with bright, pretty young women, the type that would not look out of place at a celebratory business dinner. Many were quite competent. Mira understood the implication and the threat well enough, but there wasn't much she could do.

Three years had passed. She had spent a huge amount of time and energy finding a place for Gregor Volkov, then furnishing and decorating it with exquisite taste. She often went there, slept there, but always as transient guest, never with anything more than the hope of permanence. She herself still resided in her decrepit house, with her children living with her every other week, Alicia now verging into adolescence.

She had modified her body, changed her life for Echelon and Volkov. The only tangible result was that her life had come to a dead halt in every *area except the relationship with Volkov. That had become a tangled mess of anger, ingratitude, and resentment, over growing the ruins of whatever affection they might have possessed a long, long time ago. She persisted because there was too much pride and ego invested to let go—but also because there was no alternative left for her except persistence.*

*

I didn't know what it was that was different about her body as I held her that night after the movie, just how exactly she'd changed since I'd embraced her as a lover. The surgeon did a good, if completely unnecessary, job. The implants were small and proportionate. It's the attitude they represented I would have despised.

I didn't know much of anything, really. Mira never left my thoughts during those long years—but those thoughts were that Mira's life was well in hand, that she was heading where she wanted to go. It did not occur to me that she needed love—the real kind—needed me—or that she might be on the way to desperate trouble. Subtle trouble, but no less desperate for all that.

And Mira? Though the walls of her life may have been shuddering with pressure, though the ceiling might have been groaning with stress, she gave no sign. Grace under pressure, as always—her defining characteristic.

I interpolated some ruminations about love and its various methods of possessiveness in this chapter. There is in my view no such thing as unselfish love. Flesh and blood does not permit it. But I suppose I do believe in the possibility of pure, whole-hearted love. The thought that any man could know Mira, possess her, and not appreciate what he had, recognize her preciousness, was a thought that was literally inconceivable to me. In the truest sense of the word, I found the idea unimaginable. If she was with someone, by definition that someone must be treating her well. It was impossible that he could not. Q.E.D. So I remained in my blissful, invincible ignorance.

If there is such a thing as pure love, I think it must be blind in this way—without the ability even to contemplate any other feeling. Perhaps that is the principal indicator of its existence. Perhaps it is the only one. At any rate, this particular blindness of mine, as naïve as it might appear in cold print and hindsight, is one of the few aspects of Mira and me about which I have no regrets at all. None whatsoever.

CHAPTER 13

▼

All these various currents in my life and Mira's came together in one extraordinary week about nine months later. The week was extraordinary in two ways. The first lay in the confluence of events, the sort of simultaneous, interdependent flow of happenings and coincidences that no one would believe if they supposedly took place in fiction. It was not the end itself—that lay another ten months in the future. But the wave that would break then definitely crested during that week.

And the second? Those of you who have stuck with me this long are undoubtedly way ahead of me. As usual, I was completely oblivious to everything of importance. I knew of the events, of course, or most of them. What I did not know or even sense was their interdependence. The one particular factoid of which I remained typically completely and invincibly ignorant was the essential one. It was the last time Destiny was definitely on our side. After that week, it began to toy with the thought that there might be other, more interesting ways for the story to end.

*

The tumult of coincidence actually began with a letter I received some three weeks or so before. It was from the business that had unexpectedly paid my ancient legal fees a year earlier. This one was delivered by Fed Ex to my condominium. What it contained was an invitation to an extremely important shareholder's meeting the Monday morning three weeks hence.

The intelligence of Albert Einstein was not required to figure out what was going on. My old client was finally about to make a public offering of its shares. As I owned a modest number of them—2,000 out of a million issued—I was pleased. I was not overwhelmed. I'd had a couple of big hits in the '80's. I wasn't expecting anything but some modest good news this time around.

Nonetheless, that Monday morning I clocked off a couple hours of personal time with the District Attorney's Office—I was always scrupulous about that sort of thing—and went over to the shareholders' meeting. There I learned that the obvious conclusion had been the right one—the company was indeed planning to go public, with the offering being handled by one of the major investment banks, a quality underwriter. The stagnant little tech company had become a hot property. The price per share of the initial offering was set at $10.00. That was pretty much the modest enrichment I had expected—and while it wasn't going to change the world at all, learning you're twenty thousand dollars richer is a nice way to start any week.

There were shouts to high heaven from the assembled throng as this glorious news unfolded, and the meeting ended. I went up to greet the CEO, my old client of some 20 years before. I hadn't seen him in over a decade. The dot.com bubble produced a lot of fly-by-nighters, but he'd earned his shot. He'd treaded water for most of the '80's and '90's; now his ship had finally come in (a nice metaphorical twist, that). I sought him out to congratulate him.

"Walt!" he exclaimed. "Compadre! Nice you could make it. How are things in the justice biz?"

"Never better." I grinned back. "So. You've finally managed to con 'em all. I always knew you would."

"Hey, don't let 'em know all my secrets," he answered. "You're doing o.k. here yourself."

"Twenty grand for sure doesn't hurt," I agreed. "A nice thing to hear on Monday morning."

He grinned more broadly, too broadly, and turned to the man at his side, his veep for finance, another long-time friend. "Told ya," he said. "Told ya he wouldn't figure it out." He turned back to me. "Once you're out of something, you're *really* out, aren't you?"

"I'm not following," I answered, a bit perplexed.

"Walter, me lad," he continued, putting his hand on my shoulder, "guess we forgot to include that info in your mailer. The million shares we have on the books aren't enough for a usable float. We need a lot more shares than that—as you would know if you'd thought at all about it, since I learned this stuff from you. We're splitting the shares 75 to 1, dear Walter. You don't own 2,000 shares. You own 150,000.

"And there' still goin' out at ten bucks a pop. You're not twenty grand richer, boyo. The number is one-and-a-half million dollars richer.

"Now," he continued, noticing that I had gone completely pale, "how's *that* for a Monday mornin'?"

✳

I felt as if a magnum of champagne had exploded in my bloodstream. I literally did not know what to think; I could not put two coherent thoughts together back to back. My old client grinned more widely; his little joke had succeeded beyond his wildest expectations. He felt he owed me—I suppose I had been a smug, know-it-all, sonuvabitch in the old days. How I did it, I don't know, but I managed to get myself together, thank him, and weave my way to the car, where I drove with unseeing, deliriously blissful eyes back to the office, a mortal danger to everyone else on the road. Somehow we all survived.

I groped toward an understanding. What fractured, happy thoughts I did have were about the kids. Gradually, as the framework of rationality was slowly restored, I began to think again. The new-found money made no difference to me. I already had `drop dead' money, and I was in no mood to retire. In this day and age, even a windfall of that magnitude doesn't make that much difference in life style. I wasn't exactly going to be running off to Tahiti and sitting on the beach. I could buy a nicer house, but I liked where I was living. Maybe I'd remodel the kitchen, but that was about it.

Elizabeth? It wasn't a real difference maker there, either. I had already taken care of college, and her basic adolescent expenses. The intangibles had always been the worry there—the effects of divorce, anger and abandonment. I had felt for some time those issues had become history—not that the separation would not always have an impact on her, but I had managed to reduce the effect to the normal dimensions of one difficulty among the others of everyday life. It was a goal that I'd worked quite hard to achieve, and I was proud of it.

The more I thought of it, the more I realized the big impact was going to be felt with Nick. His long term security was—had been—my one remaining waking nightmare. He had made remarkable progress, but it was more and more apparent he was going to be a life-long dependent. The realization that slowly glimmered through my foggy brain was that my old client had solved that problem, too. Between what I had already accumulated and this new windfall, Nick would be all right. He had reached the same plateau I had—not rich exactly, but safe.

But for all this microscopic introspection about trees in my life, big (Nick) and little (remodeled kitchens), the reality of the forest completely eluded me. What the new money meant was that I was free— finally free. I don't mean I was free to walk away from those responsibilities; I would never have done that. What I mean is that I had gained enough space and momentum, with the extra boost of this new equity, to carve out a new life that allowed me to discharge them on my own terms. In fact, other than a dim realization that anxiety for Nick was a thing of the past, I didn't give the possibilities for my own life much thought at all. I was too used to the walls, to the fortress, even to dream of a world beyond them.

But something had begun to stir deep within my being. As I pulled into the office parking lot, I suddenly felt the damndest impulse to call Mira—of all people—and tell her what had happened. It seemed to come out of nowhere—I hadn't spoken to her in a few months. But there it was—she was the person with whom I wanted to share the good news, not the woman I was seeing, not Linda, not any of my friends—Mira.

Mira! The name suddenly exploded in my brain, the second detonation of the morning. The moment the thought of calling her occurred to me, it was instantaneously transformed into an irresistible impulse. An overwhelming gladness seized possession of me, a blinding primal joy, the sort of feeling that used to come over me when I was seventeen, on a bright spring day when the whole world was open to me and anything was possible. These were not emotions that had been frequent visitors to my middle years. It was not the good news itself—that was already history. The delight I would have in sharing it with Mira, *that* prospect was the cause of all this uncluttered happiness.

But before I could get to my office, get organized, and do it, I ran into Mark Carroll, the chief investigator of white collar crimes in the office.

"Where have you been?" he asked.

"At a shareholder's meeting. I signed out."

"Turned out to be the wrong morning. We've got a trade secret complaint. Sounds major."

The prospect of a major new case would normally be a flawless way to start the week. But this morning, I was more than a little impatient with it. Nonetheless, I followed him towards the big conference room where we handled intakes of criminal referrals of that type.

*

Right at that time Mira was sitting down to a mid-morning meeting herself, coincidentally (if anything that happened that week can be called a coincidence) at the same place where we often met. Her emotional state was the polar opposite of mine. She had received a call that morning from one of the trophy girls that now populated the Echelon offices. The girl wanted to see her as soon as possible, and suggested coffee. Mira agreed to meet. She had no more difficulty deducing what the subject was going to be than I had with the shareholder's meeting. She went to the place at brunch time with her stomach in knots.

"He sleeps with everybody," the girl said. "Or tries to."

"I really didn't need to hear that," Mira said. On this particular occasion, she wasn't merely eating lightly. She wasn't eating at all.

"I know. I don't mean to hurt you." Mira realized suddenly that this girl had sought her out because she pitied her, felt sorry for her. The realization was as demoralizing as any of the revelations. "I'm sure you probably have guessed as much. But you have to know the way he talks about you."

"What do you mean?"

The girl summoned up her breath and nerve. "He calls you the Board—because you're—you know—not full figured. And do you have a daughter who—you know—has some sort of problem? Like the way she talks or"—the girl was searching for a euphemism for `retarded', but couldn't think of one—"something?"

"Yes," Mira answered evenly. "My daughter has a form of autism. You can hear it in the way she talks."

"He calls her the Dummy. He makes fun of the way she talks—like this"—the girl produced a flow of garbled sound, which bore a faint resemblance to Alicia's mangled syntax and elocution, with a Russian accent. Mira felt a rush to tears, but somehow remained dry-eyed. It was the eyes of the trophy girl in which tears suddenly welled up.

"He's an absolute pig," she said. "To everyone. You don't know when you first meet him. You think he's just foreign and colorful. But he's a pig. Nobody likes him. Nobody trusts him. Did you know his two friends left?"

"Yuri and Ilya?" Mira asked, surprised. "They're gone?" Gregor had said nothing of this.

"Yes. They started their own company. Ilya said it was because of Gregor." Her eyes were suddenly flooded again. "I didn't mean to hurt your feelings. I didn't know about you when I got involved with him. He said he wasn't married, but he didn't say anything about an understanding. I didn't find out about you—that he even had an understanding with anyone—until Christmas. Then I asked him, and he said these awful things. I didn't mean to hurt you, but if you're counting on him I thought you should know. That you had to know. I'm sorry."

"Don't be," Mira answered vacantly. Her thoughts were already elsewhere. "Thank you, in fact." She paid the check. The two women left in opposite directions. The girl went through the front door and out into the sunlight. Mira went to the restroom area, where she tried to phone Volkov. His secretary told her he was at the district attorney's office and therefore not available. She then put down the phone, went into the restroom, opened one of the stall doors, knelt down, and vomited the contents of her stomach into the toilet.

*

I had no recollection at all of ever having met Gregor Volkov. He seemed distantly familiar to me, but in the way someone who resembles a known acquaintance can seem familiar, not familiar as a memory. He was there along with two of the Echelon lawyers, and one of the directors of the company. As it happened, the director was Mark Stewart, the person that Mira had contacted about Echelon some two years before, the contact who had started the venture capital ball rolling. Having a huge personal stake in the success of the company and

Volkov, he had become its guardian angel. I knew none of this at the time.

There were the usual handshakes and mutual introductions, and then we got down to business. I haven't written very much about my practice as a prosecutor, as that aspect of my life has not to this point been very important to the story. But the care and handling of trade secret cases is one of the most sophisticated areas of criminal law, and—not to put too fine a point on it—not something that every garden-variety litigator can do. The theft of trade secrets is an extremely serious crime. But it's also the easiest crime in the world to imagine or exaggerate, since the taking is not of any tangible thing. When physical goods are stolen, something that used to be in one place isn't there any more. But the owner of an idea still has possession of it, even after it's taken.

The big problem is distinguishing the genuine complaints of theft from bogus complaints made by executives crying wolf about some key employees leaving and going into competition against them. The first is a crime. The second is the American way. Separating the sheep from the goats is the trick, and I do believe I had become fairly adept at that—terrific, in fact. All that work I did in the 80's helped a lot.

The initial interviews on these cases are fairly heavy stuff. Unlike more conventional crimes such as rape or burglary, local police departments don't have the experts on hand to evaluate them, so they nearly always come straight to the D.A.'s office. Usually, the CEO or head of engineering comes in, with company counsel, sometimes a director, often a witness to the taking if one exists. I always start with the business aspects—what's the name of the company? How long has it been in business? What are its annual sales? Is it public or privately held? And so on. The reporting parties almost never expect this approach. The idea is to calm everybody down, and also to get some down and dirty idea of just how the supposedly stolen technology fit into the actual business operations of the victim. The process has proven to be a very useful reality check.

That's what I did at this particular meeting, or rather tried to do. But I could barely finish a question without Volkov interrupting. Before I had even said ten words, he had broken in excitedly to tell me that he had been betrayed, how terrible the situation was, that something had to be done at once, that he was the victim of a monstrous conspiracy, and all the rest. This would have been annoying in any case, but might have been tolerable if he had actually answered any of the routine questions I was asking during the course of his babbling. But he didn't. Instead, all we got was a reiteration of the same hysterical monologue, with minor variations, as if we all hadn't heard it right the first time. After 20 minutes, we were exactly nowhere.

I would have thought it was impossible for anyone or anything to transform the ecstatic mood I was in that day. Not so. The blind joy that had filled me just before I entered the room dissipated rapidly. After a remarkably brief acquaintance, I had just about had it with this guy. I glanced about the room, and noticed that my investigators had stopped taking notes. These are a group of serious, middle-aged guys, mostly good, alert street cops who became interested in computers and technology and made their own way into this esoteric area of law enforcement on pure curiosity and street-smarts. They are too shrewd a group to write off any complainant quickly, since there are a lot of eccentric personalities in the business. But they had written off this one.

Volkov was completely oblivious to all this, but his lawyers and the director were not. Stewart finally cut him off and took over. He introduced himself as a partner in one of the local venture firms. He was in his early forties, very smooth, with a presence, Stanford, Harvard, or Wharton MBA, I guessed. From him, I learned that Echelon had developed a unique firewall product, the Firebird, and that it was doing very well. The company was planning its initial public offering—the well-known IPO—in about ninety days. From him I also learned that the problem was that the two other co-founders, two other Russians named Yuri Razumaev and Ilya Grischuk, had left the company late the week before and were organizing a competitive business. This information came through despite and not because of Volkov, who kept on making frantic, irrelevant interruptions.

That, however, is where the process ground to a complete halt. Yuri and Ilya had left the company, and that was terrible, we all understood that…but what exactly was it that they had *stolen*? No, no, we didn't understand, Volkov would respond, they have left the company, they are going to go into competition, it's terrible. Yes, I repeated, I understand, but this is supposed to be a complaint about stolen technology. What *exactly* have they taken? You don't *understand,* he repeated, becoming more agitated, hands waving, voice strident, they have left the company, they are going to compete. I tried again, then my investigator tried, then Stewart tried. It was no use. After 30 or 40 minutes of this, the plain truth of the matter had become apparent to everyone in the room, lawyers and Stewart included.

There was no theft; there never had been. Nothing had been taken. Gregor Volkov was worried about competition, nothing more. The entire process was a preposterous, boondoggling farce.

Which the time had come to end. I am careful of my own time, but ferociously protective of the time of my investigators, which is one of the scarcest resources of the criminal justice system. "Mr. Volkov," I said, "I don't think there is anything we can do for you."

His eyes bulged. "What!!" he said, "you mean you are not going to arrest them?"

"They have not committed any crime," I replied evenly.

"But they have *betrayed* me," he whined.

Good for them, I thought, because my good mood was completely gone now and I had frankly had it with Gregor Volkov. I was certain that sentiment was shared by the entire staff. "That's not a crime," I said, evenly again.

Volkov opened his mouth and was about to dig an even bigger hole for himself, when Stewart took over. I liked him—he was smooth, but not schmarmy, and he completely understood the problem. "I don't think that Mr. Volkov has done himself justice," he said. "I think what he means to say is that there is so much proprietary technology in the Firebird that it is impossible to believe that Razumaev and Grischuk could create a similar product without making use of it."

"That may be," I answered, "but it's pure speculation at this point. There's not enough here for a search warrant or anything else. We're not going to open a file here." Out of the corner of my eye, I noticed the relieved expression on Mark Carroll's face.

"Couldn't you at least talk to them?" Stewart suggested. "At least ask?" I understood his plan at once. The most modest police contact would discourage the new company from using anything that could conceivably trace back to Echelon. At the same time, I could see some advantages for them—they'd be on notice of what Volkov had tried and could steer clear of the reefs. It is much better to prevent a crime, even a largely imaginary crime, than to prosecute one.

"I think we could do a knock-and-talk," I said. 'Knock-and-talk' is police-ese for an on-site interview without a search warrant. I could see Carroll roll up his eyes. "It might avoid another session like this," I added, and then my investigator understood my thinking fully. He nodded affirmatively.

Volkov was unmollified and started to protest, but Stewart and his counsel understood the lay of the land. Give him a minute's leeway and he could easily whine himself out of the minor league commitment I had made. In a moment, they were up on their feet, shaking hands, thanking us, for our time, and out the door.

I post-mortemed the referral with Mark Carrol. "Can you get out there tomorrow?" I asked. "I want to put this one to bed as soon as possible."

"Absolutely," he said, agreeing. He shook his head.

"That asshole is some kind of world's record."

I had no argument there. By that time, I had some hazy notion that I had seen Volkov some place before, but not in any way that troubled me. His was just one case among others, with the twist that it came with an unusually obnoxious victim. Out of sight, out of mind—the amazing thunderbolt that had struck that morning was too wonderful a development for an irritant of that scale to matter long. My thoughts returned to that happy subject almost as soon as Mark had closed the door—and with that subject, by automatic pilot to Mira.

I was engulfed in memory. Mira taking off her glasses as she stood in my hallway—Mira laughing as she pronounced her real name 'Elmira'—Mira delicately separating one cauliflower blossom from all the others—Mira dressing, Mira undressing, Mira smiling, Mira speaking, beside me, beneath me, with me, mine. It was an intoxicating tidal wave of memory, besieging me, deluging me, coming out of nowhere. I was a fairly useless prosecutor that afternoon, lost in a torrent of remembrance and daydream.

Why this should have been, I had no idea at that time. Mira was never far from my thoughts, never far from my heart—that I did know, even though (I thought) everything was impossible. But why the sudden, unexpected acquisition of this new wealth should trigger all these recollections of her, I had no idea at that time. What I can see clearly now is that my heart had become aware, long before my duller, rational faculties, that she was now feasible, that things of which I had not permitted myself even to dream were now in the realm of the doable. The flood of memories was the voice of my better self, pounding on the walls of the cell in which I had imprisoned it for so long, demanding to be heard. That is crystal clear—now.

Thus I did no work that afternoon, between all the remembrance of things past and—I have to be candid here—wave after wave of raw lust. Finally, I decided to call her that evening—partly to clear my head, partly to check in on her.

But also—for the first time in five years—to obtain some idea from her of what might be possible.

*

Mira passed one of the most dismal days of her life that day. It is bad enough to be confronted with infidelity—but it is even worse when the possibility of infidelity has been obvious, self-evident, and doubts and misgivings overcome by sheer willpower. The self-condemnation of double folly lies there, first for the initial trust, second for ignoring all her better instincts. She had to confront the fact, not merely that she had been made a fool of, but that she had been one of the major architects of the fraud. She had to recollect the long series of concessions, acts of trust, broken and renewed promises. All her adult life she had been confident in her power to command the loyalty of the men to whom she gave her own loyalty. Now she did not know what to think.

Above all there was Alicia, her baby (even though her eldest), her precious. Here, too, there had been a foretelling in Volkov's indifference and inability to relate—and yet the degree of cruelty implied in his mocking speech to a stranger was something of which she had never dreamt, which she could not fathom. What had Alicia or she ever done to <u>him</u>? Another doubling, for the act of cruelty to her daughter was a declaration of hatred of her. He knew perfectly well where her major point of vulnerability lay. Now she had to reconcile that nightmare thought with memories of befriending him, sleeping with him…loving him, for the word and concept did apply, however strange and corrupt the process had been.

What I had always prized in Mira was her lack of self-consciousness, her simplicity. I don't mean by 'simplicity' simple-minded or naive; she was anything but simple-minded or naive. I mean simplicity in the sense of directness, the free and unaffected natural gesture that was her greatest gift. But now she was caught in a racking, relentless inner turmoil entirely alien to her.

She had thought she had known Volkov. She had thought she cared for him, and he for her. She did not want to believe what she had been told was true. If it were true, he did not care for her—despised her, in fact—

and she should have no more to do with him. In her younger days, the act would have followed directly on the thought and that would have been that. But now the thought of ending it was wrenching, tormenting. Why? Because she cared for him so much? Or because he had become the repository of all her hopes and dreams? Was the cause of her anguish love? Or frustrated ambition? She tried to forget the money, but found she could not. Did she love him? How could she have loved him? How could she not love him? What did she really know, anyway? She tossed about in this whirlwind of emotion and second thought, punctuated every so often by gusts of anger and humiliation on Alicia's behalf, not knowing what to believe, not even knowing what she felt.

She was in this frame of mind when I called, about 9:00 that night.

*

At that time I had not seen Mira in nearly five months, since Thanksgiving the November previous. That has never been one of my favorite holidays, and I often travel or take vacation time over that weekend. For whatever reason, I made no plans that particular year; the kids were going to be with Linda, and the woman I was dating would be with her own family. That left me at loose ends, which was hardly a new experience and one with which I coped fairly easily. But thoughts of Mira, who also shared custody, popped into my mind, and I called to see what she was doing. As it happened, Alicia and her brothers were going to be with their father that day, and Mira had decided to host an orphans' Thanksgiving for any of her friends who might have nothing better to do. That sounded like me, the implied invitation quickly became express, and I was happy to accept.

It was a nice occasion. Twenty or so guests crowded into the front room, and made small talk. If ever there was a mismatched group, that was it, with different ages, different backgrounds, different reasons for being there. Yet it was an oddly convivial gathering, with a lot of laughter and high spirits. The cause certainly wasn't wine and song, for we were a largely abstemious bunch. The two exceptions were a couple of Russian émigrés who brought their own vodka and celebrated the holiday in the traditional Russian way, becoming happily but quietly besotted. The memories of that slight encounter are still vivid. Mira presided over the table in her hovel with regal informality, as if it were palatial—gracious, charming, poised.

Later, after the dinner was done, I drove her to the airport, for she had planned her own holiday trip to North Carolina and her mother. I wondered then where the significant boy friend was, whom I would have thought would handle that chore. It was not an inquiry I felt comfortable making out loud, but she sensed my curiosity and mentioned that one special friend she'd invited was too busy with COMDEX and CES preparations to come. This was supposedly a comment in passing, but she meant me to understand something, and I did. There was to be no repeat of the spontaneous passion of our movie date. There wasn't. When we got to the airport, we exchanged a quick, friendly peck, and then she was into the terminal and out of my sight.

But now I was going to speak to her again, with terrific news and for some purpose towards which I was only groping. I was as breathless as a school boy. I waited an eternity, until nine o'clock, when the children, if it were her week, would be settled down. Mira picked up on the second ring.

"Hello?" she said. Even though it was only a single word, her voice sounded curiously dull and flat, somehow listless.

"Mira," I answered, already a bit apprehensive. "This is Walt."

"Walter," she acknowledged, but in the same flat manner. Very unusual—normally, her enthusiasm in hearing from me would be open and obvious.

"I have some really great news," I continued, a little worried but basically undeterred, and then I told her what had happened that morning.

"That's wonderful, Walt," she said, with a touch more life, but not much more. Then I became really concerned.

"What's wrong, Mira?" I asked.

"Nothing," she answered quickly. "Nothing at all. I have my bad days, too, like everyone else. You just never ran into one before."

"You were the first person I wanted to share this with," I said truthfully. "In fact, the only one." That was also true, but one of those truths I didn't know myself until I said it out loud.

"Oh, Walt," she sighed.

"And you're the only one I want to celebrate with," I plunged ahead recklessly. "I was sort of hoping I could talk you into coming away with me this weekend. Drive up to Tahoe. Watch some North Carolina basketball"—this was the first weekend of March Madness—"see some shows. Be together."

Now, this must seem completely out of character and at the time it seemed that way to me as well. I felt like a mad, impetuous fool as I spoke. Yet I do believe this was one of the few moments when my heart spoke to me clearly. Something was wrong in her life, really wrong. I could sense it, what with her mood and the absent boyfriend and everything. This was also one of the rare occasions when I knew—or, more accurately, allowed myself to feel—how much I wanted her, desired her, needed her, craved her, and who cared what the cost might ultimately be.

"Walter!" she said, astonished, "I thought we were just friends." But there was in her voice something close to its marvelous normal tone.

"I don't know what we are," I answered, "I've been confused by that for a long time." I never spoke truer words. "I know you've been seeing someone—"

"Yes," she interrupted, "but we've hit sort of a bad patch."

"Well, then maybe you need a break. I don't know what happens long or short term with us. All I know is I want to be with you this weekend."

"Oh, Walt," she said. "I don't know. I mean, that's a whole new level for us."

"Not exactly new," I reminded.

"New enough."

"But will you think about it?" I pressed.

"Yes," she sighed, "yes, I will. Think about it." We chatted a few minutes more, her mood entirely altered, and then I hung up the phone in a great mood of my own. The promise `to think about it' in Mira-speak was as good as a promise to go. And I very much wanted to go. At that moment, I knew exactly what I wanted. It was the one occasion, unique among all the other occasions, when I was close to being in complete touch with myself.

*

The conclusion, however, was not nearly as foregone as I took it to be. When Mira hung up the phone, she did not even know what to think, let alone what she was going to do. Her lightness of manner concealed a considerable gravitas of soul. Commitments to her were serious matters, and what she had with Volkov was still a commitment, no matter how badly it was going. All I had suggested formally was a dalliance, whatever the sub-text, and I couldn't have said myself what the subtext truly was— whether what I had in mind extended beyond the weekend or not.

But I was right about one development. The lift in her voice was for real. My call had totally changed her mood and outlook. She had one thing that evening that she hadn't had at noon.

An alternative.

*

It is astonishing how quickly human beings assimilate events, good and bad, no matter how unexpected and out of the ordinary. It's great to win the jackpot, but one day later it's just a few more digits in the bank, another fact of life, and not all that different from all the other, more prosaic facts. I was back at the office the next day, with trials to prepare, warrants to issue, and justice to do. The good news about the newly-found money was rapidly becoming history, one more part of the landscape.

And yet I remained hyper-elated, in day two of the grip of a delirious bliss. It had nothing to do with the stock. It had everything to do with Mira. I awoke with her on my mind; I went through the morning on automatic pilot with unseeing eyes, with my gaze fixed on the horizon.

I would like to report that those visions were of a far-off horizon, with a cottage with a thatched roof and ivy and rosebushes in the front, and Mira and me in rocking chairs in front of the fireplace. That would, however, be a flat-out lie. The visions were of an immediate horizon, that very weekend, and they had nothing at all to do with rocking chairs. They were about what I could do to her and with her in a bed. All I could think of was Mira in her white nightgown, Mira in her naked slenderness, Mira's small, light hands on my shoulders, with her eyes open and expectant as she awaited penetration, those same hands clutching at my hair in her own ecstasy. The real world seemed pale and insubstantial in comparison.

I was finally awakened and shaken out of my erotic torpor in mid-morning by the jangling of the telephone, which had much the same effect as does an alarm clock at dawn. The caller was Mark Carrol, reporting from he scene of the knock-and-talk to which we'd agreed the day before. "They called their lawyer," he said. "Edward Raymond, from the Wilson firm. He says he knows you."

Indeed he did, as our paths had crossed a few times in the 80's. He was one of the few big firm guys I respected. Most of them are totally unable to function without two paralegals and a legal secretary jotting down every deathless word. Their version of a start-up is almost always a client company far enough along that it would succeed with or without them. Monstrous overhead will cause that sort of self-delusion. But Ed enjoyed hands-on work with raw start-ups himself, and he was good at it. I picked up the phone.

"Long time, Ed," I said.

"It sure is, Walt," he said warmly. "I've followed your second career with interest. I sort of envy you."

"It has been interesting," I answered.

"I'd better get to the point. I represent Yuri Razumaev and Ilya Grischuk. I have for a few weeks now, since they decided to break away from Echelon. You know me, Walt, and you know I know what I'm doing. Almost the first words out of my mouth were not to take anything from the Echelon offices—not even the stuff that belonged to them. Not so much as a paper clip."

"Go on," I said. Ed Raymond had quite a bit of credibility with me—plus what he was saying pretty well matched my own intuition from the meeting the day before.

"There isn't anything here. This is a clean start-up. I know you believe me, Walt, we go back too far, but I'll put my money where my mouth is. Your guy can make back-ups of all the hard drives here—and he can search wherever he wants to. Furthermore, we'll sign a consent to search anytime you want for the next year. What I mean is you guys are welcome to poke around any time. Drop on by. Don't feel you have to call first."

"They picked an odd time to spin off—right before an IPO." Ed Raymond had sold me—as a matter of fact, I'd been sold since I learned Raymond was involved, but I was touching all the bases.

"You evidently haven't met Gregor Volkov."

"The first one that you've called wrong, Ed. He came in personally to make the complaint."

"Then I shouldn't have to tell you why they left." I laughed, because he was right. "Volkov is a grade-A asshole, a jerk's jerk. My guys came up with the Firebird all on their own. Volkov latched onto them at a trade show in Hamburg, and claimed to have all kinds of connections with the venture capitalists in the U.S.—complete bullshit. He did do a good job promoting them, but he's stiffed everyone who helped them—including them. They quit because they're very, very tired of Gregor Volkov and all the nonsense."

"I see," I said. "Walking away from—what is it?—ten—twenty—fifty million dollars? That's pretty tired."

"Indeed it is," Raymond agreed, "but to cash in you have to create an operating company. Volkov is going to piss once too often in the soup for Echelon to succeed. Plus we're going to blow it away when we get organized." He paused. "Look, I'll bring them around for an interview if you like."

As he spoke, all of the preposterous machinery of the whole preposterous farce playing out that week began to creak and groan and shake. The wheel came as close to breaking right then as it ever would, the whole ridiculous contraption blowing up in the face of whatever sneering, malignant deity had concocted it—for Razumaev and Grischuk were, of course, the two vodka-challenged Russians who had been at Mira's orphans' Thanksgiving dinner. Had I met them face to face, the game would have ended right then and there. But it was not to be—I didn't want to waste any more of my time or anyone else's.

"No, Ed, I said, "that won't be necessary" I said. Luck, not the Empress but the Court Jester this time, the Practical Joker, was rolling on the floor. Big joke, but forgive me, I'm not laughing. I hope Luck the Practical Joker does have a persona and there's a hell somewhere that he can fry away in. "Put Mark on the line." My investigator took the phone, I told him about the offer to furnish back ups and to search, and I asked him to follow through. This was one case that wasn't going anywhere, but I wanted the reasons thoroughly documented. Raymond asked for the phone back.

"Just one last question," he said. "You *do* know you have to split stock in these little companies before you take them public, don't you? I mean, if you need some sort of refresher course—"

"Oh, knock it off, Ed," I said, and I began to laugh. "I assume that little story is going all around the valley?"

"Indeed it is," he agreed. "Too rich not to share. But, Walt, you going to do anything more about this Echelon thing?"

"No," I said, because it was the truth and he deserved an unequivocal reply. "To be candid with you, it was almost dead on arrival. But we do have to check everything out. I'll call you if it heats up at all."

"Thanks," he said, the relief evident in his voice, and rang off. He'd done a good job for his clients that morning. Both common courtesy and basic professional responsibility required I notify the victim of these negative developments. I wasn't up for another confrontation with Volkov, so I phoned Mark Stewart, and described the recent events. He also knew Ed Raymond.

"I'm going to close the file, Mr. Stewart," I said. "I don't think there's been any crime committed here. Frankly, if it weren't for the sensitivity of the company with the IPO coming up, I wouldn't have done this much."

"I understand," he sighed. "I'll pass the word along."

With that task done, I went back to daydreaming, delicious musings about Mira.

*

Mira was certainly not prey to any delicious musings of her own about me. Her life remained on hold within the same narrow confines. It had descended by degrees into a deep rut, to which she'd become accustomed and from which it was difficult to escape. Yet the simple event of my phone call and invitation—all right, proposition—had produced cracks in a landscape that had appeared to be unweatherable. She tried several times to reach Volkov, to confront him with his faithlessness and his cruelty. He could not be contacted; he was involved in long sessions about damage control of the defection of Razumaev and Grischuk.

Although her thoughts continued to center on Volkov, scraps of daydreams involving the Alternative—me—began to appear on the periphery of her consciousness. These were happy thoughts, which gave her pleasure to think, with the result that she thought them more and more and began to give the idea of weekending with me serious consideration. This day, though still edgy and difficult, was much, much better than the day before.

*

Directly after lunch, my phone rang. I expected it would be Mark Stewart, and indeed it was. Referrals that come with all the emotion I'd observed the day before don't die easy deaths.

"Is this decision final?" he asked.

"Yes," I answered.

"Well, Gregor Volkov demands to see you before it becomes absolutely final," he said.

"It is final, whether Gregor Volkov likes it or not. He can demand this and demand that," I said, "and huff and puff and blow my house down, for that matter. But he has no right to another conference, and I really don't see the point."

"Look, Mr. Kelsey," he sighed, "I know we don't have any right here. And I fully understand your thinking. But I've checked you out, and I know you know the turf. We have a public offering only 90 days away, and a CEO who's about as hinked up as Sylvester the Cat. I'd appreciate it if you'd hear him out, just so he can get all this behind him. There's a lot of money for a lot of innocent shareholders at stake."

Well, when he put it that way…I would much rather have spent the afternoon in a delicious amorous haze, but duty called and there was a limit even to my post-adolescent adolescence. I agreed to meet them an hour later, about two o'clock.

At exactly that hour, they were announced, I greeted them in the lobby, and ushered them into my office. Volkov's agitation was apparent at first glance, as was Stewart's embarrassment.

"I have been informed correctly? You are not going to pursue criminal charges against these hooligans? "Volkov had not even seated himself before he spoke.

"You have been informed correctly," I answered neutrally. "We will not."

"But this is outrageous!" He sputtered. "These men are thieves—traitors!"

"My investigators and I spent quite a bit of time with you, Mr. Stewart, and other representatives of Echelon, sir. None of you were even able to say that anything was missing, let along that something valuable had been stolen. We are not proceeding with criminal charges because there is no evidence of a crime."

"How can there not be a crime? They have betrayed me, they have betrayed everyone at Echelon!"

"It is not a crime to start up a competitive business, Mr. Volkov. It is only a crime to steal something. You haven't been able to tell of us of anything that was actually stolen."

"Then I am not going to get justice?" he retorted as he sat, and we were off. I had him fairly well pegged from the day before, and the meeting went in the direction I had foreseen. He added no new information or basis for complaint; I hadn't thought he would. What he did instead was posture at victimization, as if victimization were a given fact and it was up to me to justify the lack of response. I will give him credit. It was a superb, well-practiced act. I was sure it had been performed often before, with success. It took an effort of will not to become defensive. But I was now two years past my fiftieth birthday, into my 28th as a legal practitioner, and that game wasn't going to work on me.

What did begin to get to me was that there was no shutting him up. Personalities of that type never admit error, so I did not expect that. But I did expect him at some point to wind down. He did not. Instead, he moved relentlessly from tack to tack, retreating back to ancient points when newer ones were disposed of. All of this occurred in a reedy, whiny, self-righteous tone of voice that increasingly began to grate on me.

"Why did you send an investigator if you did not believe there was a crime?" he demanded to know.

"To eliminate suspicion, Mr. Volkov," I answered evenly. "As much for their protection as yours." *Not that I owe you any explanations*, I thought to myself. We had then been at it a good fifty minutes, and I was becoming extremely annoyed.

"And this investigator, this Carroll, what did he do?"

"He went to their offices and discussed this situation with them. Warned them not to make use of any information that was the property of Echelon. They said they would not—in fact, they offered proof that the core concepts of Echelon were invented long before they met you."

"And this Carroll accepted their word for this?" he sneered. It did not escape my notice that he did not deny the claim of prior invention. He almost certainly assumed I wouldn't notice.

"No, he did not, Mr. Volkov. Your former associates also provided him with cloned hard drives of all their computers—plus they opened their offices for him to search as he liked. They telephoned their lawyer—a guy named Ed Raymond, a first rate guy, who I've known for fifteen years. He doesn't get involved with thieves."

"Ah!" Volkov exclaimed, sitting back in his chair. He turned to Stewart and gestured. "The lawyer is a friend of his. The prosecutor has a friend. Now I understand." He turned to me imperiously. "So how long has this Raymond been a friend of yours?"

I haven't written much about my own physique during this narrative. As it happens, I stand about six one and weigh 205 pounds. For aerobic reasons, I work out daily with light weights. They aren't strength builders as such, but it sure hasn't hurt. The bottom line is that I was a strong kid and I have remained a strong man. I have developed a little osteoarthritis in my hands and knees from all the basketball in my teens and twenties, but I'm still a fairly powerful guy.

Before I even knew what was happening, my right hand had shot out and I had Volkov by his tie and collar. I hoisted him out of his chair and pulled him over my desk into my face. Volkov was too astonished to react. Stewart straightened up.

"I don't know whether you know this, Mr. Volkov, but it is a serious crime in this state to make a false police report. And that it is exactly what you have done. You haven't suffered any injustice. You've perpetrated one. You haven't the slightest idea how close I am right now to having you arrested." His eyes went wide with fright; he knew instantly what that sort of scandal would do to the Echelon public offering and his dreams of wealth. "I have absolutely had it with you."

All this was extremely unusual behavior for me. I am a non-violent individual both by nature and principle. I hadn't laid hands on another man in anger in my entire adult life. I have never spanked either of my children, and Nick can be enormously provocative. Even when I was a kid, I was the original anti-bully. I was solid enough that the bully types left me alone, and I had no interest in throwing my own weight around. I hadn't been in a fight since second grade.

Yet there I was with my hand clutched around Volkov's tie, completely infuriated, ready and willing to turn him into cream cheese. That was odd enough, but what came next was absolutely extraordinary. Even after I'd spoken, after I knew he'd heard me, I had the strangest impulse of my life—an urge, then and there, to *kill* Gregor Volkov, to raise my arm and shatter his larynx, and then gloat over my deed as he writhed and strangled in his own blood. The electric spark of rage in my soul jumped the gap to his. He could feel the primordial rage in my grip, see the fury in my face, and he knew with an instinct as primitive as mine that it was a murderous rage. He went pale with fear. Stewart sensed the same thing and straightened up out of his chair. For a short but definite instant of time, I hated Gregor Volkov with my whole soul, and my hatred was homicidal.

For an instant only—then, shaken to my core, I thrust him back against his chair and released him. I had never experienced an emotion like that in my life, and I never wanted to again.

These days I wonder how much I knew or sensed about him and the way he'd treated Mira. I'm not talking about ESP or paranormal stuff, in which I have no belief whatsoever. I'm talking about a type of instinctive faculty, mostly subliminal, only partly conscious (if that), that recognizes the connection between faint and scattered points of data and organizes them into a coherent whole—not the antipode of rationality, but its better angel, a faculty that leaps fearlessly ahead of all the painfully slow logical reasoning to the ultimate conclusion. I don't believe in clairvoyance. But I do believe in that type of intuition.

Whatever the cause, at that moment, I hated Gregor Volkov.

He composed himself as best he could and tried to resume. "This is intolerable," he said, correctly. "You had no right—"

"Get out," I said. I might have been shaken to the core, but I was not about to let him know that. "I have had it. You are the criminal, not the others. One more word and you'll be in cuffs."

"I will complain—"

"Complain to whomever you like," I said. I turned to Mark Stewart. "Get him out. Now."

Stewart put a hand firmly on Volkov's shoulder and almost lifted him out of his chair. Volkov began to protest, then thought better of it. In a second, they were out of my office. I did not see them down the corridor to the elevator. Instead, I sat, trying to still my racing pulse, trying to clear the adrenalin out of my system, my good mood completely shattered, my amorous haze gone.

*

At about the same time, the sun broke through finally into Mira's world. The casual invitation I had issued of a sudden burst through the overcast and shone forth as a full-fledged alternative. She did not have to be with Volkov; she could be with me—and the prospect delighted her.

I doubt Mira ever gave articulate expression to her feelings about the situation. She never rethought or double thought her feelings. She acted on them. Considering herself committed to Volkov, she had been at first inclined to dismiss my invitation out of hand. But she could not dismiss the prospect entirely from her mind, and gradually it took hold. Finally, the thought broke through. Spending some extended time with me struck her like a warm shower on a bitterly cold blustery winter day. The reason was simple enough.

I loved Mira. She delighted me; her company contented and soothed me; and the sexual possession of her seemed to me a treasure beyond comparison, literally priceless. She knew all that. Thus time spent with me would be free of recriminations, complaints, second guessing, and the tormenting miasma of doubt that had clouded her last few days. Call it a necessary tonic, call it an irresistible temptation—I prefer the former—but there are few human beings who would not have felt the attraction.

So it was the sun broke through, her entire disposition began to change, and the acceptance of my invite—which I had assumed was a done deal— now actually did become inevitable. Mira began to daydream herself of what the weekend might be like, and her afternoon became very pleasant.

*

I thought I'd be alone for a while, but in a remarkably short time Mark Stewart poked his head back through my door.

"Can I come in?" he said.

"Sure," I answered, although I was still brooding, and he stepped into my office with light tread and closed the door softly behind him.

"I'm sorry," he said, which was nice to hear. With all my brave talk, I wasn't all that keen on Volkov complaining to the brass about the assault, particularly with a witness. "I didn't know it would go like that."

"He's impossible," I said. "It's not my problem. But if you leave a man with a personality like that in charge of a public company, you're nuts. You may be able to make him presentable for the dog-and-pony shows to the institutionals, but sooner or later he's going to alienate all your vendors and your entire customer base."

"We know we have a problem," Stewart answered, "but he's not really that bad. He's under a lot of stress. This spin-off has really spooked him."

"I wondered why Razumaev and Grischuk would quit when they're just about to get rich," I said. "What they answered is that they don't trust him—and now I can understand why. These companies develop a lot of centrifugality as they go from rags to riches. You have to have honor all along, top to the bottom, or nobody trusts anybody when the real money starts to show up."

Stewart was quiet himself, and I wondered if I'd said too much. It really wasn't my place to give him advice.

"I'm sorry," I said finally. "I'm talking my own philosophy."

"No, no," he answered quickly, "you're absolutely right. I was just thinking this is chickens coming home to roost. We've let Volkov get away with stiffing a lot of people who helped him. He started out without two dimes in his pocket, and he promised stock to a lot of people. The finder who brought him to me never got anything, and now it's coming back. Now we're going to have to compete against ourselves, in effect. We should have insisted on some simple integrity a long, long time ago. But what we do now I don't know."

Once again the machinery creaked and wobbled, for the finder that Stewart mentioned obliquely was, of course, Mira. It was one of those coincidences, supposedly stranger than fiction that occurs with surprising frequency in real life. But I truly wish it had happened in fiction, so that I could edit events, re-arrange them, casually ask the names of all those anonymous victims Stewart had mentioned, and then alter all of the now irrevocable events when I learned that Mira led the list of Volkov's victims. But there was a reason in real life why Stewart did not volunteer their names, and it was the same reason I didn't ask—because the specifics were a private business problem of Echelon's that was none of the business of the district attorney's office. For the same reason, I wasn't even curious.

Stewart and I made a little more small talk. Then he left, lost in his own reflections. My bright mood was totally destroyed. I sank into brooding thought myself, along the lines of the importance of loyalty and the danger of believing in your own personal rationalizations for your own personal desires.

And so the wheel remained unbroken and turned again.

*

Stewart went down to the parking lot, where Gregor Volkov was waiting in the passenger's seat of his BMW. The moment he opened the door, Volkov began—this was worse than Moscow, he thought he'd left the KGB behind in Russia, and on, and on.

"Shut up, Gregor," Stewart answered as the car exited the lot, in a tone that froze the flow of speech in mid-syllable. Volkov remained deathly afraid of his board of directors.

"You made a complete ass of yourself," Stewart went on. "You're just lucky you weren't dealing with the KGB. Yuri and Ilya didn't steal anything," he continued, warming up, "as you damn well know. What happened is that they got fed up with you. As I am now. As the entire Board is. As everyone who has had the misfortune to do business with you or befriend you is. What I am saying," he continued his voice rising," is that I have HAD IT!! One more complaint, one more incident, one more whining word, and I will pull he plug on this IPO, and I will rehire Yuri and Ilya, and I will reorganize the company without you, and cut you out without a share, then turn you over to the INS and let them turn you over to the KGB or the GPU or whatever goddam secret police they've got going over there now. I will then get the best night's sleep I've had in whenever. So just shut your fucking mouth up if you have any idea what's good for you."

I could have told Gregor Volkov that what Stewart was saying was entirely bluff. So could any competent securities lawyer. With the technical muscle having departed, there was no way Stewart and the Board could dump the CEO without writing off the company and the investment completely. So Volkov was in no danger himself. In fact, he'd become essential, at least in the short tem. But he didn't know that.

"What can I do, Mark?" he asked timidly.

"You could start by doing right by Mira Watson, for one thing," Stewart answered, and they drove on.

*

The good mood had disappeared, the froth was gone, the door was closed, and I was mired deep in glum and grim. The deepest needs of my soul were once again obscure to me.

The direct experience of the coarse, raw undiluted ego of Gregor Volkov had set me off on ruminations about my own egotism. What I was pondering was the possibility that I might be doing my own personal bit of rationalizing. Mira, I knew (or thought I knew) had been involved with someone for some time who was important to her; to whom she had given enormous devotion; which she had pursued for quite a while; and who—this was the bottom line—was close to essential to her long-term future. It was obvious to me that the relationship had hit some reef or shoal—but don't they all? Was it fair, was it right, to exploit whatever temporary frustrations she might be feeling to enjoy her company—and her favors—for a weekend—and do irreparable damage to her more important long term prospects? Yes, something might revive between us, yes, there was a certain possibility, but was it right to tempt her with this 'maybe' against the solid potential of whatever and whoever it was she had been cultivating?

My God, to this day I amaze myself! I had an image of Mira's phantom boy friend as someone rich, solid, urbane, good-looking, younger than I—someone a great deal like Mark Stewart, come to think of it. The thought that she might have been embroiled with the other man who had been in my office was beyond the realm of my imagining.

So—after reflecting on this situation and my own would-be selfishness, acting on this utterly pea-brained train of thought, this pot-pourri of addled common sense, could-not-love-thee-half-so-much honor gone stark, raving mad, I phoned Mira that evening. The option was still mine. She had not formally accepted my invitation.

*

She had her suitcase open. She was already planning her wardrobe and beginning to pack.

*

"Mira"—when I'm nervous or ill at ease, I get straight to the point—"I've been thinking."

"Yes?" Her tone of voice is etched in my memory, light and eager. But that night I was too bent on doing what I had decided to do to react to it.

"I'm not so sure this weekend is a good idea. I mean—"I plunged relentlessly ahead—if it was done when it was done, it was best done quickly—"I know you've been seeing someone. I know it's someone important. I really don't want to interfere."

"I'm not sure I know what you mean, Walt," she said, but of course she did know, and the disappointment was already drooping into her voice. It is agony for me to remember this, let alone record it.

"What I mean is that nothing really has changed in four years. I'm not sure where we go, or what we'd do. I'm not sure—if you really have some solid possibilities in your life—in fact, I *am* sure—screwing something good up for a week-end—maybe isn't such a great idea." There was a dead silence on the other end of the line. "Even if you have hit a bad patch with is guy, whoever he is," I finished. I sounded awkward, nervous and stupid to myself, mostly—I can see now—because I was acting awkwardly, nervously and stupidly.

"I see," Mira said quietly. There was another long silence. "That's a very sensible way to look at it, Walt," she said. "I have always admired your good sense." Her tone was a curious blend of wistfulness, irony and respect. It cut straight through to the bone of my soul, past all the intellectualizing, past all the barriers of cold reason—I had hurt her, I knew, and I wanted to undo the hurt.

Yet I would not go back, for I had persuaded myself that the agency of the hurt was the misguided invitation in the first place, and that to renew it would be to compound the wrong.

"Mira, it's not that I don't want you," I said. "I want you more than anything," realizing as I spoke exactly how true those words were. "But I don't know where it leads, beyond this weekend. I don't know where we'd go, or what we'd want to do. And I don't want to upset something that might be real, and important, on that kind of whimsy."

"I understand," Mira answered simply and I think she truly did, that this was not a rejection of any kind, but something, in its demented good will, far, far worse. "Perhaps you're right," although I am certain now—was probably certain then—that she knew, or at least sensed, full well how wrong I was.

I was still searching for the right words of explanation, comfort. "I care about you—a lot," I said softly, truthfully. "Probably more than any one except the kids. I want to do the right thing by you. That's why." This stands to this day, and I hope to God will always stand, as the stupidest thing I have ever said in my life. It was the stupidest precisely because it *was* truthful.

All we had done was talk about a weekend. We had been lovers once, but friends for a much longer time. Her emotions about Volkov were still unsettled. We were not in a place where everything could have come out in one grand eruption—it would have had to unfold, in stages, gradually, if I'd simply had enough trust and courage to take her away that weekend. Everything would have been different, we would have come together, and we would still be together.

But it didn't happen like that.

"All right, Walt," she sighed, "there are plenty of things I have to do this weekend anyway. Maybe it's for the best."

"I'll call you for lunch next week," I said. I did not like the flat tone in her voice.

"Sure," Mira said, as flatly as before, and a little while later we rang off.

*

She sat down on her bed, completely deflated. The brightness of the Alternative had vanished as suddenly and completely as it had appeared. She wondered bleakly what would happen next. But the wheel had not finished turning. There was one small ratchet left.

Five or ten minutes later, Volkov phoned. He was full of remorse, tearful, apologetic, almost—it seemed to her—terrified. He had done wrong, he was sorry, so sorry, he would never do such a thing again, could she ever forgive him? As with most of us, forgiving for Mira was easy. Forgetting was the hard part. But now it seemed as if fate itself had spoken. So forgive him she did, with her usual grace and poise, and they agreed—he tearfully, she with her habitual nonchalance—to begin again. If there was more weariness than exhilaration, more exhaustion than excitement, more past than there could ever be future, she did not let that sub-text show.

Thus the week ended.

*

Why?

A question that repeats itself in my head again and again, a bell tolling, calling me to account. It will haunt me to my last day on earth. I have answers. I don't have a good answer.

In one sense, it was the dancer's art, the dancer's illusion, the apparent effortlessness of the gesture. I had known Mira four years then, and I had yet to see through it. Each time we met, every time we spoke, she was calm, poised, nonchalant. Yes, she had problems, but the solutions were close. Yes, her involvement might have its transient difficulties, but it was a serious relationship that held promise for her future. Not in so much as the whisper of a syllable any time in the four years did she let slip how difficult her life had truly become, how bleak and desolate the landscape that I thought was full and rich.

Added to that was the persistent self-doubt of maturity. The course of true love never did run smooth. For the youthful, the obstacles arise from the indeterminable future. But for those a little further along—read 'middle-aged', they arise out of the all-too-determinate past. I was not afraid of pain. I was not afraid of loss. I have had enough experience with both not to be intimidated by either. What I did not have was the certainty that what I really wanted to do—hurdle the gate on my valiant white steed, seize Mira from whomever she was with, throw her over my saddle, and ride off towards the sky—was the right thing to do. Those acts are the stuff of romances, bodice rippers, juvenile fantasy.... it's kid stuff. Ninety-nine out of one hundred adults who believe in that sort of thing are grown-up teenagers in need of a keeper. Nine hundred ninety-nine out of a thousand of those hyper-romantic gestures result in nothing more than a huge mess of smashed crockery and a colossal quantity of spilt milk.

But this time the romantic gesture *would* have worked. This time it *was* the right thing to do. I was the hundredth person. This was the thousandth occasion. My resistance to those facts was the paradoxical proof of their truth.

Mira would have grabbed the bridle in an instant and been in my arms. She was already rejoicing at the thought of the knight. And what difference should it have made whether the man behind the wall was a good man or a bad man, or who he was, or what his deservings were? Worthy or unworthy, the hell with him—why should any of that have mattered? Mira was my destined true love, mine to have, mine to hold, mine to possess, mine to defend. Together, we could have ridden off, and together we could have built our castle—no fortress, that castle, but something made entirely of fresh air and sunshine. What is so rarely possible in real life was possible for us, that day, that week, any time. The one, the only difficulty, was the one that always defeated us—the difficulty of belief.

Volkov hovered in the atmosphere, a dark angel, as I brooded in my office on that far-off, ghost haunted afternoon—Volkov, with his grandiose sense of entitlement, his delusive belief in his own importance, when what he truly was was a useless, obstructive, destructive parasite. I compared my own egotism to his; I measured my own sense of my just deserts in relation to his absurdities. He, too, in the depths of his pygmy soul, probably saw himself on a white horse. Was I any different? What it finally came down to was that I was not willing to declare myself the hero of my own story. That seemed to me to be an act of supreme effrontery and arrogance. Somehow, at some time—even now, I don't know exactly when or where—all this crossed the line from pondering to rationalizing my abandonment of Mira.

I really don't know the exact reasons, I don't remember the precise moment, and actually, I don't really care that much. Ultimately none of that matters. All that does matter is that Mira and I did *not* go to Tahoe that weekend, we did *not* begin again that Saturday, and it would have made all the difference if we had. But it didn't happen— and no matter how many times I relive that week, recount those days, rethink that afternoon, it never does. Nothing changes.

Thus it happened that, with my responsibilities to my children well in hand, with more than adequate financial resources, with my dues paid and my vistas entirely uncluttered, I left my true love to live in her wretched little house, and to be courted by her wretched little suitor and to see all her high shining hopes become wretched and little in their turn.

And in so doing, I squandered the best of the last chances. Destiny threw up its hands completely and gave up. Maybe it even switched from friend to foe. From then on, if the game was to be won, I was

going to have to do it on my own—and I hadn't even figured out what
the game was or even that there *was* a game.

*

That weekend was the first of the NCAA basketball tournament.
Usually that is one of my favorite weekends of the year, but this time I
found it listless and weary. Mira preyed on my thoughts. I could trick
my conscious mind into believing that all was well with her, that I had
done the Noble Thing by clearing off—but not my intuition, that
dot-connecting faculty that understands so much more than daylight
reason ever can. It knew that something was terribly, terribly wrong.

Mira did go off with Gregor that same weekend, and I believe even
to the Tahoe Region. She had accepted the turn of events with her customary resilience. She was determined to make the relationship work.
All was thus forgiven, because necessity required that all be forgiven.
She did her best for him the entire weekend. For his part, on that
weekend, he was as bright and lively as she had known him, with only
mild, occasional lapses into moody sullenness. Despite the uncertain
past and the disastrous present, Mira began to renew hope that they
might have a future after all.

Eight weeks later, the Echelon IPO launched on schedule.

CHAPTER 14

▼

Mira returned to her miserable house after the weekend, hoping that something workable, a new beginning, would emerge, phoenix-like, out of this train wreck of a week. But there were no beginning left in the whole tangled mess—only fresh disappointment, frustration, powerlessness, and an ever growing distance between where she was and where she wanted to be.

Even so, the dancer kept her balance for the longest time—long after anyone else would have fallen flat.

✳

Gregor Volkov had encountered his nemesis that week, the *bete-noire* of all narcissists—a blunt, unforgettable, unrationalizable confrontation with independent, powerful personalities who saw right through his bullshit and had no patience with it or him. He felt reduced, petty. He writhed at the memory of my hand on his throat. He trembled with anger at the recollection of Stewart's contempt.

Nothing had worked out as he planned. He had expected to find freedom with wealth, fame with success. But the wealth had not been liberating. Stewart and the underwriters had shackled him to his shareholding until the company's performance justified its price. His fame was rapidly descending into the worst kind of notoriety. With the financing for Echelon *done, his narcissism could no longer be disguised as ambition. Its continual manifestation exasperated everyone who had to deal with him. He could feel silent contempt all around him. The tantrums he threw in response only increased the ambience of ridicule. But he could not stop himself from being himself.*

The defection of Grishuk and Razumaev made his situation worse. Those of the Echelon staff who had been willing to tolerate his excesses on the ground of cultural eccentricity now learned that his countrymen didn't like him any better than Americans did. Disapproval became constant, universal. He could sense it everywhere. But there was never any open display. There was never anything he could directly confront.

He was frightened. The fear became malice, the malice, vindictiveness. Since he was no more capable of monstrosity than he was of heroism, his vindictiveness took the form of whiny spite. His luck there was good. Fate had provided him with an easy, accessible target, someone close enough to Stewart and the faceless, jeering audience to be identified with them, yet powerless to retaliate.

*

A few weeks after the debacle, I ran into Mira again, at the Open House that signaled the beginning of the end of the school year as much in Special Ed as it did in the regular classes. It had been three years since Nick and Alicia had been in the same class, but they had been rejoined this particular year. As a result, I had actually seen more of Mira's daughter that year than had Mira herself. She was growing up wonderfully, maturing into a marvelous little girl, bright and alert, with the touching, invincible innocence that is so often characteristic of these children. She was not nearly so badly off as my Nick, a statement I can make without envy or jealousy of any kind. There is no competition in that environment.

Mira was there. I could hardly look her in the eye, which should have told me more about the actual quality of my recent actions than all my nobly worded rationalizations. We made awkward chit-chat for a few moments about inconsequential stuff, and then the subject turned to our children.

"Alicia is marvelous," I said. "Her progress is just astounding. You must be very proud."

"I am, Walt, I am," she answered flatly. I noticed then that she seemed much more harried and distracted than at any time I could remember. She seemed to be considering her next words carefully. "She's going to be living with her father this summer."

"What!" I answered, genuinely astonished. I thought of all the petitions, all the court appearances, the long, lonely fight she'd carried on with such wonderful resourcefulness. "Are you sure?"

She nodded forcefully. "Yes. Alicia, and also the boys. For the summer. No longer," she added firmly.

"But why?" I said, truly perplexed.

"Because I think—well, I hope—well, no, I am—I'm getting married," she said. I felt my heart seize at this. "And my—friend—my fiancé needs—what would you call it?—a period of adjustment. He isn't that used to children."

I felt complete confusion. So it seemed my noble instincts in March had been correct after all. I had apparently done the right thing in not tempting Mira out of her involvement. This was supposedly what I had wanted for her. Thus, I would have expected to feel the kind of wistful self-congratulation that is typical when some act of mature selflessness has worked out. Not so—instead I was hit by a raw, territorial anguish with a terrific hormonal oomph to it. The higher brain can be deceived over and over again. The lower brain always knows what it wants.

That was cause enough for confusion right there. But also Mira did not appear to be nearly as happy as I would have expected. She seemed to be far more anxious than she was ecstatic.

"Congratulations, Mira," I said, trying to sound sincere, being sincere from the neck up. "But...you know...the kids."

She took my hand quickly and squeezed it gently. "Not every man has the paternal instincts you do, Walt. Some men need to get accustomed to the idea. He's a good man. It'll work out."

"O.K," I said. "When's the happy day?"

"Oh, we haven't set that yet," she answered quickly, too quickly. "In fact, it's all up in the air. Very much up in the air," and she changed the subject at once. Another parent caught her eye, and she smiled, and then evaporated, leaving me standing alone, burdened with thought.

For the first time I worried for her. The decision she'd made about the kids was totally out of character. For the first time, too, I wondered about the man in her life, the type of man who would insist on a separation from her children for any period of time, no matter how brief. She seemed distracted and uneasy, bereft of the casual grace that was her hallmark. The thought crossed my mind that the decision, the anxiety, and the man might not be entirely unrelated. I made up my mind to call her, to find out what was up and what I might be able to do about it.

I did call her, several times during the next few weeks. She was never in to take the call, and she didn't return any of them. Gradually the concern slipped to the bottom of the agenda and the back of my mind. Everyone has a bad day now and then.

*

Her time had run out. Alicia was now thirteen, the boys eleven and ten. The miserable, idiot house from which she had struggled to escape for five years had claimed its revenge at last. It was too small, obviously, intolerably too small. The fact was inescapable. The court evaluators knew it, the judge knew it, and Mira knew it, too.

Volkov had a house, the one she had found for him. It was more than large enough. He held out that carrot, made her promises, or promises to promise, or something. But there was a catch. He explained it. He loved children, wanted children. But he was not ready to cope with hers. He was particularly not ready to cope with Alicia. Her children had always been there. They had always been an obstruction. He had never really had a chance to know her. Perhaps—he suggested—perhaps, if she gave them over to their father for a summer, perhaps in that period he and Mira could find themselves. And if they did? Volkov would do…something.

The Mira I had known five years earlier, the Mira I had fallen in love with, whose action was as swift as thought, would have dismissed him without a single backward look. The real affection she felt for him had never dulled her instincts as to the basic weakness of his character. But this was a Mira weakened by abandonment and disappointment, burdened with worry. So she swayed in the wind in an agony of indecision. Ultimately she rationalized it in the only way possible. She knew she was lovable. She had been nothing but loving to him. Surely in the end this bedrock reality must prevail.

It was only for the summer, she told Crockett firmly. They would revert to the traditional arrangement when school started in the fall. Crockett smiled and made no reply, but left the courthouse with the children in his car.

Perhaps it was for the best, Mira said to herself, heart in mouth, as she watched the car disappear. She and Volkov would have a good summer. She would have the opportunity to use all her wiles to win him over. He had been truthful when he said he was uncomfortable with her children.

Particularly Alicia.

✴

June became July and that Humpty-Dumpty week, a mess of eggs broken with nary an omelet in sight, faded further and further into the past. In July, the Internet finally tossed up on shore the woman I had been searching for—a warm, companiable, sexy lady a year or two younger than myself, in search of a friend, but with commitments of her own.

Her name was Naomi. She was the recently separated, not-yet-divorced spouse of the chief financial officer of one of the major banks in the area. She had her own income, her own house, and two late adolescent children of her own. She needed nothing from me, except my time and companionship. She was intelligent, alert, and so physical she was almost too physical. I liked her a lot.

Thus my life settled into place. During the week, I did justice for the Great State of California. On the weekends, I took Naomi to the movies or the theatre or whatnot, and afterwards to bed. Elizabeth and Nick moved gracefully and securely through their childhoods. I had finally rebuilt the life that had gone to ruins six years before. All of the building blocks were firmly, finally mortared down.

It was as safe as I had imagined, as secure, as unthreatening—and as unchallenging. It was also dry, desiccated, and tinged from the outset with the gray shades of boredom. I should have felt safe and content. But that whole summer long I could not escape a nagging sense of disquiet. My own small house of bricks might be safe enough, but somewhere in the distance the wolf still prowled, and from far away I could hear its faint howls.

*

Mira and Gregor had a good summer, with much time together and one long trip, to the Canadian Rockies. September came. Nothing had changed. He repeated the promises—or the promises to promise—he'd made. He spoke of fulfilling them at some vague, undetermined date in the future. He made sure that the carrot could be seen and equally sure that it would remain dangling, just out of reach. In the meantime, he lived in his house and she stayed in hers.

Gregor did speak explicitly about Alicia. In fact, he spoke constantly about Alicia. He never let the topic drop. How was Alicia doing at school? Could the good reports really be trusted? Perhaps her teachers were simply trying to keep Mira at bay. Perhaps there was something that could be done medically? Had Mira really exhausted all of the alternatives? Perhaps she should have done more.

In mid-September a secretary quit Echelon, threatening a suit for sexual harassment. Stewart, speaking for the board, told Volkov that the directors had adopted a zero tolerance policy for him. Mira met him as planned that evening. She knew nothing of these developments.

That night he talked of nothing but Alicia. He brought up all the old themes. He raised a new one. He was concerned about how her needs might impact Mira's career. He knew she was finishing—at last—her business plan for Gifter's Anonymous. He was troubled. How would she be able to manage a start-up and cope with Alicia? There were only so many hours in a day. She herself knew how demanding the launch of a new business. Mira left the next morning with her stomach in a knot.

The rawest wound was Alicia's emerging womanhood. Her adolescence had begun—she was naively and eagerly interested in boys, in romance, in sex. How would Mira cope? Volkov wondered. Perhaps birth control pills should be given to her with her vitamins. Perhaps she must be chaperoned. Perhaps… perhaps…he knew of many thoughtful caring parents who had had their daughters sterilized. He spoke with apparent sympathy. Mira's blood chilled at the words. He saw that and pressed on, even more sympathetically. But surely it would be a worse disaster if she became pregnant? He was only trying to be helpful.

It was a Chinese water torture with an acid drip. Mira endured it. She hoped—or rather rationalized—that all these expressions of concern were genuine, rather than a subtle mode of torment. Perhaps the concern would metamorphose into affection. It was only necessary to do a little, more, just a little bit more, and all would be well.

The family court date came. Mira went to court and explained in her most winning way that her new housing arrangements were not yet in place, that she would consent to Crockett as primary custodian The judge grunted, far less sympathetically than she had hoped, and extended the order without comment. Outside the court, Crockett told her that all the kids were doing well, but that he was a mite concerned about Alicia. She was having many more silent and morose moments than he'd expected for a child who had been so outgoing a few months ago.

Later she mentioned this to Gregor. He became somber and thoughtful. Then he said that he had heard that often children like Alicia regress badly with the onset of puberty. Perhaps this was what was happening to Alicia. Perhaps she should be re-examined. Perhaps Mira had been slightly neglectful not to have seen to this already.

She felt as if she was being torn in two.

*

School started the week before Labor Day. I took Nick to the first day of school, with the pleasant thought that I would see Mira there, since for the second year running Nick and Alicia had been assigned to the same class. Not so; it was Crockett who dropped off Alicia and gave me a cheery wave as he departed. When Nick brought the directory home, it was Crockett's address that appeared as Alicia's primary address.

Now I was really perplexed—I remembered how firmly Mira had said 'no longer' than the summer when we were talking of the changed arrangements. I placed another series of calls to her in late August and the week after Labor Day. She did not return any of them.

*

The faith of parents such as Mira and me in their children is a defiant faith. I can't produce good, solid, Rotary Club reasons why Nick matters in answer to some sneering skeptic. Good Lord, I can't produce them for myself. My son, Mira's daughter, don't compute; they don't quantify. But the trace elements they add to the human solution are supremely important. They exemplify what makes the human soul real and substantial, a thing of beauty beyond our trivial superiority of survival capacity as a species. As such, they redeem us, both as individuals and as a species—the reason we might just have more claim on the Universe than Tyrannosaurus Rex. They are the living embodiment of God's promise, the rainbow reflected anew in the iris of their eyes.

But I can't explain this faith to doubters. They either know it or they don't. I—Mira—none of us—can escape the shadow of doubt ourselves. The Devil whispers constantly in our ears, that the ultimate word is truly 'no', that we are fools deluded by love. We do our best to ignore him, but it is not possible to be entirely deaf to this. It is the one point of vulnerability in all our lives that is beyond fortification, the one constant open wound. It makes for an easy target for those in need of targets.

*

Naomi had all the qualities that I was looking for in a woman. But she was not without her own baggage. No one our age is. She had been a social lioness in the upscale community where she still dwelt, in a two million dollar house that would be hers without encumbrances when the divorce was final. She had also been a lioness of a mother. The baggage took the form of an excessive insecurity about both her social status and her relationship with her children. She worried constantly that the mutual friends she and her husband had had would all desert her in favor of him. She agonized that the kids would prefer his new girlfriend to their mother.

I did my best to assert the plain, prosaic truths about these matters. Every woman in their social circle was secretly on her side, terrified that the same fate could befall her. The only person who could alienate Naomi's children from her was she herself. Sometimes this reassured her, sometimes not. Sometimes she would rest her head on my shoulder and agree in a soft voice that she was being foolish. But as often she would find the open statement of this obvious stuff infuriating. She did not want my comfort, she would complain, all she wanted to do was vent, and what the hell did I know about it, anyway?

I had had too much experience in my life with angry women to become exercised over these incidents. These were small spats that arose suddenly, and were gone as quickly. But my thoughts at those times would go to someone I knew who did not have a two-million dollar house, and who did not share a cordial custodial relationship with the father of her children. Once or twice I mentioned the wonderful nonchalance with which a woman I had once known had handled a lot more adversity than Naomi faced. She would usually quiet down then and become thoughtful.

*

Mira went often to the house she had found and furnished for Volkov, spent the night there, then returned to the empty home where she dwelt. They spoke of past and present, but never future—except Alicia's future, a subject he would not let drop. The fall wore on. Nothing changed. The promises were always firm and always vague.

One rainy October night she confronted the issue directly. 'Is Alicia a problem?' she asked. 'Is that the problem?'

He noted that she was the one who had brought the subject up. Therefore she should not blame him if he had to say unpleasant things. Alicia disturbed him. He did not know what to do with her. He knew boys, liked her sons—but Alicia bothered him. Perhaps…? Crockett was a fine man and a good father who could manage her well. Perhaps…?

So there it was. Her openness had solved nothing. Once more she felt herself being torn in two. She loved Volkov, or thought she did. But Alicia was her oldest and neediest, the key to her soul. There was no way she could ever abandon Alicia. For the balance of the fall, Mira writhed and twisted on this bed of coals, searching for a solution. She worked with intense urgency to finish the Gifter's Anonymous business plan, hoping that might provide a solution.

And in the short term kept on sleeping with Volkov.

*

That was a good year for tech stocks, the last good year. My newly-found equity holding soared with the rest of the market. By early November, it was worth six times what it had been in March, and that had not been inconsiderable.

These developments naturally pleased me. But I didn't sell any of the stock, or change any aspect of my life. There wasn't anything I could think of to do with the money. So it sat in the brokerage account, getting larger and more useless with each passing day.

*

I remember the last few months of my mother's battle with breast cancer vividly. She drooped, then drooped again, a declining curve that suddenly became a dead drop to death itself. I am told that is the way most fatal, wasting illnesses go—a slant down, then a steeper slant down, then a final, precipitous drop off the table. Perhaps the same pattern applies to all the processes of moribundity in human affairs—a challenge for the chaos mathematicians, if any of them want to take it up.

That was the pattern with Mira, and the end of the affair with Volkov. November came. She finished her business plan; threw a small party for the other founders, and sent it off into the void, hoping. Volkov did not attend, for some apparently unimportant, apparently understandable reason.

A few days passed with no contact from him, which was not significant. The days stretched to a week, then two, without sight or message. That was significant, and troubling. The phone remained silent. She called herself, casually at first, then with some urgency. There were no calls back. The realization dawned on her that it was over, as cruelly, as crudely, as that.

Mira might have been angry, except that she could not afford anger. She had too much investment in time, energy, and self in Volkov for that. She wondered—hoped—that she had misunderstood something. She tried call-

ing again. There was no response. There had also been an unnerving silence about Gifter's Anonymous, which further sandpapered her nerves.

Now, finally, her marvelous poise had reached its limits. She called Volkov again, and again and yet again, desperately, until finally, by random chance, she connected. He was distant, random, evasive. Nonetheless, he agreed to see her. Even he must have realized that one last meeting was unavoidable.

It was the Wednesday night before Thanksgiving. He met her in the living room. She was dressed as always, stylishly but not provocatively. Nonetheless, he eyed her greedily, and began to undress her. His pleasure in her body, both before and after the cosmetic surgery, was undisguised. But now she stepped away.

'Not tonight, Gregor,' she said. 'I don't want to go to bed with you. I want to know what's wrong.'

'Nothing is wrong', he said, but she persisted. He realized that he could not evade the issue.

'I care for you deeply, Mira,' he said. 'I want you. We have been through a great deal together. But I do not believe I can ever win your heart."

"I care for you, too, Gregor. You know that, I've done a great deal for you.'

'This is what I mean', he said. 'This is exactly what I mean. You always make me feel guilty, as if I must be permanently in your debt. You expect me to care for you out of gratitude. You have no concept of true feeling, of love with an open heart.'

'I do for the people I care about,' Mira said. She was regal and calm. There was no trace of either damnation or plea. 'I did for you. I gave you space when you had no money. I helped you with your plans and dreams without asking anything in return. That is what love is.'

'No, it is not,' he said. 'This is what makes debtors and creditors. This is not the true love of the heart. In your heart, you belittle me. You have contempt for me. You are no different than all the others.'

'What others?' she asked.

'Never mind', he said hastily. 'The point is that you never let me forget what you have done for me. This is not the generosity of love.'

'You made me promises' she said, with the same detached dignity.

'You made promises to me,' he replied. 'That you would change some things in your life. I cannot keep mine if you do not keep yours.'

'But I have done things for you,' she said. 'I gave up my children. I even thought of surrendering Alicia. You asked me to do this.'

'You have thought of this, but you have not done it. And giving you the strength to do this, this was my greatest gift to you. The dummy is the great curse of your life. I hoped to accomplish this for you, to do this favor.'

She knew Gregor. She knew he had chosen the word 'dummy' to inflict as deep a wound upon her as he could. She wondered if he had also chosen it to convey to her the awareness of the full extent of her folly, that that girl at the lunch had been right about everything. The same flash of insight carried to the next level. At once she was certain that the rearranged custodial arrangements, the talk of permanence, had all been some sick game to see how far he could goad her off her true path in pursuit of a will o' the wisp. Their eyes met; there was a quick flash of triumph in his that he did not successfully conceal; she knew she had been right. She wondered how much else of her life he had deliberately damaged.

'You hate me,' she said, without rancor, stating a newly-discovered fact. 'Why?'

'You are being ridiculous,' he answered. He had a superbly developed instinct for when to advance, when to retreat. 'I don't hate you. I love you. I chose the ugly word to open your eyes—tough love, you Americans call it. I want you to see the child not through a mother's eyes, but as the rest of the world sees her. She should be in an institution, far from you, where she can be helped and you—we—can live the life we deserve.' He took her hand. 'But if I spoke too cruelly—please—forgive me. I did not speak to insult or hurt. But to enlighten.'

She felt a weary familiarity with this stop-and-go. It had been standard operating procedure for three years. Volkov was not without his flashes of warmth and tenderness; they always appeared at these times. At the begin-

ning, she had been confident the true Volkov showed through in those flashes. She had believed that with enough warmth and reinforcement from her, that that self would emerge unimpaired. Her greater wisdom told her that that was not so, that he was a fundamentally flawed human being, but she deliberately ignored that insight.

She was next to certain he was pretending. But she could not be sure. His explanation was plausible. His explanations were always plausible. So much was at stake—what if she had misjudged him? Suppose he had meant well? What if she were wrong? Second thoughts of that type are what had ensnared her. Tonight she was too tired, too dispirited to indulge them.

'I'm going to go home now', she replied.

'Please do not, Mira,' he said. 'Not yet. If I am wrong, I am sorry. I only want what's best for you. You know more about these things than I do. I can learn. Don't go. Not like this"

So another battle in the long, exhausting war between her better judgment and her sense of self was joined. There had been no such divisiveness when I knew her. Her better sense knew him for what he was—and yet to walk out and write off completely five years, all the time, all the energy, all the sacrifice, all the deserving—she did not have the strength to form that resolution on this night. Perhaps, she reasoned to herself, with his attitude about Alicia finally completely in the open, they had touched bottom. Perhaps this time she would be able to find the word, articulate the feeling, which would finally open his heart.

'All right', she said. This time, when he reached for her, she did not step back.

She knew it was a mistake almost at once. It was hasty, dismal, unilateral sex that changed nothing. Later she invited him to Thanksgiving dinner. He was noncommittal. She was certain he would not be coming.

Afterwards Mira drove home. She had spent her twenties in a theatrical troupe. The sexual indiscretion did not particularly prey on her. But she wondered when and how she had become so indecisive, so uncertain. Once home, she took an endless, hot, inadequate shower. Had she taken stock at the time, she would have concluded that her career track had been totally obliterated; her investment of time and self in Echelon had disappeared without a trace; her social life was non-existent; her precious, one-parent family lay in ruins. But closure of that type is only for accountants and storytellers. Real life goes on, and Mira Watson was a creature of movement. As she tried to wash his touch off her body, she automatically began to plan, to consider what she would do to restore her life. Later she searched for, and found, the MBA curriculum guide for the course of study she had abandoned three years before. It was time to move on.

Her attitude about Volkov was a wild, confused tempest of contrary gusts and gales—anger, frustration, love, or what at that time she called love—actually a yearning to restore her own integrity. As she jotted down the school number, she wondered what she really felt about him. An experienced emotional geologist would have noticed that deep down, far beneath the constantly changing winds that blow over the surface of the earth, a small, fierce pool of hot, liquid hatred had formed.

*

On the same Wednesday evening, Naomi and I had one of our own periodic quarrels. This one was occasioned by the Christmas vacation plans her soon-to-be-ex-husband had made for their children and his new girlfriend. These were for two glorious weeks in some ritzy warm-weather place—the Bahamas, as I recall. She was worried, as usual, that the glories of this splendid holiday would cause their children to forget all about her, and embrace the new woman in their father's life in her place. I explained, as I had so often, that this was a psychological impossibility if she simply kept her cool—that is, kept her mouth shut and let the kids develop their own resentments of the woman who had replaced their mother without her help.

On some occasions Naomi allowed herself to be consoled by this perspective, but this was not one of them. She was just too nervous, and maybe she knew she had no ability at all to keep her mouth shut under this provocation. Whatever the reason, she blew up. She had intended to spend the night with me, but decided on the spur of the moment to go home. All that had happened often enough before, but this time there was a twist.

"I think maybe we should cool it for a while," she announced.

"You surprise me," I said, smiling.

She did not smile. "We're not going anywhere. All we do is go out and stay in. I need someone to love me. I don't think you can."

I stopped smiling. Naomi had always been supremely practical and physical. She had never spoken like this before, of needs of these types. "Why do you say that?" I fished.

"Because you already love somebody else."

"I'm not in love with anybody."

"I didn't say you were in love. I said you loved somebody."

"Who?" I was actually curious.

"That girl you're always talking about. The graceful one. That balle-rina." I had described Mira to her, but never mentioned her by name.

"Modern dancer, actually. I've barely mentioned her. I haven't seen her in months."

"As if that matters?" Naomi gave me a look of withering contempt that I had to come know well, one of her specialties. She was one of those wise persons who have no sense of their own wisdom, instead view people who possess less as foolish. "For such a smart guy, you don't know a damn thing about yourself. You love her. I wish you loved—never mind." She struggled into her coat. "Maybe when you've figured it all out, we can pick it up again."

Then she vanished through my door and into the night, leaving me alone with a lot of surprising and confusing thoughts.

CHAPTER 15

▼

I will now tell you how all this ended.

∗

Since the separation, Christmas had been one of the drearier days of
the year for me. The Big House was the ancestral home, and the kids
would have been distraught if they'd spent the Night Before any place
else. So I would pick them up at about noon on Christmas Day to take
them to my own family celebration. It was not a good deal; Christmas
Day, to my way of thinking, has the same relationship to Christmas
Eve as a nutshell does to the nut. I usually spent that evening on my
own, warding off self-pity by reminding myself that the actual Christ-
mases of my past hadn't exactly been feasts of White Chistmas-y sentiment in keeping with the mythical popular tradition. They had been
feasts of much different sentiment in keeping with the actual Irish
Christmas tradition—the time to reckon up all the slights, misunderstandings, and resentments of the past year and demand payment in
full.

That particular evening was lonelier than any of those in the years
that had gone before. Naomi, who was Jewish, might have kept me
company on the Eve. But she and I were still on the outs. The Christ-

mas Day celebration had been postponed two days because two of my brother's children had caught bad cases of stomach flu that was going around. The upshot was that I was going to spend both days entirely on my own, which was a pretty depressing prospect. I am not that interested in televised sports.

Sometime in the early afternoon of Christmas Day, the thought crossed my mind that Mira and Crockett probably had the same custodial pattern as Linda and me. Her kids had likely spent Christmas Eve with her, then departed for their father's house at about noon. I was in real need of company. I had wanted to touch base with her for some time. It seemed like the right time. So I played the odds and called her at home.

My luck was in. She answered on the second ring. "Walter," she said. My heart leaped as it always did at the sound of her voice.

"I thought I'd call, wish you a happy Holiday, and catch up on the news. Have you and the lucky guy set a date yet?" I tried to make this sound casual.

"I don't think there's going to be a date, Walt," Mira answered. "It looks like I've been bamboozled. Or dumped."

"What?" I said, and straightened up in my chair. Her tone seemed as casually nonchalant as always. But there was a difference. It was likely imperceptible to most, but not to me. I heard an edge, a tightness, a stress that put me instantly on alert. Somewhere deep in my subconscious, something began to happen. Sparks began to fly. "I thought it was all set. I thought that was why you gave up primary custody to Crockett."

"So did I," she said, with the same close-but-not-quite-right tone. "But I guess I misunderstood. The guy and I weren't on the same wave length, I guess."

"Some guy would have you give up on the fight and then pull the rug out?" More sparks were flying wildly now. A small firestorm had already ignited, getting larger and fiercer with each passing microsecond. Emotions I didn't know that I still had began to take possession of me, a full-fledged visceral rage. Even in this early stage, I was infuriated. I had not given up this priceless woman so that she could be used like *this*. "What do you mean, not on the same wave length? He asks you to rearrange your life and he doesn't *understand?*"

In the whole time, I had never once asked the name of the man in her life. Mira and I had always had a tacit understanding that those details were in a zone of privacy that was none of my business. But I was too angry now to stand for that sort of nicety. "What man has done this to you? *Who is this guy?*"

"Gregor Volkov," Mira answered.

∗

Before she had finished pronouncing the name, I had erupted out of my chair, with a roar and a bellow. I had always thought that the phrase 'seeing red' had only a metaphorical meaning. Now I learned that it was literally true. A red haze clouded everything in my field of vision; the room swam before me. I was engulfed with raw fury, a naked, undiluted rage that burned through every corpuscle of my being. I felt an anger of a purity that I had never experienced before and would never have imagined that I could experience. It blazed from the tips of my useless hair to the bottom of my blind, ignorant soul. I had some loose awareness of seizing something nearby, and smashing it, again and again and again, against the desk at which I'd been sitting.

Several second elapsed. When consciousness returned, I found myself holding what was left of a vase that Naomi had given me, in one of her attempts to brighten up my condo. It had no relation to the cause of my fury; it had simply had the bad luck to be near at hand. It had been a fairly sturdy item, but I'd reduced it to shards and smithereens. The shelves into which I'd smashed it had been knocked apart, as if a hurricane had blown through them. I was sitting in the chair where I'd been, with the phone receiver still in hand, wet from the vase water and covered with bits of broken glass and the stems and petals of what a moment before had been a half-dozen red roses.

"Walter! Walt!" Mira's voice sounded in my ear. "Are you o.k.?"

"Yes, I'm fine," I lied, because I was *not* fine, I was anything but fine, and already I knew that it would be a long, long time before I was fine again. My arms and legs were trembling; the thump of my heartbeat drummed in my ears. The savage anger that had arisen was not subsiding, but cresting and cresting again, like the gusts of a cracking forest fire. The vase had died in vain. "Mira, how do you know Gregor Volkov? How long have you known him?"

"For about four years. Walt-" her voice sounded concerned—"do you know him? Is there a problem?"

Oh, God, is <u>there</u> a problem! "Yes I do," I answered—it took an effort to keep my voice from shaking. "Look, I'd like to see you tonight, right away. Right now. Neither of us has kid duty. Let's see a movie. It's been a long while since I've taken you out." I didn't know what I was going to say or do, let alone what should be said or done; I hadn't any plan or even the inklings of a plan. All I could think or feel was a terrible, inarticulate sense of wrongness, about all my ideas, all my preconceptions, everything I had said, thought, or done with or about Mira Watson for the past five years. Something was out of whack with the entire order of the universe—something that had to be put right immediately, without losing another second.

"All right, Walt," she agreed, after a momentary pause. "It would be fun. I'm a little puzzled why all this urgency. After all this time." She did not speak pointedly, with any sense of rebuke, and yet I felt stung, cut to the quick.

"I'll see you in ninety minutes," I said.

*

By the time I showed up at Mira's place. I could no longer hear my heart beat, but I was still reeling. At the same time, I had become fully alert, alive to everything around me. I felt as if I were completely awake for the first time in a long time—not like a man shaking off a deep sleep, like a man startled awake by an alarm bell, who wonders how long it's been ringing while he drifted uselessly in dreamland. Gregor Volkov—I repeated the name again and then again. Gregor Volkov, Gregor Volkov, Gregor Volkov—how was it possible?

The house was another physical jolt, a taunting, sullen presence in my eyes. I bit my lip. She was still living there, wasn't she? At that moment Mira was out the door, moving briskly, before I could start up the walk. My heart raced slightly as it always did when she appeared, but my focus was on that miserable house. *I won't be there long*, she'd said…five years before. Five years, during which nothing had changed, nothing had happened. Five years that I'd left her there; five years she'd had to put normal dreams, reasonable ambitions, on hold; five years that I'd done nothing, while my fat, stupid, useless wealth had grown fatter, stupider, and more useless.

What had I been thinking? I would have that phrase constantly ringing through my mind the next few weeks. Mira sat across from me in the front seat of the car. We made the most miniscule and irrelevant kind of small talk possible. She was obviously curious about my reaction to Volkov, but biding her time; I myself was lost in a tumult of thought, all themed around that taunting refrain. *What had I been thinking?* No healthy courtship drifts on and on over four years, without movement, without finality. Predators abound in this world; I knew on what a fragile base her life rested; for what possible lunatic reasons could I have blithely assumed that she would be treasured as I knew she should be, that she somehow would be magically immune from envy and spite. *What had I been thinking?*

The Cineplex to which we were headed was set in the midst of an attractive business park, with large, spacious tree-lined avenues and gracious, open buildings. The theatre matched the setting, gracious and spacey, with an unusually large, airy lobby. A small, coffee bar was set up at the front, with a number of small tables and chairs. I had taken a number of my Internet blind dates there. It was an ideal place for a heart-to-heart talk, like a bar without the alcohol.

This was Christmas night, with a lot of new movie releases that everyone wanted to see. The lobby was thronged with ticket-holders waiting for later shows. I bought a couple of tickets myself to justify our taking up space, then found us a table. I doubted very much we'd get around to seeing the movie.

"How do you know Gregor?" Mira asked, forgoing the small talk and getting directly to the point the moment we were seated.

"That's my question to you, too," I smiled, but I didn't evade the issue. I told her, about Volkov and the false accusation against the other Russians, Volkov and the investigators, Volkov and Stewart, the universal impression of an absolute, unrepentant, raving asshole and me-firster. Mira listened thoughtfully. She did not interrupt, either with comment or defense.

"Your turn," I said simply, when I was done.

It was then, that Christmas night, that Mira began to tell me the story of deceit and betrayal that I have retold here. The lobby was jammed; there was a constant hubbub that stopped just short of clamor; crowds of theatergoers milled about around us, circling nearby and occasionally jostling against the table. Mira leaned forward and spoke softly and directly to me, so as not to be overheard. I listened and watched, nodding, for a long while saying nothing.

She told me about Echelon, the business plans, the search for financing, the rounds of interviews, the presentations, the final success, the dismal aftermath. She recounted her own role matter-of-factly, without any hoopla or embellishment. But I knew her, I had met Volkov, and I had spent ten years developing start-ups of my own. I didn't need the fine print to know who had provided the ideas, who had infused the energy, who had created the style, found the contacts, breathed life and credibility into a project that had none at all before she arrived. I listened and nodded and seethed.

All at once she blushed slightly and became shy. "I didn't have a deal in place that day we had lunch, Walt. I was embarrassed when you asked me. I lied to you. I'm sorry."

In an instant all of the emotional turmoil peaked, and I came close to losing it. *She* said *she* was sorry. I wanted to burst into laughter, I wanted to weep into my hands, I wanted to howl with rage—actually, I wanted to do all three at once. But this was about Mira, not me. There was too much at stake for such self indulgence. Instead, I looked away for a long moment. Then I met her eyes.

"Mira," I said, "there's one thing I've got to insist on, tonight and forever. Don't ever—*ever*—apologize to me again. For anything. Ever."

She looked puzzled, then smiled. "You mean, love—or whatever—means never having to say you're sorry?"

"No. That's one of the dumber things ever written about love—or whatever. What I mean is that I owe you. Not the reverse. You have nothing to apologize for. So please don't. It tears me up."

Interwoven into Mira's story of Echelon was the personal story of herself and Gregor Volkov. It did not take me long to realize that I was hearing a classic description of the mechanisms by which a weaker personality ensnares a stronger—the relentless narcissism, the resentment of gratitude owed for favors done, denial as a form of revenge, the constant, eternal manipulation, games within games within games. Listening to her describe it matter-of-factly was knives in my ears. From time to time, the ferocious rage of the afternoon gusted and roared in my veins. But I gave no sign, other than the occasional whitening of my knuckles underneath my folded arms.

"What do you think about all this?" I asked when at last Mira was done.

"I don't know, Walt," she said, after her own long moment. "I don't know, I'm a pretty confused person, if you want to know the truth. I never thought I could get all mixed up like this. Sometimes I think Gregor is the worst man on earth, and other times I wonder what I did wrong. Sometimes I really want him, Walt, I have to tell you that. Other times I wish I'd never met him. There are times when I think I still love him, and other times"—Mira paused, wondering how much to say, then decided, and leaned forward.

"—other times I want to kill him. I have all this mess with the family court now, that I never had before. And then there's the master's program, that's all messed up—and the stock, of course. I even had surgery for him—I even altered my body for him.

"But all those things are the small things. The big thing is he tried to separate me from Alicia—and I went right on seeing him. *Being* with him. How could I? How could I even have stood the sight of him? I was never like that. Then I wonder what sort of woman I really am, that I'd even wait two seconds to show him the door. What's wrong with me, anyway? And I wonder whether I should hate myself instead of him. Maybe it's my fault for not saying something. Then the whole thing gets very muddled and I don't know what to think."

"The problem isn't you, Mira. It never was you. The whole problem has to do with Volkov and the kind of personality he is. There's no winning with that type, no matter what you do. He's been playing a game with you, a real simple game. It's called You Lose. It has only one rule, and the rule's the same as the name of the game—You Lose. Do nothing and you lose, you get nothing. Try appeasement—you lose again, your offering is never good enough. Protest that the game's unfair, and that's the worst of all. Obviously you're an undeserving person for saying such awful things." She was listening intently. I wasn't saying anything she hadn't intuitively understood, but she had not heard them expressed aloud."

"You know, there's a saying," I said, "that living well is the best revenge. It's not true. Living well isn't the best revenge—it's the *only* revenge. Looking back either for love or revenge is putting one foot in the quicksand. It's something you have to get behind. The first move in any game is deciding to play. You can't win this game, any more than a basketball player could score a touchdown. You winning is not in the rules. The only thing you can do is not play. Living well is all that's left."

"I know you're right, Walter, but it's advice that's a lot easier to give than to follow." Mira shook her head and smiled wanly. "Like I said, I'm still trying to sort it all out."

She was as dazzling as ever that evening. It was Christmas night, and there were few people in that crowded lobby who were not feeling its effects, digesting one of the big slabs of raw emotion, good or bad, that the holiday generates. Mira spoke too softly for anyone but me to make out anything but her intonation; her gestures were small and delicate; she was no more conventionally beautiful than she had ever been; we were only two people at one inconspicuous table—but I could feel a ripple of attention run through the crowd, heads turning, persons who thought they had no time or energy for anything but their own problems and preoccupations wonder for a second or two about what was going on between us. Mira was eye-catching even when she was trying to be inconspicuous. Nothing that life dealt her was ever going to damage or corrupt that style, of that I was certain—and I was glad for that one thing at least.

And yet…and yet…

The chestnut hair that had cascaded gloriously down to her shoulders when I first met her was still glorious, but tinged with gray at her temples now. Embryonic crow's feet had appeared at the corners of her eyes. She was still a striking woman—she always would be—but the signs of the stress she'd been living under were everywhere, now that I was looking for them. She'd been 35 when I first met her, at the sunset of her youth, and blessed with the radiance of sunsets. Now she was unmistakably into her middle years with its inevitable accountings, its disillusionments. Five years had passed while she remained stranded in her dark, detested house, watching all her dreams and ambitions crumble into dust. Mira might have glorious reserves of style and class, but she was no more immune from the ravages of time and disappointment than any other human being. *What had I been thinking?*

"What do you think about all this?" Mira asked, as if she could hear the refrain playing ceaselessly in my head.

"That it should never have happened," I answered immediately. "That it's all my fault."

"You don't have to rescue me, Walt," Mira said. "I got myself into this mess. I'll get myself out of it."

"I didn't mean fault like that. It's that I haven't been true to myself or to you. I can see that now. I don't know why I didn't before."

"I always understood your commitments. Nick means as much to you as Alicia does to me. I never blamed you."

"Nick and Alicia. You and me." The moment spurred me. On the nonce I decided on my point of departure. "I wonder sometimes if the life after this one really is the way the nuns told me as a kid. Maybe the moment after it's all over down here, I'll find myself standing before the throne of God. Before He asks me to account for anything, I'll ask him to account for something. I'll ask him why He did what he did to my little boy. I imagine He'll point out to me all the good Nick's condition has done, how it drew me away from alcohol, how he's enriched the life of everyone who knew him, how it led me to my true love, although I have screwed that one up but good.

"And I'll listen and nod, and when God's finished explaining all of His good and many reasons, I'll step straight up to the throne and punch Him in the nose. Because none of that's good enough reason, and He damn well knows it. So I guess I'll go to hell, and that'll be that."

Mira laughed, a subdued version of her laugh of delighted surprise, but still a wonder. "Maybe I'll be there with you," she said.

"I tell that story a lot. But I added something tonight—'leading me to my true love'," I said quietly. These were the first words I ever spoke to Mira from the heart, although she had never deserved anything less. They were the most honest words I ever spoke in my life. The revelations of the afternoon had had the effect of a nuclear blast on me. It had utterly vaporized the fortress I had worked so long to erect; that had vanished as if it had never been. Gone, too, were all my monochromatic rationalizations, my one dimensional logic, my noble posturings, my articulate, beside-the-point philosophizing, my insane hesitations. All of that had disappeared under the sea, forever. I saw the realities of my life with the clarity with which I have seen them ever since. "Those were the most important words."

"Yes. I heard you."

"Do you mind me talking that way to you?"

"That's sort of ancient history, Walt." She met my eyes. "I thought that's the way you wanted it."

"I've been a fool, Mira." I met her gaze, with—I hoped—a calm dignity, without challenge, without shame. It would not do to beg her forgiveness. Mira had no use for beggars. "I've wasted years of my life and yours that we can't get back. Some real harm has come to you that I could have stopped.

"But do you mind now when I speak to you like this?" I laid my huge misshapen paw on the table beside one of those delicate hands that had caught so many eyes. To my enormous relief, she did not pull hers back.

"There was a time," she said after a long pause, "when I wanted more than anything to hear you talk that way."

"And now?"

"It still sounds very nice. But like I said, Walt, it *is* ancient history— and I really am pretty tangled up right now."

"That should never have happened." I took a deep breath. "It's not you who needs rescuing. It's me—from not being who I am and what I'm supposed to become—because that's just not possible without you. I know that now. Nick and Alicia, Elizabeth and the boys, you and me—I was crazy to ever think those were choices, that it was one or the other, that there was any division between them. You and Elizabeth and Nick and all the people I care about—you're all strands in the same large fabric. My life means nothing apart from it—from them, from you. I should have known that all along."

We had attracted a little attention now, even though not a word of this could be heard by anyone but Mira. Some of the bystanders had caught a sense of the intensity at our table and become curious. I pressed on despite that. "You're my second soul, Mira," I said very, very softly. "There has never been a moment since we met when you didn't enchant me. There hasn't been one time when the sound of your voice didn't delight me. You know that—but I don't know if you know how much I admire you—respect you—as well."

"Not everyone sees me like that, Walt," she answered.

"I know that. But that's the whole point, that's the way I see you. That's what's important. That's all that's important. That's the proof to me that you belong to me, and I to you, and we belong to each other. Because I cannot stand the thought—I can't stand even the bare possibility—of all that astonishing personal quality, all the loveliness at your core, being endangered by anyone or anything—including neglect, including me. Until this afternoon, I had no idea how protective of you I really was. I actually thought there was some other man who could do a better job for you than I could. But I was the goddamndest fool to ever think that."

"Are you sure that you're not just being jealous?" Mira asked, testing.

"I'm quite sure. I've wanted you from day one, Mira. More than anything. But I decided long ago that I wasn't going to be jealous of anyone who made you happy. I'd have envied him, sure, I'd have wanted to trade places with him, I'd have thought he was the luckiest guy in the universe, but I wasn't going to be jealous. I don't hate Volkov. My only beef with him is that he hasn't been good to you. If it weren't for what that means to you and what it says about me, and what an idiot I've been, I wouldn't give him two seconds of my time. He doesn't mean that much to me. It's you I'm interested in, not him."

She started to say something, but now I took her hand gently in mind. Praise be to God, she did not withdraw it. "Truth be told, I never thought I was worthy of you—and if you want even more truth, I still don't. That was the ulterior motive for my Great Renunciation— I didn't think I deserved you. But I can see now—what I always should have seen—is that that kind of false nobility is really the worst kind of moral cowardice. Because if I don't try, if I don't at least try, what happens is that there are real good odds you'll end up with someone who doesn't appreciate you enough to feel the same respect and admiration—someone who's envious and jealous instead of appreciative. It took me a long, long time to see that, but I see it completely now. And that's why I asked you here."

I let go of her hand gradually and sat back. I had said what I wanted to say. Perhaps I had said too much. Perhaps way, way too much. Mira sat thoughtfully apart from me for a long moment, then turned her head away from me. "What do you want of me, Walter?" she asked, without looking up.

"Just a chance. Just the opportunity to erase these whole ridiculous five years. To get us to where we always should have been."

There was another long silence. Then she glanced up at the marquee and all at once was in motion. "Our movie's starting. Let's go." She picked up her purse.

"I didn't really care about seeing a movie," I said, astonished.

"Neither did I, but now I want to."

"Was what I said that far out of the ball park?" I said. I was more than a little disappointed. I was close to crushed.

She took a few strides in silence, then looked up at me. "I'm not going to answer that. You know, Walter, you can be a very overwhelming personality. Did you know that? You gave me a lot to think about, and I will think about it. But right now I am not going to be overwhelmed. By you or any one. Right now all I want to do is see this movie."

And so we did.

*

It was probably a pretty good movie, but I don't remember too much about it. Afterwards, I drove Mira home. Most of the way she faced the window. Occasionally, she'd glance my way and flash a quick, shy smile, before returning to the window. She said nothing; I didn't dare.

I walked her up her walk, heart in mouth. We reached the door. She turned to face me. "What are you thinking?" I asked at last.

"That's what I've been trying to figure out." She became as serious I had ever seen her. "I have to tell you the truth. I'm sick of men, Walt. I'm just weary of the whole lot of you. I don't mean anything personal, because you're an awfully good man. I think the world of you. You know that. But I'm tired of all of you. I've always liked feeling womanly in my love life—which means you give a man a little room to operate, you have to. I like men with a little macho in them. But I never really lost control. I was always in charge of my own life and my time. I made some decisions with Crockett I regret, but they were *my* decisions.

"And now it seems like I've been hoping, and compromising, and pleasing, and begging forever, for some man to decide what he's going to do. Part of me wants Gregor in the worst way, and part of me wishes he'd drop dead tomorrow. I don't know which is right, and I don't care. What I'm sick of is wanting and wishing and not *doing*. I've never been dependent like that before in my life, and I never will be again. I hate it."

She paused, then went on. "Now you're here, and you want to make everything right. I won't lie to you—there was a time when I wanted that a lot, when what you said tonight would have been music to my ears. But now it's just talk, and one more man who wants to take over my life. I know you mean well, and I'm certain you're a better man than Gregor. But I don't want my life taken over by anyone. I'm sick of it.

"When I was younger I used to think I could dance on clouds. I thought I was all air and fire—all spirit—like I could fly and fly, and nothing and nobody could ever catch me. But now I think I'm the same earth and water as everyone else—the same mud. No different. Just another frumpy middle-aged woman with a lot of problems and no solutions."

"You're no frump, Mira, "I answered "You were more right than wrong the first time. There's a fire there that burns bright."

"Thank you, but I'm not going to let anyone take over my life. Ever again."

"I don't want to take over your life." I put my hands gently on her waist; again, she did not pull back. "I never did. I've got no preconceptions about what you should be, or do, or anything. The way I see it, the people who care about you are supposed to enable you, give you wings, and maybe a place to perch when you need rest. It's the whole rest of the world that supplies the force of gravity, the mud and earth. I don't want to kill your dragons for you. I want to forge you the sword so you can kill them yourself."

Mira looked down at her feet, then straightened, and looked up at me. "What do you want, Walt?" She looked away from me again. "Practically speaking, I mean. In the near future?"

"I'd like to take you away, for a week or so. Talk, sort things out. New York City, if you're in an urban mood. Kauai, if you want warm weather. Just take a shot at putting things together."

"You mean, like Tahoe?" Mira said quietly. I winced, and dropped my hands from her waist. "I'm sorry," she said.

"I told you I don't want to hear any apologies from you," I said, and held her again. "Ever. I had that coming, I know it. A lot more than that. All I can tell you is that it may be a cliché, but I know now what a fool I've been, what an absolute idiot. And all I'm hoping is that it's not too late."

"If we did go—if I went with you—would it bother you if you had to take two rooms? Because I'm not ready for *that*. I don't know when I will be."

"You can decide the conditions," I said. "I'm in this for the long haul. We were lovers once and I hope we will be—and more—again. But that's entirely up to you. Of course, it does bother me a little to know how sisterly you've come to feel about me. But I'll live."

At this, she suddenly stepped through my light embrace, put both hands on my face, and kissed me, a long wet kiss, Hollywood bobby-soxer style, with one foot raised. "Walt," she whispered, "there hasn't been one second when I've ever felt the least bit sisterly towards you. That's not the problem."

She stepped back and reached into her purse for her key. For the first time I felt a spark of optimism. Perhaps it was not too late to redeem everything. Maybe, just maybe, I could pull this off. Then she looked up.

"And you can kill all the dragons you want for me," she said. "There are plenty to go around. Trust me on that."

"Can I call you Monday night?"

Mira nodded instantly. "Late. I'm starting my classes again. If—and it's very much 'if', Walt—I did take a trip, I'd have to take my books along.

"But I'd like it if you called that night. Very much."

*

I sent her flowers that Monday—not a big, ostentatious bouquet, for I took those comments about overwhelming her as seriously as she meant them, but just large enough (I hoped) to indicate how absolutely serious I was, small enough to confer no sense of obligation. Late that night, as arranged, I called her.

"I was hoping you wouldn't forget." She said. "Or change your mind."

"There's not the slightest chance of either," I said. "I was hoping you liked the flowers."

"Yes," she said immediately. "They were very nice. Just right."

"Only for openers, Mira," I said quietly.

Every night I would call her, sometime between ten-thirty and midnight, and we would talk, often as late as one or even two a.m. This was Mira's unalterable condition—I tried to persuade her to let me take her to dinner, or back to the movies, but she would have none of it. "Not yet, Walter," she would say. "For now this is about all I can handle."

We had come full circle, for this was how we had begun five years before. Back then we had been tentatively exploring one another, trying to flesh out the first impressions each had made of the other. This time we were trying to sort each other out, trying to determine what was possible, what was not, what was of the essence, what an accident, what shadow and what substance. This was far more complex and profound than our beginnings had been. The processes of recovery are much more difficult than the processes of discovery. That sounds more like a rap rhyme than I would like, but I believe it is the truth.

So we talked. We began about the time I'd normally go to sleep. Our respective bedrooms, miles apart, were completely dark. Enveloped in night, with the details and distractions of daylight gone, without random thoughts of errands and urgencies suddenly streaking through the firmament, speaking in whispers and stillness, an openness, a oneness could come to be only in moontime. From the moment of first meeting, Mira and I had shared a unique rapport, one that I had nearly caused to die stillborn. But now it lived, and developed easily and inevitably into what it always should have been. We talked naturally from the heart, as if that language were the only language. These were the best nights of my life.

I began making love to her—in the old-fashioned, nineteenth century sense of the word—almost at once. "The man who possesses you is one of the luckiest men in the world," I whispered into the phone.

"He's been gifted with something priceless. The man who sleeps with you is blessed by God. I can speak to that personally. If I were to find myself, the instant after my last breath, holding you in my arms, with that little white thing you wore to Asilomar, and your eyes meeting mine, with April sunshine all around, I'd know my soul was saved. I'd know I was in paradise."

"Would you still punch God in the nose?"

"Oh, yes." Her light laugh sounded in the receiver in the noiseless background of her house. "Because I'd be willing to pay almost any price, but not Nick."

"You may be overrating me, Walt," Mira whispered, serious.

"No. We all of us can become an infinite number of different personalities and beings, avatars, if you will, of our real selves. You've been a scullery maid for too long. I want to remind you of your nobility, the regality in you. Don't worry, I haven't forgotten the earth and water. I know you have your flaws."

"Such as?"

"Rotten taste in men, for one thing," and was rewarded—for the first time in forever, so it seemed—by her full-throated, surprised, delighted laugh.

"You can say that again," she said.

We talked of practicalities and banalities as well, the state of the world, people we knew, industry gossip. We discussed our children, our pride in their past and present, our anxieties for their future. Nick's progress was compared with Alicia's, Alicia with my own Elizabeth, Nick with her Wesley and Charles. I brought her up to date on my own situation, the unexpected windfall I had come into. It was important that Mira be certain that my determined, unambiguous courtship of her was not the result of some pea-brained adolescent decision to abandon everything else in pursuit of her—Mira would never have tolerated that—but rather a recognition that she was, had always been, a necessary part of the universe in which I lived—that that universe would be incomplete and desolate without her.

Occasionally, when time had run out and we'd said good night, I'd step to the computer and send her an e-mail. Sometimes I'd send her a poem.

*

To love one woman, or to sit
Always beneath the same tall tree
Argues a certain lack of wit,
Two steps from imbecility.

A voyager, therefore, sworn to feed
On every food the senses know,
Will claim the inexorable need
To be Don Juan Tenorio.

Yet if, miraculously enough,
(And why set miracles apart?)
Woman and tree prove of a stuff
Wholly to glamour his wild heart?

To chance and change I took a vow
As I thought fitting. None the less
What of a phoenix on the bough
Or a single woman's fatefulness?

Two or three minutes after I dispatched this, well after two in the morning, my phone rang. "Did you write that for me?" she asked, without further ado.

"I would have," I answered, "except Robert Graves beat me to it."

I heard her light laugh, and then at once she was deadly serious. "Walt...you are on level here? You're not just playing games? You're not toying with me?"

"I've never been more on the level in my life. Why do you ask?"

"Because"—I waited—"this is beginning to get to me." She disconnected on the last syllable.

I slept little that night. I was too exultant for sleep.

*

But there were other nights.

"Walt, I'm not worthy of this," she whispered, after another poem—Byron, I think.

"Why would you ever say that, my precious darling?" for I had begun using endearments by then and she didn't seem to mind.

"Because," she said, and her voice took on the resonance of steel, "because Gregor tried to separate me from Alicia. And I didn't break it off. I went right on sleeping with him. I'm not worthy—of the poem, or you or anything. I don't know why you bother."

For this, too, had become a constant theme, the other side of our dialog, the dark side of the moonscape. Mira had spoken truth that Christmas night. She didn't know whether she loved Volkov or hated him. Sometimes, at the outset of our wanderings, she would speak of him wistfully and longingly, wondering where she had gone wrong with him. These were not pleasant moments for me, but I wanted her to open her soul, and those were among its contents. So sooner or later, she would return to herself and Volkov and her children and, above all, Alicia.

I did not have to endure too many unpleasant moments, because her expressions of affection towards Volkov diminished to the vanishing point with tremendous speed. But the subject of Volkov did not disappear—not hardly. We would be discussing some unrelated subject or event, or I might even be whispering my deep heart's wisdom, and a stray phrase or thought would bring back a recollection of an incident, an occasion—often some rather trivial misbehavior of Volkov's—and she would of a sudden be enraged. Mira being Mira, she didn't tear her hair, rent her garment, or rant and rave. There were no Lady Macbeth or Medea acts. The only hint was a perceptible hardening of her tone when she recalled whatever incident it was. Her anger might not even have been apparent to someone who didn't know her as well as I did. But I perceived it, and it bothered me a lot.

Mira was not by nature a mercurial personality. She was not at all a moody person. The speed and intensity with which these memories overtook her gave me another measure of how truly enraged she was. The precise point on which her anger always turned was not so much Volkov's conduct as her own acceptance, her passivity, in the face of it. What galled her was her failure to react. Having met Volkov, I knew all too well that she had good reason for her rage. But I also knew there was no hope of ever setting the scales right. The only thing for it was to live her way through it and out of it, hopefully—if I could persuade her—with me. The way back led nowhere. Mira could see that as clearly as I could, and yet the anger would not relinquish its grip on her. To me, that anger—not Volkov—was the great opponent, and I was determined to defeat it.

I never became angry myself with Volkov. To become so would have been to give his actions a moral content, and my contempt for him went much deeper than that. I might as well be angry at a poisonous snake or a scorpion. What I felt for my part was not anger, but a profound, pointed exasperation, that such a trivially warped, transparently damaged personality as Gregor Volkov had ever been permitted to find a place on Mira's radar screen. I felt this exasperation most keenly when a memory of some bland compromise suddenly took possession of her in the midst of a discussion of some happier topic, and she was lost to me for a while. It was at those times that I most easily recognized my enemy.

*

It was an entrenched foe, solid, fortified, with four years' inertia behind it. But the murmurs of our whispered night songs were too rich, too intense not to have their effect. Gradually Mira relaxed, listened, and began to find her real self again. Interruptions of cold fury occurred less frequently. I did not have to swear that there would be no more mind-changing, no equivocation, no desertion, no change in course.

"You've won my heart," I said. "You know that. All I want in return is one little thing."

"Which is?" Mira asked rhetorically, knowing the answer.

"You," I whispered. "All of you. Always. Heart and soul, and—of course—body as well. Way back when, I didn't think I deserved you. I still think that—"

"I'm not so sure, Walt."

"It's what I think, anyway. But the simple truth is you're too precious to me to leave the job to anyone else. That's what I've learned. What I would always have known, if I weren't such an idiot."

"The way you talk, Walter," she sighed and murmured. "I don't know what to think."

"But do you believe me?" I said, heart in mouth—for the moment of decision had at long last arrived. A long silence ensued.

"Yes," Mira breathed at last.

During the daylight hours, I had begun systematically clearing my calendar, to free up the first week of February. I told Mira this at the beginning. I made it clear to her that she should feel under no obligation, that I'd find something to do with the time regardless of her decision. But now—it was late January—the time had come to find out what that decision was.

"That trip I've been talking about—would you come with me?"

She did not tease. She did not hesitate. "Yes. I'd like that very much. I've been clearing my own schedule."

"Where?"

"Kauai, if you don't mind. New York's too cold—and there are too many people there."

"Would you like me to get two rooms or one?

"You know, Walt, I've been thinking about that, too." She paused, let me twist for a long, long moment, and now I knew for certain she was teasing. "It seems to me that two rooms would be an awful waste of money," she said at last. "Don't you think?"

I was momentarily lost for words. My discomfiture, and her anticipation of it, amused Mira. She giggled—something I had never heard her do before—into the phone.

"Didn't it ever occur to you, Walter, that I'd find two rooms as frustrating as you would?"

"No," I answered immediately. "I'm an Irish Catholic boy. The thought never crossed my mind—" and that produced her rich, delighted laugh.

"Oh, dear me, what am I going to do with you?" she sighed. "What am I to do? You're still a closer, Mr. Kelsey. You always were."

I knew then that she was feeling 'womanly' (to use her word) about me again, and finally looking away from the past and towards the horizon. I whispered my 'good nights' and hung up the phone, happier and more content than I could remember being in my entire life. I had redeemed the past, so I thought; I had erased all the history; I had brought the future to life for myself and for Mira.

When I hung up the phone, I was sure I was going to pull it off. I was certain of it.

CHAPTER 16

▼

Friday, January 30th, was my last working day before the trip. Mira and I were to leave for Kauai on Sunday.

It was not a good day. The whole week, the weather had been in a particularly obnoxious winter pattern—Arctic high pressure producing a succession of cold, bright, dry days. The unknowing called them beautiful, but those of us who have lived here for a while know it to be a type of drought pattern, not good during what was supposed to be our rainy season. That Friday was more of the same.

Before I went to court, I opened up my newspaper, looked at the front page—an act of courage beyond me most days—glanced at sports, then turned to the business page. There, staring out at me from the middle of the first page was the proud, smiling, four-tone-color face of Gregor Volkov. There had been a recent spate of business success stories by companies founded by emigrant entrepreneurs, and the business editor had decided to run a feature on it. Volkov had literally become the poster child for all this achievement.

"Christ," I muttered to myself. "Not today. Any day but today."

*

From the night she decided in my favor until the day before, everything between Mira and myself had gone from good to better. We had talked nightly, with the same richness as earlier, but in a more relaxed, broader vein. We had crossed the big river into a new country that was both native and strange, and we both knew it. I had found a first-rate beach front condo on Kauai on the Internet. I e-mailed her pictures of the interior and beach area, and she became really excited. I wondered how long it had been since Mira had had a really good vacation. Without making a big deal about it, I privately decided that this trip was going to make up for all the ones she'd missed.

Mira had relaxed her ban on dating in view of these developments, and allowed me to take her to dinner the Saturday night preceding. We had a great time, then saw the movie we'd sat through on Christmas, this time actually watching it. I tried to talk her into spending the night at my place, but she was having none of it. My impression was that she wanted our first night in the Islands to be a very, very special renewal. I was more than a little disappointed, but I had invested too much of myself, and made up too much ground, to take any chance on blowing it at that point. Her chaste resolutions did not prevent her from sliding into my arms and necking with a teen-age ferocity for a good half-hour or so before she went in. Everything was going well. Everything was going perfectly.

Then, abruptly, the clock turned completely back, when Mira had her appearance in Family Court.

*

"The change in primary custody was never intended to be permanent," Mira had said. *"It was only while I worked out some problems in my life."*

"I understand that," the judge replied. "But the primary concern here is the welfare of the children. And stability is an issue. The boys seem to be doing very well with their father. And Alicia is adjusting too, I believe."

"She needs her mother," Mira said. "I think I have been a very good mother."

The judge took off his glasses. "You've been a superb mother," he said. "My comments had nothing to do with that. I can't tell you how much I respect you, and the way you have conducted yourself over the years in this court. But I have to say that I think Crockett is also a very good father, although I've never approved of his litigation methods. My comments had no implication about either of you.

"The issue is stability. As a superb mother, I know you can appreciate the importance of that. Which house is not nearly as important as one home. So I am going to leave things as they are for now, and review this situation at the end of school term." He turned to his clerk. "Marian, if we can select a date in late May or early June?"

Mira was too experienced with family court dynamics not to know what had happened. The momentum in those proceedings is glacial, in both senses of the word. It is terrifically hard to get anyone or anything moving—Crockett had found that out. But once the movement has begun, the inertia is equally hard to stop or change. Now it had moved, because she had allowed it to, and now she was on the wrong side of it.

Crockett, who was proving to be a much more gracious winner than he had been loser, tried to say something conciliatory as they left, but Mira shook him off, and continued out, tight-lipped in rage. Damn him, she was thinking. Damn him.

She did not mean Crockett.

*

When we spoke late that Thursday night, we were back at square one. Perhaps we were even at square minus one. Mira sounded more distraught than I had ever heard her. The theme of worthiness had diminished considerably as she gained confidence in me and regained it in herself. But this night it reemerged in a full-throated roar.

"I let him ruin my school, I let him screw up me and my children, and even after I knew it was happening I kept sleeping with him. Like any other dumb floozy. I never stood up to him. I never confronted him. Not once. What's wrong with me? Where did I stop being me?"

"Nothing's wrong with you, my precious darling. These things happen little by little, one tiny step at a time. You have no idea of how much you're giving up, until you look back. Believe me, I know. I've been there." As indeed I had.

"Oh, Walt, I believe you when you talk like that. But I believed Gregor. And I know you're a totally different man than Gregor, a much better man, a wonderful man, but I don't know how or when my life ever came down to believing men. I feel like I lost my self—like he stole the real me somehow. I don't feel worthy of you, Walt—or Alicia, or Wes, or Charles, or anyone in my life. I let everybody down."

"You didn't. That's simply not true. You did your best under impossible circumstances. You couldn't expect more of yourself."

"I could have done a lot better. I saw through him at the beginning. What happened to me? Where did my judgment go?" She paused. "I don't deserve any of you," she said.

"It's not that bad," I said. It was difficult to offer her much in the way of hard consolation. I would have loved to tell her that there was some magic solution to the family court situation. But it wasn't true, and she knew it. Urging her to make the best of it was simply a condescending method of belittling genuine anguish—and no way, ever, would I tell her how guilty I myself felt about these turns her life had taken. My guilt was real enough, but expressing it aloud was simply a means of contorting her anguish into sympathy for me. That was the Gregor Volkov style, the narcissist's manner. No way.

"Nothing horrible or unchangeable has happened. Crockett's a pretty good father. The kids haven't moved to Zanzibar. We'll talk about that, next week, how we go about setting it right, little by little, step by step, the same way it went wrong."

"I *know* Crockett's a good father, and I know my babies are safe. But…I kept on with him—after he interfered, after I could see it was useless. I let him get away with it. I forgot all about who I really am. How can I ever face my children when they get bigger and ask me what happened? I am completely ashamed of myself."

"Mira," I said gently, but with a trace of firmness, "dwelling on all that history doesn't rectify the mistakes. It compounds them. There is no winning that way. You have to get beyond this."

"I know you're right, but—see, there I go again, going along with you, just accepting you." There was real torment in her voice, a throbbing frustration that blazed through her customary nonchalant pose. "The same way I just went along with Gregor. He interfered with my children, he cheated on me, I'll bet he ruined my business plan, and what he said about Alicia—I won't even repeat that to you, Walt. And I just accepted it. I went along with it."

"Mira-"

"I know what you're saying, Walt, and I know you're right. But it's so difficult to get over it. I never challenged him on it. I never called him to account. I just went along with it."

We continued talking, and finally I was able to soothe her slightly. We even ended on a romantic, upbeat note. But normally, after we were done, I went instantly to sleep, calmly and peacefully. That night, I tossed restlessly, well into the morning. We had crossed the Big River. The country was new. The old myths—Orpheus and Eurydice, Lot's wife—gave the warning. The one mortal sin, the only mortal sin, was looking back. The ultimate siren song is made up not of fond memories, but unfinished business. That was the tune that Mira was hearing, and could not stop herself from hearing. I couldn't sleep because I had a lot on my mind. The sooner we were in Hawaii, the better.

And the next morning the puff piece on Volkov. The timing could not have been worse.

*

I would have liked to start my vacation at noon, but I had been unable to change one court appearance, a preliminary hearing set for that Friday afternoon. It was routine stuff, a case of receiving stolen computer components, which could be done in an hour or two. The plan was to finish it up efficiently, get the office ship-shape, leave some notes for staff to perpetuate the illusion that I would be missed, then take off to meet Mira for dinner at six. I had some slight hope that she would be willing to start the honeymoon that night, but the more likely scenario was that she would insist on waiting until we reached the Islands.

As it happened, the hearing was more prolonged than I had anticipated and I did not get back to the office until four. I began to straighten up the clutter on my desk. At the same time, I turned on the speakerphone to retrieve my voice mail. I had three messages. The first two were routine. Mira's was the third.

"I'm going to be a little late for dinner, Walt. I have to take care of a couple of errands that have come up. Can we say, oh sevenish?"

I had my car keys in hand and my coat on before the message had finished playing. By the time I reached the front of the building, I was in a dead run. The alarm bell that had kept me awake the night before was now a siren blasting away. Mira and I had done too much talking in the last month, I had become too alert to the meteorology of her being not to read the weather report. The 'errand' she tossed off so casually was some sort of settling-the-score confrontation with Volkov. I was certain of it.

The distance between the County Center and Mira's house was about ten miles, a quarter hour's drive in good traffic. But this was rush hour. How I knew that was where whatever was taking place was taking place I couldn't have said, but I knew. I roared out of the parking lot, onto the freeway, and drove north like hell. I considered cheating into the commuter lane, but thought better—they're pretty well-patrolled and the time I might lose being ticketed was too big a risk to take.

I had no idea of the details of what Mira had in mind. One thing for sure, I wasn't a bit concerned that that pathological relationship would be miraculously reborn. It had been some time since she'd expressed any confusion about how she felt about Gregor. But it was true that there is no winning with a personality like Volkov. What worried me is that she'd end up even more frustrated, more in emotional debt, than she already was. There was no way it could end well.

I tried her phone a couple of times on the road with my cell phone, without an answer, which meant nothing except that she wasn't answering her phone. It was forty minutes before I reached her house. I drove my car into the curb, hurtled out of the door, and sprinted up the walk. As I neared the door, I could hear two voices, a woman's, calm and low, and a man's, loud and edgy. I knew my instincts had been correct. Then the door was in front of me, and I burst through it and into Mira's pathetically small living room.

I had thought I'd prepared myself for the worst case. But I saw at once that the actual case was far, far worse than anything I'd envisioned. Gregor Volkov stood cowering on one side of the room. Mira was on the other side, about eight feet away. Her right arm was extended toward Volkov at eye level. In her hand, she held a Glock semi-automatic handgun, pointed right at his head.

*

"Hello, Walter," she said, as if she'd been expecting me—not that my entrance into the house had been any model of stealth. "I was hoping to take care of this without delaying our schedule. But it just wasn't possible. I didn't really think I'd fool you. You know me too well."

"This is a big mistake, Mira," I said quietly.

She shook her head ambiguously, whether in agreement or not I will never sure. "I have to get myself back, Walt. I have to be me again. I can't be anything for you, or my children, or anyone until I've done that." She was speaking to me, but she never turned her head or took her eyes off Volkov.

I tried to match her composure. "Where did you get the gun?"

"In the wall safe, Walt. I'm a Southern girl—and a single woman. It's a useful thing to have around the house." So that explained the new safe—one more thing I hadn't known and hadn't guessed. I was clueless to the very end. She shot me a quick glance. "I want to go away with you, Walt, I want that more than anything, but I can't do it until this is taken care of."

"Mira—" Volkov began to croak brokenly, but she cut him off. She had only taken her eyes off him for a split-second. Now he had her entire attention again.

"I just said I was a Southern girl, Gregor. I do know how to use this—and I will if I have to."

"But what do you want of me, Mira?" he begged. He was terrified, and with good reason. "I have apologized to you over and over, as often as you have asked, for whatever you wanted."

She leveled the gun, and he froze. So did I. I noticed he had soiled his trousers. "I want you to apologize as if you meant it. I want to hear you get the point."

"But I *have* got the point. I always meant for the best—"

Mira flicked the safety off with an audible click. My blood froze. "This is what I mean, Gregor. An apology for accepting what I gave you and thinking I was a fool for giving it to you. An apology for mistaking kindness for weakness. An apology for not knowing I did what I did out of caring for you, Gregor, not because I didn't know who you were, or what you were but because of what I thought you could be. An apology for making me beg for what was rightfully mine. An apology for all of that, without telling me at the same time how it's really all my fault, without twisting everything into someone else's problem. An apology that tells me that you've done wrong and you know you've done wrong, to me and my babies."

There was a long, long silence, while he groped for words and Mira studied him calmly. The thought suddenly struck me that she had regained herself. Somewhere along the line, during all the nights, all the outpouring of soul, she had been restored. The unity of act and resolve, of thought and action, that had dazzled me on our first night, when she began weeding through my clothes without a moment's hesitation or a single second thought, was once again hers. But these were the wrong thoughts, the wrong action. The restoration had done nothing to undo the damage to her life, or erase three years of continual insult and humiliation. From her old again, new again perspective, the memory of that studied, unredressed contempt had become intolerable. Not for the first time, not for the last, I cursed myself, that the thoughts that had inspired this particular action had ever come to be.

"That will never happen, Mira," I said quietly.

"Please don't, Walt," she said.

All at once, something flashed in Volkov's eyes, and I knew he'd recognized me. "Listen to the policeman, Mira. He can tell you that I have nothing—"

"Shut up, Volkov," I said, without taking my own eyes off Mira. "Look at him, my darling. *Look* at him. He's worthless. He's literally a piece of shit—excrement you flush down the toilet and forget." Volkov forgot his fright for a moment and reddened with indignation. "He's locked into his own ego— just another pathetic creep whose idea of the world stops short when it goes beyond him. He doesn't have the capability to understand how he wronged you. He can't apologize—that's the reason, the exact reason, why he's worthless."

I could see her waver; she was listening. "The only advantage he ever had over you was that you have the capability of trust, and he doesn't. You deliver and he can't. It's not that he doesn't—it's that he can't. That's a comment on *him*, not you. *Look* at him, Mira. *Look*—through my eyes, through everybody's, the way everybody sees him." Now she was studying him, regarding him, thinking. "Then just flush him away, like everyone else does, and forget him. It's what I told you Christmas Night. The only smart thing to do is not even be involved. We have things to do, you and me. Great things."

She did nothing for several seconds, perhaps half-a minute. But at long last, the gun wavered in her hand. I could see the aspects of her smile return to her face—and slowly, all, too slowly, she lowered her arm gun. "You always give me good advice, sweetheart"—the first time she had ever used that endearment. I believe she wanted Volkov to know something—"and you're right. He *is* worthless. I mustn't play this game.—but it's not just because you said so, it's what *I've* decided to do. I'll always wonder how—and why—but I have what I wanted— what I needed—now." The tension left her body.

"It's over. Just please go, Gregor. I never want to see you again. I will soon forget you ever existed."

With the gun lowered and the tension eased, Volkov forgot his fear immediately. He had played czar to serf with Mira too long for that pattern not to reassert itself by automatic pilot the moment the stimulus to fear had disappeared. Indignation came sputtering forth "What! Mira, you think you can do this to me, and then simply tell me to leave!" My impression is that he had been more outraged by the source of the threat than by the threat itself, the inconceivable indignity of being menaced by a woman he was accustomed to bully and ridicule. He had never had any notion of her real nature. "Even in this Wild West country, I do not know how many laws you have broken this afternoon. Do you think this policeman will do nothing?"

"Shut up, Volkov," I said wearily. "I'm not a policeman, I'm a prosecutor. And get this straight, completely straight. *Nothing* happened this afternoon. I was here when you came over, and nothing happened. You and Mira talked, you were hoping to begin again with her, but she was disinterested, and so you went away. Nothing happened."

His eyes got big. "What! You mean she threatens to kill me with a gun and you would do nothing?"

"What gun? What threat?" I shrugged. His face hardened and reddened, but I went on. "Who's going to believe you, Volkov? You're a liar and a promise breaker. Everyone who's met you knows it. Mark Stewart knows it. Razumaev and Grischuk know it. I'm a deputy district attorney. Everyone believes me. No one believes you. So nothing happened. Now put yourself together and get out. And count yourself lucky that it didn't get any worse."

"So," he said, still groping, "you would lie on your soul for this woman?"

"Gimme a break," I said. "I'd swear on a stack of Bibles for her. I'd perjure myself before all the saints. I'd sell my soul for her a dozen times over and think I'd got the better of the devil. I know her worth, friend. You never did."

"*Aaah*," he said, at last comprehending, "so—when did you know Mira?"

"Long before you," I answered. "My son Nick was in the same class as her daughter Alicia."

Volkov's mouth dropped open. I believe there was a streak of peasant in him that no amount of education or civilization could erase. He was fearful of me. He remembered my hand on his throat, and he knew (and probably overestimated) my power in the justice system. But he was contemptuous of Mira, whom he despised for what he perceived to be her weakness. In some crudely naïve fashion, he had seen Alicia as the symbol, the living embodiment, of that supposed defect of hers that gave him the moral right to be contemptuous ofher. Thus to learn that this sign, this showing forth, of a hidden flaw, was one that I, the fearsome one, shared with Mira, the despised one, struck him with naïve astonishment.

"What!" he exclaimed. "You, too, have a dummy?"

He spoke artlessly, almost innocently. Normally, passive aggressive narcissists like Gregor Volkov develop a sure sense of limits, of just how far a given individual will bend to their manipulation before he or she has had enough. Volkov had for certain displayed that instinct often enough in the past. But the traumas of the afternoon had unhinged him. This one time his speaking was uncalculated, words straight from the heart, at the worst of all possible times.

The last word had infuriated me, but I had no time for my own rage. Instinctively, I knew what was coming. I turned to Mira, took a step, and put my hand up. I was too late. I had seen Mira move with a marvelous, natural grace on many occasions in the past. But I never saw her move with more elegance, with more beauty, than she did at that moment. There were no separate movements, just one magnificent, continual flow. She had begun to face me. Her back had been partly to Volkov. On the sound of the word 'dummy', as if that word were a starter's signal, she swung back around on her right foot in one smooth, unbroken, swift but unhurried movement, simultaneously raised the handgun up from her waist to eye level, leveled it without pausing, sighted, and fired.

*

The perfection of grace, the stillness of the gesture, can quiet time itself. But this is only the most profound example of the dancer's illusion....

*

...because time began again at once, in a terrific echoing roar of smoke and thunder. Blood and sinew spewed across the small room, spraying the walls, the furniture, the lampshade, some even splattering into the kitchen. Volkov reeled back, grabbing at his throat and gagging, then collapsed. Mira was thrown by the recoil towards the other wall, but I caught her by her left arm, literally as she flew by me, and brought her to her feet. She and I stood silence for an instant, but for a moment only. Then we both stepped to where Volkov lay.

The bullet had struck him in the throat, at his larynx. It could not have been more than a millimeter off from where I had seized him that day in my office. He was bleeding profusely and already gasping for breath. "I know some CPR," Mira said. I suppose she'd learned it as part of her building management responsibility. "Go into the kitchen and get some towels."

I did just that, and brought them back to her. She knelt down besides Volkov and applied them calmly and efficiently to staunch the bleeding. It was not much help. Later the coroner would determine that Volkov had died of asphyxiation, that he had literally drowned in his own blood, but we hardly needed an expert to tell us that. What was happening in his throat would have been obvious to anyone. He kept gasping for breath and attempting the impossible task of clearing his wind passages of the rising tide of blood. This was the way I had envisioned killing him that same day, but I had no time to ponder the coincidence. Complete panic showed in his eyes and face. He didn't want to die, and yet he knew he was about to. I did not hate Gregor Volkov at that time—that came later. But even if I had hated him, I would have felt sorry for him. Nobody should die like that. No one.

Mira never said a word as she tended to him. His eyes appealed to her, again and again. He was begging for something from her—for what exactly I have never been sure. At the time, I thought he was appealing for some sort of sign of regret, of remorse, on her part. Later I wondered if he might even have been beseeching her forgiveness for the wrongs he'd done her, though that was not something that occurred to me at the time. Either way, she offered him nothing in response—no apology, no explanation, no prayer, no blessing, either for body or soul. She remained entirely dry-eyed. She tended to him with an impersonal care she would have extended to any stricken animal. I may not have hated Volkov at that time, but she did, and she would not even offer him the consolation of regret as he suffocated on her floor. I had known her in many roles—as courtesan and lover, as friend and businesswoman, as wife as well, for in my heart that had already occurred. But that afternoon what I saw before me was an avenging angel. As she knelt beside the dying man, she was awesome, and terrible and not a little frightening. I should, I suppose, have been put off or even frightened. But nothing of the kind—we were bonded now; what had passed between us was now confirmed in blood. I had never loved her more.

The police arrived almost at the same time as I came out of the kitchen with the towels. As luck, good or bad, would have it, a patrol car had been near enough in the vicinity to hear the shot. The patrol officers had sense enough not to disturb Mira at her task. The paramedics did not arrive until near the end. One of the pros knelt down gently beside Mira, and wordlessly signaled her to rise. She turned the scene over to him at once. He did what he could, but Volkov died about two minutes later.

It was nearing six o'clock, the time when we were to have met for dinner. Mira was probably wearing the outfit in which she'd intended to meet me. We would not be going to dinner. We would not be going to Kauai.

She came over to me. No one stopped her; the room hadn't been organized into a crime scene yet. Silently she put her arms around my waist, and buried her head on my shoulder. I could feel the wetness of Volkov's blood on her clothes, then on mine. Then, silently, very privately, face pressed against my coat, she began to cry, a flood of tears soaking the lapels of my suit coat.

"Oh, Walter," she whispered against my chest, so softly only I could hear, "now it can never, ever be." The tears continued to flood. "I'm sorry, sweetheart. I'm so sorry."

"I told you once," I said hollowly, clutching her, staring sightlessly at the present, but contemplating the ruins of past and future, "never to apologize to me."

*

A few minutes later, the homicide detectives arrived on the scene. A few minutes after that, we all went down to the police station.

CHAPTER 17

▼

Knowing police interrogation techniques, even having worked with police on interrogations, isn't all that helpful in the face of an actual interrogation. I am in a position to know that as truth.

Mira and I were separated at the police station the moment we arrived, and taken to separate rooms for questioning. I was in the most unusual state of mind of my life. I had seen the gunshot, felt the blood and flesh spatter on me, heard Volkov's death rattle—and yet I could not accept the reality of it. The incident was as far off and distant to me as a war report in another country or last week's television show. It could not be the case that the Mira I knew and loved had shot her former lover, with an echo so loud the house shook. Such things do not happen in ordinary suburban houses, to me, to mine, to people I know. Since it could not be real, it was not real—I could not grasp either the fact or the immediacy of the fact.

But paradoxically my thought processes were almost unnaturally clear, in the way a fever delirium or forceful dream can produce a glittering, angular alertness. I was not at all confused. I was thinking with manic speed, but at the same time with a weird, icy precision.

I first formed some wild-eyed, heroic notion of taking responsibility for the shooting—'riding the beef', in convict jargon. But it wasn't possible—not in this day of electron microscopes, DNA, and crime scene analysis. Almost the first thing the detectives did was administer a paraffin test. There had been only one shot fired; Mira had fired it; and the only thing I would accomplish by claiming otherwise was the destruction of my own credibility.

I also considered fabricating a self-defense story. I'd come onto a frantic scene of assault and aggression, and Mira had saved herself with a single shot. But the patrol car had shown up almost immediately and the crime scene showed no evidence of struggle. It just wouldn't wash. The ultimate bottom line was that Mira was somewhere else in the building—and, I was certain, telling the whole truth as she knew it in her calm, artless way. The truth for its own sake meant nothing to me. I was going to put the best spin for Mira on the incident that I possibly could. But all of that effort would be useless unless what I said was believable. If I was going to lie for her, therefore, which I was, I was going to have to do it subtly, in a way that matched the actual facts and her recounting of them, but bent them to her favor to the maximum extent possible.

Thus, in my version, Mira was the true founder of Echelon. She had never received her rightful due. When she read the puff piece about Volkov in the paper that morning, she'd snapped. She never meant to kill him. She merely wanted to humiliate him. I arrived and defused the situation. But Volkov could not resist one final, sneering taunt, once he thought he was safe. Mira raised the hand gun—I thought—to fire it into the ceiling, as a rejoinder to his insult. But unfortunately it discharged and Volkov died.

"That's not what she says," one of the detectives said.

"What does she say?" I asked.

The detective smiled. "Give us some credit, counselor." They were solid and professional, and—to give them some credit—they didn't try to game me. As it happened, her story roughly matched mine. She admitted to aiming the gun at Volkov while denying she meant to kill him. But she also described Volkov accurately, as the sniveling, whining coward he'd been, rather than the arrogant monster of my fiction.

"She sure is composed," the same detective remarked.

"She wasn't composed at the scene," I said.

"That's not what the patrol guys say."

"They got there too late, and they weren't watching. She sobbed like a baby on my coat. Check it for tear stains. They're there—and, "I continued, improvising, "you should have seen her with Volkov before the medics got there. She was like a ministering angel. She held his hand, and whispered to him. She even prayed with him, with the tears running down her cheeks. It was the most touching thing I'd ever seen." This particular outright lie gave me enormous pleasure. I hoped somehow, somewhere, the ghost of Gregor Volkov was listening. I may have pitied him in death, but I had no use for him in either life or afterlife. *Fuck you, bastard,* wherever you are. Perhaps I had begun to hate him.

"What were you doing there?"

"I've known her for years. I've dated her from time to time. Our kids went to the same elementary school. We're very good friends."

"Nothing more?"

"Nothing more." Our first term as lovers had been five years before, archeological stuff. I had made our traveling arrangements in my own name. I could trust Mira to be discrete on that point, because she'd want to protect me. What had been solemnized in blood and death that afternoon was known only to her and me.

"What exactly did he say that made her raise the gun?" one of the detectives asked, resuming the hunt.

I knew then that Mira had refused to tell them exactly what Volkov had said that triggered his death, that she would rather go to her grave or to prison for life than see Volkov's word for Alicia appear in a police report or—worse—newsprint. I had been counting on that. *Good for you, girl,* I thought, and remembered again why I loved her.

"Some sexual thing, about how if she'd been better in bed, she'd have her stock." This, too, was a slander—if how Mira behaved in bed was the decision point, there wasn't a man alive who wouldn't give her the sun and moon—but one I knew she'd forgive.

Sometime after midnight a detective returned from a search of Volkov's home. They'd recovered the message Mira had left on his answering machine, about eleven o'clock on what was now the day before. It was replete with sexual innuendo, intoned in her most seductive voice. All had been going well until that point, but the inference that she lured him over to her house with the intention of doing him harm now came into play. This was ugly evidence, very bad stuff for Mira, and my stomach twisted into a knot of worry.

The detectives had counted on that, and I had to endure a whole new round of questioning, on the pretext that the whole event had been a conspiracy of some sort. It was easy stuff for me to deal with personally, because it wasn't true that there was a conspiracy. But they knew that. What they really wanted from me was a concession that Mira could have acted with premeditation. This I absolutely refused to do, reiterating my version of events again and again and again. We butted heads into the wee hours, until at last they gave up.

Finally, at about 5:00 a.m., I was released. The detectives had decided I was a material witness only. Mira stayed, held with no bail on charges of first-degree murder. The answering machine tape was devastating.

*

The case received huge publicity at the outset. At that time, everyone was interested in the doings of the high tech community. Gregor Volkov had appeared on the front page of the business section on the day of his death. Mira wasn't as well-known, but she had been around and about, and a surprising number of people were aware of her.

The initial press spin was `Jilted Mistress Kills Lover', which was not a good spin for Mira. In an age as free and easy as this one has become, the public has less and less sympathy for people who kill for love. There was a lot more to be said on Mira's behalf than that, and the first task I set myself was seeing to it that it was said, loudly and often.

A few days after the initial flurry of press reports had died down, I phoned one of my own contacts in the business section, someone who I had befriended frequently in the past. "Ah, Walter," he said after he recognized my voice, "the eyewitness. I'm surprised you haven't been suspended."

"They don't exactly call it a suspension. I'm merely relieved of all trial responsibility and switched to writing motions and doing whatever scut work comes around. Nobody speaks to me, or even acknowledges I exist. But, please, let's not call it a suspension. Such an unpleasant word. What I'd like to talk to you about," I continued, "is the Mira Watson case."

"*Really?*" he replied, and I could hear excitement in his voice. "An exclusive interview? With the eyewitness?"

"You wish," I answered. "I'm saving that for court. And we'd better get clear right now that we're on deep background. Just call me Mr. Informed Sources."

"Rats," he said.

"Don't sound so damn disappointed. I've got a much better story for you—about how the real entrepreneurs, the little guy—or in this case, the little gal—get stiffed by the establishment, and how nobody gives a damn. It's about what really happened with Gregor Volkov, who is maybe the biggest jerk I ever met, and Mira Watson, who deserved a lot better than what she got. And I will give all this to you chapter and verse, and I'll tell you how and with whom to confirm it."

"*Really!*" he said, and I noticed that some of the excitement had returned to his voice.

I told him the whole story of Echelon as I knew it, beginning with Mira's befriending Volkov by letting him squat on the property she managed, through the financing campaign, the indifference of the establishment to the justice of the matter, Volkov's toying with the custody issue, of the bad news she had received in family court only the day before. I omitted any mention of the special qualities of Alicia. I knew which parts of the story Mira would want told, which ones forever untold. Then, as promised, I told my reporter friend how to verify everything I'd said.

"Give it a day or so" I said in closing. "I'll let all these people know you're coming."

"It's a good story," he said, still with excitement. "There are lots of people around here who are going to identify with her."

"That's the idea," I said.

Ed Raymond was next. "I think you might want to prep Razumaev and Grishuk for a call from the editor of the business section"

"How interesting," Raymond said. "About what subject?"

"Gregor Volkov."

"Aaah," he sighed. "As I surmised. And for what purpose?"

"Their purpose might be to take a shot at Echelon by telling the world everything it really didn't want to know about their former colleague." I paused. "The achievement of which purpose of theirs would, as it happens, further one or two of my own."

"I see," Raymond said thoughtfully. "Actually, I think they'd be rather happy to oblige. I don't believe their budget was overly impacted by flowers for Volkov's funeral. And they loved that girl—I mean, loved her. Razumaev was in tears when he heard she was in jail. She's quite a dazzler."

"Yes," I agreed quietly. "She is that."

There was one more call to make, to Mark Stewart. I was worried about him. Venture capitalists are famous for talking the talk without walking the walk. Behind all the super stud publicity, what they really are are glorified portfolio managers. They're all for entrepreneurial risk, just as long as someone else is taking it. Stewart was typical. He'd been too concerned about his own standing with the firm to deliver for Mira when it really mattered. I wondered if he'd even take my call.

It turned out not to be a problem. He asked about my interest, and I gave him the usual song-and-dance, a concerned friend who had known her through elementary school connections. The full extent of my relationship with Mira, I was not disclosing to anyone. Stewart was on board immediately, still another man with a bad conscience. "I could tell him a lot more than that, if you want."

"What do you mean?"

"Just this. Last November, Mira sent us a business plan, for a little dot.com b-to-b business she called Gifter's Anonymous. It wasn't the greatest prospect I've reviewed, but it wasn't the worst, either. The plan was terrific. You could see how much work she'd done with it. I thought it had a chance."

"And?"

"Volkov killed it. He didn't have much credibility, but in this business a negative from any direction is enough. Besides, everyone knew they'd been an item, so naturally his opinion carried some weight. He could have given it the high sign, but he dissed it, and he dissed Mira as well. He was his usual idiotic self. It was an opportunity to throw his weight around, and he couldn't resist. He was a real piece of work, that guy."

"Yes, he was," I said. So Mira's instincts had been right about that subject, too. Volkov had left no area of her life unscarred. "But I think you'd better keep that story to yourself."

"Why?"

"I want the story to present her side of all this. She guessed at that, but she didn't know. That's too good a reason to kill him. I don't want it to get the prosecution thinking about additional motives."

"I see," he said.

*

Throughout all those long days and weeks, I lived on air and adrenaline, thinking non-stop about Mira's defense and doing little else but working on it. Most of the time, I was possessed by an unnatural giddiness. I was often exhilarated; I laughed frequently, and I made terrific jokes. People wondered about me. It was not unlike the false euphoria that occurs in the aftermath of a major family death, when the funeral is planned with a manic energy that burrows as far as possible into the depths of the present, to keep the future as distantly at bay as possible. It's an emotional state only a degree or two removed from hysteria, if it's removed at all.

In all that time, I neither saw nor spoke to Mira. It half-killed me, but that was the way it had to be. She was in jail, where the visitors are noted and the calls are monitored. The most precious gift I could ever give her was my own credibility. I was the only witness to the actual shooting, and I intended to give the most favorable and compelling testimony on her behalf possible. So what I did do for her had to be done indirectly and covertly. I threw myself into those tasks with a gusto I had rarely felt in my entire life.

The most important of these, much more significant than the media spin, had to do with her assigned counsel. Mira did not have the means herself to afford one of the superstars in the local bar. I would have loved to loan her—hell, give her—the money for the retainer. But it was just too dangerous. The result was that she ended up with the public defender. That's not the end of the world—the public defender's office is much more competent than most people realize, particularly in major cases. But there's a huge gap between competence and brilliance.

The case was assigned to Charlie Towne, a decent guy but something of a plodder. The good news was that the jury would respond to his likeability and earnestness. The bad was that he was not likely to produce any flash or imagination. There was no way I was going to leave it at that.

A few days after Charlie was appointed, I ran into him at the clerk's office, accidentally on purpose, while I was doing some filing. I did not know him all that well—the public defender's office didn't pick up the defense of the sophisticated while-collar stuff that I handled all that often, and in any event Charlie Towne would never have been delegated to that type of case.

"Hi, Walter," he said, a bit sheepishly. "You know I'm going to have to talk to you."

"I'm looking forward to it," I said. "A little bit awkward for me, you know—being a D.A. and all. I'm surprised you haven't moved to recuse the office."

"Ah, geez, Walt, all you are is a witness. And you're kind of well-respected over there. I don't want to make waves. What chance is there?"

This was even worse than I had expected. "Charlie, it's the theoretical possibility of prejudice that's important, not the actuality." The thought then crossed my mind that research on this stuff, maybe even text or moving papers, could be provided to Charlie in unmarked manila envelopes, and that the source would be absolutely untraceable. "You really should think about it."

"I will," he said, then looked at me harder. "Hey, Walt, you don't look so good. Have you lost some weight?"

"Oh, maybe a pound or two," I said.

*

I had actually lost some fifteen pounds in six weeks. My days may have been maniacally upbeat, but my nights were a different matter.

Dreams awoke me in the middle of the night, every night. I could not return to sleep afterwards. It was not one recurrent dream, but a whole series of recurrent dreams. The setting of all of them was the same. I was back in Mira's living room, with Mira and Volkov and the gun, before anything had happened. Then the events would unfold again, with some variation on what had actually occurred.

Sometimes Volkov had a gun of his own, fired first, and Mira fell. Those were horrible. Sometimes he produced his gun and shot back after he had been wounded. They weren't much better. A few times,

Mira would shoot and shoot and Volkov could not be killed. On occasion, he *would* be killed, but would arise as a zombie and pursue us
both. Those were true nightmares. Once Volkov had a gun and fired
and fired as I took Mira by the hand and we fled to safety. I liked that
one quite a bit, but it only happened once.

The worst—the very worst—were the revisits to something very
close to the actual event. Over and over Mira would make that beautiful half pivot, at the same time raising the pistol, and I would step forward, to say something, do something, somehow stop her, and I would
always be too late. As the dreams recurred, I would get closer and closer
and closer, a foot to an inch, a second to a microsecond, a warning to a
shout, but always too little too late. I would awake from these in a full
adrenaline rush, pounding the mattress in frustration.

One thing was common to all of them. I was never endangered
myself. The action was always between Mira and Volkov. One of them
shot the other, or tried to shoot the other, or something. I tried to
intervene, to stop it somehow, and nothing I did or tried worked. I was
always the powerless spectator. That was the one constant. As it was by
day, in life, so it was by night, in fantasy.

*

The prosecution had been assigned to David Rosenblatt. He scared
me. He was a quietly brilliant guy with all the academic credentials and
background; he could have written his own ticket in private practice if
he had chosen. He stayed in prosecution out of a strong moral commitment and because he loved trial work. Local D.A.'s offices couldn't
function without that type.

The good news was that Dave had a keen sense of the human
dimensions of the cases he handled. He didn't do anything by rote or
robotics. The press story I'd initiated appeared, and worked even better
than I'd hoped. It produced a small flurry of letters to the business sec-

tion and the general editor, from people who had similar stories, not exactly condoning homicide, but certainly understanding it.

Then Charlie Towne filed his recusal motion, which I knew to be in fairly good form since I'd ghostwritten most of it. That raised the real possibility that our office would be removed from the case in favor of the Attorney General's Office because of the conflict inherent in a deputy district attorney (me) being the principal witness to the offense. That motion, if granted, was commonly perceived to be a disaster for the prosecution, as the deputy attorney generals did not begin to have the trial experience that most local prosecutors possessed.

All of this I knew exerted considerable pressure on the office. I heard rumblings that the office had backed off the case considerably, and interesting rumors that the powers-that-be were seeking a resolution in some face-saving way. I began to hope. Three days before the hearing on the recusal motion, I received a message from Dave Rosenblatt, requesting I meet him in his office. I was happy to do so.

"It's about the Elmira Watson case," he said without further ado. He pronounced her name with the long 'I'. I did not correct him.

"I assumed that," I said.

"We're in a little pickle here, Walt," he said. "We're facing a pretty good recusal motion. Plus Ms. Watson has a lot to say for herself. I'm sure you've read the papers. Nobody seems to have a good word to say about this Volkov. Even his wife—"

"WIFE!?" I sat up in my chair, astonished.

"Yeah, wife. From Odessa. He walked out on her eight years ago. Anyway, I'd like to settle this case. I thought I'd talk to you. You saw what happened and the last I heard, you know a little law. What do you think the case is worth?"

I had been expecting, hoping for, this. "I think you should dismiss. I think it was an accidental shooting."

He was shaking his head before I'd finished. "I can't do that, Walt. There's the tape—and as sympathetic as all that stock stuff is, it also provides one hell of a motive. Mind you, I know what I'm up against.

Elmira Watson must be the most popular prisoner in the history of the county jail. Hell, if I convicted her of first degree murder I'd need a body guard to protect me from the sheriff's deputies. And what presence! You should have seen the way she conducted herself at the preliminary hearing. She didn't testify, but from the way she reacted—she's a very impressive person.

"But you can't walk away from a homicide like this. No matter how impressive you are, and how despicable the victim." He paused. "So I'm going to offer her a voluntary armed—which is justice, but also a gift."

"Voluntary *armed?*" He meant a voluntary manslaughter—not murder—with the additional allegation that Mira had been armed with a firearm. What it meant in practical terms was twelve years in prison, of which she'd have to serve ten.

"Walt. Settle down. In theory, Ms. Watson could even be charged with the death penalty, because of that tape. That's a special circumstance, lying in wait. That's never been seriously on the table, but that's what's possible in legal theory. Her manner is impressive, but it might come across as cold-bloodedness to a jury. And then there's you."

"Me?"

"Yes." He straightened up. "Your credibility isn't a given, Walt. We have checked a few things. You were on your way to Hawaii that Sunday with someone. I know you. You date people, but you're a pretty stable guy. I doubt very much you'd be having dinner with one woman on Friday night and vacationing with another on Sunday. It also just so happens that she'd arranged for a week off herself—the same as you. Charlie Towne says she needed the time to get her MBA studies back on track, but I'm not so sure I believe him. What makes more sense to me is that the two of you were going off together. Which makes you not as neutral a witness as you say."

"Dave, I—"

He held up a hand. "I don't want to go there, Walt, I really don't. I won't do it if I don't have to. But I think you should give that aspect of the case a little thought. I don't like Volkov and I don't like the case. I've got a pretty good idea of what really happened here."

"Why are you telling me all this?"

"Because I'm next to certain you're godfathering the defense. I think you wrote the recusal motion. I think you were the one who got the media turned around. I think you're crazy in love with this woman, and she with you—I don't blame you, by the way—kind of envy you, actually. I've got no proof of that, but every instinct in my gut tells me it's so—and so I don't think she'll settle the case without your say so.

"She can't walk totally away from this, Walt. Nobody can. Voluntary armed is justice, but it's also a gift. You may be crazy in love, but you're also a first class lawyer. I asked you here because I want you to tell her it's a good deal, and to take it."

*

I waited for the inevitable call all day in a sullen, listless stupor.

My work was done; with no tasks before me, the present had evaporated, and with it my giddiness. There was nothing left to me but the desolate past with its squandered opportunities, and the dismal future, with its leaden, joyless certainties. It was on that afternoon that my attitude towards Volkov flowered into hatred—oddly, not so much for all the harm he'd inflicted on Mira (I could have made that good), but for being an ignorant, self-aggrandizing fool who'd cluelessly twisted a tigress's tail for four years and then gotten himself killed like an idiot. Some people, they say, are natural-born murderers. Gregor Volkov was a natural born murderee. He'd probably been inspiring people to violence most of his adult life, and quietly gloating in triumph when they didn't act. Never mind the pitiful way he died, I found myself loathing him.

Finally, the phone rang at my place about 10:00 that night. It was Charlie Towne. He was ebullient.

"Walt, Dave Rosenblatt made us a tremendous offer today. Better than I thought I could ever get." He could not contain his excitement at what he clearly considered to be a major professional triumph. "Mira's got to take it. I've urged her to take it, but she wants to know what you think first."

I had been thinking about what I was going to say all day long. "Tell her this is one of those dragons I can't kill for her," I said. "I can only give her the sword. She'll know what I mean. If she feels really sorry about what happened with Gregor—what she did and how he died— then maybe she should roll the dice with the jury. But if she's not sorry, if she really doesn't feel any remorse, then she can't do better. She shouldn't be under any illusion that she can fake what isn't there. Tell her the system is set up to separate out the genuine emotions from the faked ones. Tell her she should look into her heart and see what's there and decide. And that's the sword."

*

I was in the courtroom three days later, when Dave Rosenblatt amended the information to charge voluntary manslaughter committed with a firearm, with an indicated sentence from the judge of twelve years, and Mira changed her plea to guilty. The press had lost interest by that time; the only other persons present were one reporter and a bulky Slavic woman, whom I took to be Volkov's true wife.

Mira entered her plea with a dignity that stilled everyone in court. Somehow she even made the hideous orange jumpsuit look stylish. As Mira and the judge went through the ritualistic litany of rights and waivers, one of the uniformed matrons began to weep only. Mira gave her a quick, reassuring smile; she was comforting her jailers.

Of course she knew I was in the courtroom, but she did not acknowledge my presence until all the formalities were completed. The court recessed, and everyone stood up. Mira turned to leave. There was no longer any need to be discrete, and certainly no motive for discretion. I stepped past the bar.

"Give us a second, guys," I said. The deputies like me, too.

I stepped forward, and simply pulled her against me. She came resistless, but then put her arms around me and hugged me more tightly than I had ever been hugged before, or ever will be again. I could feel her tears on my jacket as I had before, that horrible January night. Behind me, Dave Rosenblatt nodded imperceptibly to himself. He was too much the mensch to go into an elaborate 'I knew it' routine.

"You won't let me say what I want to say," she whispered.

"Please don't," I answered.

It all went on much longer than it should have, but I did not want time to resume again until it had to. There was nothing left now except the desolate reality of finality and separation. Finally, one of the deputies cleared his throat. "Counselor—"he said, uncomfortably.

"I know, I know," I said, and released her. Our moment was over. Mira smoothed her hair and straightened her ridiculous tunic.

"Good bye, Walt," she said softly, and then she was gone through the back door of the court, back into the jail, from where she would be transported a day or two later to prison.

*

My recurrent dreams began to diminish after that day, both in number and variety. But they never disappeared entirely. The basic one, the one in which I watch Mira turn, in terrible, fearful beauty, and I move forward to stop her, persisted. It recurs from time to time to this day. It may well be the last thought of my life.

The reason, I think, is that the fundamental, inescapable truth shows through in that dream—not only on that last fatal night, but for the whole time I knew and loved Mira Watson.

Always too little, always too late. As last words, as the epitaph for everything that could have happened, that should have happened, between Mira and Walt, for Elmira Jenkins Watson and Walter Royer Kelsey, they are as good as any. They speak all.

Always too little, always too late. There isn't anything more to say. I think I will leave it at that.

Epilog

▼

Echelon did not last long after Volkov's death. It was already missing its technological muscle; now it had lost its figurehead. The great winter of dot.com discontent had not yet arrived, but the market climate was already distinctly autumnal. Its stock price plummeted. Mark Stewart and the other financiers did all right. They operate on a first-in, first-basis and were long gone before the collapse. As usual, it was the public that took the hit.

Razumaev and Grischuk's new company came to the market with an improved version of the Firebird at the same time that Echelon was disappearing. There was some substance there, which was not the case with most of the companies on the technological bubble. They were bought out within weeks by one of the giants. The two engineers became very, VERY rich.

*

Two days after the sentencing, Mira was transported to the Women's Correctional Facility at T—to serve out her sentence. Of course I intended to wait for Mira. Waiting's easy when you have nothing else to wait for.

At the beginning I visited her whenever visiting was possible, which was not as often as I would have liked. T—was several hundred miles away, without any close airport. The entire weekend had to be devoted to the trip, which meant that any time some parental duty conflicted I couldn't go. Plus Mira had parental responsibilities of her own. The catastrophe had ended the long war between herself and Crockett, mostly because of his total victory. He had evidently burst into tears when he first visited her at the jail. She wanted to maintain the maximum possible contact with her children, and to his credit he saw—and has seen—to it that she does. That didn't leave much visiting time for would-be lovers.

Nonetheless, I visited her as often as I could those first two years. The visits did not go well. I tried for her, I know she tried for me—and yet we were awkward, stilted, uncomfortable with each other. The free, easy rapport we had had with each other since the moment of first meeting was gone. We could both feel the shadow of the event between us. It may be that we were both trying too hard to put everything behind us. For whatever reason, it didn't work. I did my best to be witty and wise, and she kissed me passionately, even desperately, each time I left. But nothing felt natural or right.

I still intended to wait. Perhaps all that was needed was time, which would heal this wound as it heals them all. It was clearly a mistake to continue the contact when we were both uncomfortable. So I switched, to long chatty letters, which I sent by e-mail every ten days or so. Mira obviously enjoyed getting them, and always replied, though not nearly so effusively or lengthily.

*

My darling Elizabeth grows in grace and beauty daily. She graduated from high school this year, enrolled in the college of her choice, and will—I believe—go on to lead whatever life she chooses. None of the dangers I foresaw for her ever materialized.

She knows nothing of these events, and never will, unless she reads these pages. She was not affected by them. They passed over her head like a flock of wild geese or a flight of meteors. That is as it should be. Children owe their parents respect and perhaps sympathy—for sure not curiosity. Yet some day, somehow, I would like her to discover these aspects of my life. I loved her mother once, but she does not associate that with the fiery parts of the soul. I would like her to know I am capable of passion—at this time in her life, she would more readily believe I was born on the planet Jupiter—and also of the woman whom I prized above all others.

If she does not know these things she will never have known me at all.

*

Nick and Alicia ended up in the same special ed program in high school. They relate to each other in some mute, logically inexpressible way that no one else on the planet can understand. Nick is fascinated by computer generated graphics and images, and has created menagerie after menagerie of strange, Hieronymus Bosch-y creatures. Alicia is obsessed by the young wizards of Hogwarts and has probably created more back story on their behalf than has the author. They live in two different worlds, but somehow the two planets communicate. They are both enormously valuable human beings who transform the lives of everyone with whom they have close encounters.

They have no romantic interest in each other, both preferring normal classmates in that aspect of their lives. That is Nick's bad luck, for Alicia has matured into an extraordinarily attractive young girl, more conventionally good looking than her mother. When she speaks, the crushed consonants and mangled grammar betray her condition at once. But there are also unmistakable echoes of the music of her mother's voice. She has outgrown the bewilderment and confusion she felt when the custodial arrangements were first changed. I don't know what Mira does on those visits, but it is obviously working.

*

Mira had served almost three years of her term when I received the longest letter I will ever receive from her. It was also the second-to-last. This one came hard copy. It is much gushier than her normal prose or speaking style, for reasons that are self-evident from the content. It read as follows:

My dearest, darling Walter,

There is no easy way to tell you what I have to tell you so I will just tell you. I was married last week to a man named Dwight Logan, from North Carolina. Dwight was a boy I knew back in high school in North Carolina. My mother told him about me and we began to correspond. He proposed to me about a month ago, and I accepted.

I know this is a big surprise for you, Walt, and I hope and pray it is not too hurtful. I must now write some other things that may be hurtful, although I hope they are reassuring. I have to write them because I am not going to write you again.

I love you, Walter. I love you as I have never loved anyone. I never said that to you aloud, but you have to know it now. I intended to say that out loud, in Hawaii, when we were making love again. Then I planned to call you 'sweetheart' after I was yours again, so you would know it was special and you were special. You considered yourself in need of forgiveness, my poor, foolish darling, and I intended to extend the forgiveness to you until you realized you had no need, and all was well. I wanted to be worthy to do that. That is why it all happened.

You often told me of your dreams, but I never told you mine. After I went to jail and then to here, my dreams were always that we were in Hawaii, or some other nice place, and none of it had really happened, that it was all just a horrible dream. I dreamt it over and over. But I would always wake up and be in jail, and I would know that my sleep was the dream and my waking was the nightmare and all I wanted to do was cry and die.

You have often said that you think we are true loves, that we are meant for each other. Do you know I think you are right? But Walter, none of the good things that we both meant to happen ever did happen— and the way things are is so totally tangled up, such a total mess, that there is no way to untangle it. You may despise me, but I have to tell you that I don't feel sorry about Gregor being dead at all. When I think of that awful afternoon, and I remember Gregor cowering in front of me, it makes me feel happy. The only regret I have is that I lost you. Isn't that terrible? That's why I pled guilty, because I am guilty. You gave me good advice, as always.

But if I must be a murderess in the past, I don't want to be one in the future. Every time I think of Gregor, and Gregor touching me, it makes my skin crawl. I would never have begun with him if I thought there was any chance with you. But I don't want to go on hating him. If I were to go back to you or stay in California, then I would have to go right on being that person who killed Gregor, and I don't want to be that person. We are too tangled up in this web we have made to ever untangle it. I know you know I'm right. Even though you are the sweetest, loveliest man in the world, you are all bound up with that tangle. You are a part of it all. So I must give you up.

That's why I married Dwight. I have to cut off the past, and beginning now. He is not a big clumsy wonderful bear like you, but he cares for me deeply and I intend to be a good wife to him and to learn to care for him. So please don't write me or try to talk me out of it. It will just be more painful.

I remember how you used to talk about other lives and times on those wonderful nights we had. I like to think you are right, and we will relive all this again, and make it right. It is nice to dream that somehow we would be together, and have a family, and maybe even children of our own. I love to hear you talk, Walt. I love my memories of that. I love you.

Good bye, my wonderful sweet Walt. I will always care for you. I can't write any more because I would start to cry and that is not what a new bride should do.

Love,

Mira

I gave up alcohol on a given day some 12 years ago. I will never take another drink. I can make that statement with some certainty because if I ever were going to resume drinking, it would have been the night I received that letter.

*

For some time before that, I had been obsessed with tracking down a tape of a particular live television performance. Mira had casually mentioned once that her dance company had made an appearance on the PBS Great Performance series. It occurred sometime during the mid 80's on a date and year that she had long since forgotten. I became determined to find a video tape of the telecast.

There were no archival copies existent from the official sources. But the performance had occurred at a time when nearly everything was taped by some amateur or other. It took a long time to find such a person, but the Internet is very large, my time was unlimited, and I would not give the search up. Finally I made contact with another member of the company, a middle-aged woman who had formed a sort of alumni association. She kept track of everybody. She was fully aware of what had happened to Mira, but kept the information herself—a nice person. When she learned who I was and why I wanted the tape, she was happy to lend it to me, on my assurance that I'd have a digital transfer made and return the original to her.

I put the tape on my machine with a mixture of curiosity, anticipation, and apprehension unparalleled in my life. What was the twentiesh Mira like, anyway? As brilliant, as dazzling a dancer as I assumed? Or just another faceless member of the chorus? I literally could not breathe as the tape began to roll.

She was better than I could have ever imagined. She whirled, she twirled, she moved with an exuberantly youthful version of the middle-aged grace that was stamped indelibly in my memory. All this was done with flair, a captivating gaiety, that leaped across the screen and the intervening years. For a moment I simply watched and marveled. Then the thought occurred to me that the dazzling carefree girl could not possibly know everything that lay before her—Crockett, Alicia, her sons, me, Volkov, the stone walls of the women's prison. With that came an unavoidable recollection of the only other occasion on which I'd seen her move with an equivalent elegance and beauty.

I collapsed on my couch and stared unseeing at the video. I couldn't endure any more of it that evening (though I have played it countless times since). I would have wept into my hands, but what I was feeling was beyond tears.

I had had a duplicate copy made for Mira—I fully intended to respect her wishes about communicating. But I was sure she would understand with memorabilia of this significance. The result was what I know for certain is the last letter I will ever receive from her.

My wonderful Walt,

Thank you, thank you for this wonderful gift!! Please do not send me another gift or you will break my heart. I have to forget you, my wonderful sweetheart. Help me to stop thinking of you. I will love you always.

Love,

Mira

*

After the commotion died down and the smoke cleared, Naomi contacted me and we picked up more or less where we'd left off. She's a good woman, the sort who takes good, brisk, unsentimental care of the people around her. She did the same for me. For one thing, she got me eating regularly again, as I had kept right on losing weight after the case was over. Somewhere along the line I'd picked up Mira's eating habits.

We began seeing movies again, plays, traveling, sleeping together when the occasion was right. She is fully aware of what the limitations of the relationship are. Even if I tried to conceal them, they are well nigh unconcealable. For the moment, she accepts them.

"I may not have your heart," she says, in an earthy way that only her lovers know, that would astound the delicate ears of the matrons in her social circle, "but what's left over ain't too shabby."

She is nagging me these days to write a book, to break the gloom in which she too often finds me sunk.

Everyone, she says, has one novel in them.

*

From prison, Mira put her house up for sale. It was not on the market long. A few weeks later, some routine errand took me down the street. The new owners had torn the old house down. They were in the process of erecting a rather attractive duplex on the site. It was being turned into a nice rental property, the owner living in one unit, leasing the other.

For a long time, I sat in the parked car across the street, simply contemplating the lot and the construction, and brooding.

I could have done the same thing any time during those five long years. Any time. It was easy and affordable. Mira and I might even have made a little money.

*

I never did go back to trial work at the District Attorney's Office. I resigned a few weeks later. I wasn't outraged or upset by the outcome of Mira's case. Dave Rosenblatt was right—it was a generous disposition. By any objective standard, Mira was guilty of at least second degree murder, which carries with it a much longer term. It wasn't the criminal justice system that had failed her. It was me.

But I didn't really give a damn about objectivity, and I was through doing justice for the Great State of California or anyone. My long term ambition in retirement had been to become a special education aide. With the money from my stock windfall, that had become possible. So I sold it all off, which happened to be extremely prudent investment strategy, since the deluge came not long after. But that's not why I sold when I did.

These days I spend the mornings doing my best for the special ed elementary schoolers over at the John F. Kennedy Elementary School. The 'educably retarded' is how my group is classified. They are wonderful kids; I do my best for them, and this results in pretty good mornings. How I spend my afternoons, I couldn't tell you. I don't know. I don't keep track.

I still live in the same condominium. I can afford better, but there is no point. I have spent some money remodeling, and filled it with the latest electronic toys—DVD players, HDTV, satellite television, the works. It's not a bad life. There is only one thing missing. It is embodied in a person who dwells apart from me, some 350 miles away, in a prison, and who I will never see again. I can express what is missing from my home, from my life, from my being, in a single word—perhaps not the word you are thinking of—

Grace.

I try to keep myself open for everything—I'm not going to make the same mistake three times in the same lifetime. The fortress that was vaporized that Christmas night will never be rebuilt. Anything is possible, I tell myself, but then the bell always tolls in the same instant. I am never in my lifetime going to see Mira Watson again. I am never again going to hear her voice. It is a thought that I would scarcely find endurable, except that I must find it endurable. You play the hand you've been dealt, especially when you were the dealer. That's the first rule of the game.

But I am never going to see Mira again—and there it is again, in the same intake of breath, the same movement of mind, the inescapable tolling of the bell.

*

And that's my story.

The End

0-595-29540-1